ALSO BY L.L. BARTLETT

The Jeff Res*

MURDER O
DEAD
ROOM A
CHEATED
BOUND BY
DARK . . . .

GW00716582

Short Stories

EVOLUTION:JEFF RESNICK'S BACKSTORY
A JEFF RESNICK SIX PACK
WHEN THE SPIRIT MOVES YOU
BAH! HUMBUG
COLD CASE
SPOOKED!
CRYBABY
EYEWITNESS
ABUSED: A DAUGHTER'S STORY

Writing as Lorraine Bartlett

TALES OF TELENIA
THRESHOLD
JOURNEY
THREACHERY

The Lotus Bay Mysteries

WITH BAITED BREATH

The Victoria Square Mysteries

A CRAFTY KILLING
THE WALLED FLOWER
ONE HOT MURDER
RECIPES TO DIE FOR: A VICTORIA SQUARE COOKBOOK

A JEFF RESNICK MYSTERY

ROOM
AT THE INN

by L.L. Bartlett

 Polaris Press

Polaris Press
P.O. Box 230
N. Greece, NY 14515

This edition: September 2012

ACKNOWLEDGMENTS

For many years, ROOM AT THE INN sat on a shelf. After MURDER ON THE MIND sold, my then-agent deemed the follow-up book too "cozy." She couldn't possibly know that in the years ahead I would become known as a cozy mystery author. She was right; the book is not as gritty as the two that precede it and the books that follow, but it's still a Jeff Resnick story and part of his history, and I'm pleased to share it with you now.

Over the years, many people read ROOM AT THE INN, gave me encouragement, and shared their critical eye. Sadly, I've forgotten the names of some of those who gave me input; those I do remember are: Kate Doran, Elizabeth Eng, Dru Ann Love, Janette McNana, Gwen Nelson, Yvonne Powell, Alison Steinmiller, Liz Voll, and Ed Whitmore. Thank you, all. Thanks also go to Kate Doran and Leann Sweeney for their medical expertise. Any mistakes are strictly my own. Thanks also go to my cover designer, Patricia Ryan, and to Frank Solomon for formatting this book.

To find out more about the Jeff Resnick Mysteries, please visit my website: www.LLBartlett.com

ONE

A bell over the door jangled as I stepped into the Sugar Maple Inn's living room and smelled death. Not literally, of course. It's unsanitary, and a body in the lobby isn't a welcome sight for potential customers. Besides, I wasn't sure anybody had actually died.

Yet.

I'm not paranoid, but since a mugging rearranged my brain cells earlier in the year (leaving me with lingering, often crippling, headaches), I see—absorb—more than most people.

The phantom odor disappeared, replaced by the sickly sweet scent of potpourri. It wasn't an improvement.

I took another step inside and my girlfriend, Maggie, pushed past me. The overstuffed furniture, antiques and do-dads decorating the walls and every flat surface in the living room-lobby made the place look fussy and uninhabitable. To me that is. Maggie's wide approving eyes sucked it up. Although not swank, at an average $350 a night, it wasn't within my budget.

I followed Maggie to the cubbyhole behind a Dutch door that served as the inn's registration desk. A young blonde woman sat in front of a computer, pecking away. I had to clear my throat twice before she looked up.

"Hi. Is Susan Dawson around?" Maggie asked.

"She's not available. Can I help?"

"I'm Jeff Resnick," I said, "and this is Maggie Brennan.

We're here to write an article on the inn and take a few pictures for a magazine. Is our room available?"

The young woman's face was blank. "Sorry, sir, but we're booked solid," she said, without even consulting the ledger beside her. "You might find a room somewhere else in town, but as it's coming up on a holiday weekend, I wouldn't count on it."

Was her response an omen of things to come?

"We're here as a favor to Susan and Zack," Maggie piped up. "We're supposed to stay here free."

The young woman blinked. "Susan didn't mention this to me. You're welcome to wait for her if you'd like." She indicated the porch.

I forced a smile. "Thanks."

So we headed for the door, and once again I caught that sense of impending doom. I'm not a mind reader. Sometimes I know things about people and places. I tap into strong emotions—whether I want to or not—and sometimes knowledge just follows. It's a real kick when you're making love—except on those occasions when your partner's heart isn't into it. That comes across loud and clear, too.

Maggie accepts this personality quirk of mine as one would a minor disability; she overlooks it. But I figured until I knew what was going on, I'd better not mention my premonition.

We settled on the porch swing and watched the intermittent traffic whiz by, while I tried not to think of dead bodies. "Just how sharp is this old high school buddy of yours?" I asked. "So far, I'm unimpressed."

Maggie squirmed. "Susan was voted most likely to succeed."

"Then why does she need our help?" Help, in the form of a magazine article. Maggie had been selling freelance for just over a year.

"I suppose she'd welcome any publicity." Maggie

sighed and looked away.

The afternoon sun highlighted the fine lines around her blue eyes, hinting at years of smiles. As always, she looked beautiful to me. I sensed her nervousness at seeing her old school friend again. I'd say she was three sizes more nervous. Not that Maggie's overweight. She's just about right for her five-six height. I stroked her shoulder-length auburn hair and felt bad for laying a guilt trip on her. At forty, she was older than me by four years, but her joys and insecurities made her seem—and occasionally act—years younger.

I'd known Maggie for about six months, and this was our first weekend trip together. We left the grim skyline of Buffalo behind us for a long Labor Day weekend in Stowe, Vermont for a working vacation. Maggie's editor wanted pictures to accompany her story. After losing her job some months before, and relying only on contract work since, Maggie wasn't in a position to pay someone to do it. I'm a pretty good amateur photographer. So I borrowed my brother's camera and we filled the trunk of my car with rented equipment, some of which I had only the most basic knowledge.

My gaze traveled to the large sign along the road, which announced the Triple-A sanctioned Sugar Maple Inn. True to its brochure, a towering Sugar Maple tree stood to one side of the place. In another couple of weeks it would be a magnificent example of Vermont's famous fall colors.

Built into a hillside, the inn's weathered, shingled exterior looked charming, if a little unkempt thanks to the surrounding, overgrown shrubs. Not quite a Tyrolean ski lodge, Maggie had called its gabled roof and pine green shutters on each window "quaint."

Eventually a burgundy Dodge Caravan pulled up the gravel driveway with a woman at the wheel. She got out of the van and hurried toward us. "Maggie!"

"Susan?" Maggie sounded uncertain.

With an unexciting name like Susan Dawson, I'd expected a nondescript woman, not the tall, lithe redhead with elegantly lacquered nails and a perfect body. She wasn't beautiful, but she knew how to accentuate her personal positives.

She gave Maggie a perfunctory hug, then turned to me. "You must be Jeff," Susan said, shoving her hand in my direction. Her grip was as strong as any man's, and I was relieved when it wasn't accompanied by a flash of insight I sometimes get when I meet someone.

"Sorry I wasn't here when you arrived."

"There seems to be some kind of mix-up," I said. "The girl inside said we didn't have a room. She suggested we try somewhere else."

Susan frowned. "Nadine's new. But don't worry; I've got everything ready for you. You're going to love the Sugar Maple, and you'll have the most intimate room in the Inn. Come on inside."

We followed her into the cool interior.

"This is the living room. We have five public areas available for guests," she said, which sounded suspiciously like a rehearsed speech. "This is a totally non-smoking inn. Please remember that this is our home, and we ask that you discourage friends from just dropping by. The front door is locked at midnight, but you can arrange for a key if you plan to stay out later."

"Was there ever a murder here?" I asked.

Startled, Susan blinked at me.

Maggie's glare was the visual equivalent of a kick under the table. "He means a ghost. Are there any ghosts at the inn? It could be the article's focal point."

"Oh, yeah," I agreed. "A ghost."

"No," Susan said, her eyes flashing, "we *don't* have a ghost."

One of the guests, a handsome older woman with

salt-and-pepper hair, in beige slacks and a vibrant pink print blouse, ambled into the living room. She sat on one of the matching loveseats in front of the fireplace and grabbed a magazine from the cocktail table. Her arrival gave me a chance to break into Susan's spiel.

"Have you decided what rooms you'd like to feature? Or we—"

"Why don't we talk about this elsewhere," Susan interrupted me, then motioned us to a side door marked PRIVATE. "Nadine, there're groceries in the van. Please take them down to the kitchen," she said, without waiting for a reply.

Beyond the door was the Dawson's residence, a combination office-attached apartment. A file cabinet and desk crowded their living space. The sterile room had none of the country charm we'd found in the lobby. Susan ushered us to sit at the worn Formica kitchen table. She could have at least offered us a cold drink.

"When can you start?" asked the hardened businesswoman.

"Tomorrow," I said, suddenly realizing how tired I was from the long drive.

Her lips grew tight. "Zack's not going to be happy about that."

"What did you and your husband have in mind?" Maggie asked, her tone indicating she was open to negotiation—while I was not.

"There's still time before check-in. You can take the pictures of the bedrooms today, and—"

"Today?" I interrupted.

"Is that a problem?"

"Yes. It'll take hours to set up the lights."

"Doesn't your camera have a flash?"

She didn't have a clue what photographing interiors involved. Hell, I wasn't really sure I did.

"The magazine expects professional quality photos. It

takes time to get everything just right," I said.

"But I'm booked solid for the weekend. I can't ask the guests to move out of their rooms while you—"

"Then I don't see how we can do it," I said. I didn't like her attitude and was already willing to say good-bye and hit the road for home.

Susan's eyes narrowed. "What's this all about, Maggie? You said you could help me."

"Without good pictures—" Maggie began, but I tuned out her explanation, waiting for an opportunity to speak.

"Let me guess. You went into hock to refurbish the place, you're having problems filling the rooms on a regular basis, and now the bank is breathing down your neck, right?"

Susan's gaze was icy. "Exactly."

"If we photographed one bedroom, we could concentrate on the other public areas. Is that acceptable?" Maggie asked.

Susan didn't look happy. "I suppose."

"Is your best room available in the next couple of days?"

"Ms. Marshall will be checking out Monday morning, but I've got another couple checking in later that afternoon."

"What's the time frame?" I asked.

"Check out is at eleven. New guests check in at three."

"How long does it take to make up a room? Ten or twenty minutes?" I asked.

She nodded.

"That leaves us less than four hours."

"Why is that a problem?"

"While I set up the lights, Maggie will dress the room—" I started.

"Dress the room?"

"We might need to rearrange furniture and borrow props from other rooms," Maggie explained.

"A real photo shoot would have a stylist," I explained, trying to sound knowledgeable—and feeling like a con man. The sum total of my information had come from a Google search and a magazine article only days before. "The memory card in my camera holds about three-hundred exposures."

"Why so many? I've never seen an article with more than five or six pictures."

"We'll want a number of variations on each shot, and while we can Photoshop the brightness and contrast, you want your basic exposure to be the best possible."

"After you see the results, you might want to revamp your brochure, too," Maggie put in, perhaps to get double use from my photography.

"All that costs money. Which we don't have much of."

"The girl out front said you were fully booked."

"For the five rooms that are finished. We've got seven more in various states of renovation. We'd planned on having them done before the fall colors and the leaf peepers arrive, but we've had contractor and cash-flow problems. Besides, the guests object to the constant sounds of hammering and power saws."

"We'll do the best we can," I offered, which apparently wasn't going to be good enough for Susan.

"Let me show you the rest of the place," she grumbled, and gestured toward the door that led back to the inn.

She continued the grand tour of the public areas, oblivious to the fact we'd had a long drive and might be tired. All I wanted was to kick off my shoes, use the bathroom, and catch a few Zs before dinner.

The inn's lower level was decorated in the same—although somewhat more restrained—country charm as the lobby above. Eight or ten tables were scattered throughout the large dining room. Two picture windows, one to the south and one to the east, overlooked the vast gardens outside. A professional coffeemaker, with a full pot, and a glass jar filled with homemade chocolate chip cookies beckoned guests.

The game room boasted a stately old pool table. Game boards decorated the walls, and shelves filled with books, puzzles, and a large-screen television could entertain bored guests. As we walked through the maze of rooms, Susan rolled out the rest of her canned speech.

"What time is dinner?" Maggie asked innocently.

"We only serve dinner during ski season," Susan said.

Maggie gave me an uncertain glance, then looked back at our hostess. "I just assumed that since we weren't here as guests—"

"There're a lot of nice restaurants in town. We have a blackboard by the kitchen where guests rate them. Take a look before you go out tonight. Breakfast is served from eight until ten. You won't go hungry," she said.

As we hadn't had lunch, and weren't going to be offered dinner, I had my doubts. Our freebie weekend was beginning to look like an expensive venture. Would Susan present us with a bill when it came time to leave?

We followed her back to the cubbyhole where Nadine had given us the brush off. She grabbed a key from the desk drawer. "Follow those stairs to the second floor. You're in number six. I'll be here in the office if you need me."

Guests had to haul their own bags. Maggie and I went out to the car and grabbed as much as we could carry for the first trip, leaving the bulk of the camera equipment in the trunk.

Susan wasn't kidding when she said we'd have the most intimate room. Intimate as in small, and also one of the inn's unfinished rooms, although the tiny bathroom did have a working sink and toilet. The shower stall was half-built—the tiles still in a box on the floor. Freshly spackled walls awaited a fresh coat of paint. Fine plaster dust coated the sink and edges of the room that someone's hasty clean-up had missed. One battered, hard-backed chair sat next to the double bed, which was covered with a faded floral spread. The closet had no hangers. We'd have to live out of our suitcases.

Maggie held up well until we finished unloading our stuff. She looked around the tiny room and her eyes brimmed with tears.

"What wrong?" I asked.

"Everything. Susan's welcome was anything but warm. We have to fend for our meals. This room is so small we can hardly turn around and—" she bounced on the mattress, "—the bed is uncomfortable."

I sat beside her. She was right. The mattress felt like concrete. "So we'll eat cheap." I tried to sound light-hearted, like the whole thing was an adventure. I wiped away her tears and kissed her. "Of course, we could just go home."

She sniffled. "Home?"

"If the town's booked up we might have to drive another hour or two to find a room for the night, but it can be done."

"I don't want to go home. I promised the magazine a review of a Vermont inn. I can't set up anything else before my deadline."

"Okay," I backed off, "it was just a thought. We'll finish the work as soon as we can, and in the evenings we'll take advantage of whatever the inn has to offer. Okay?"

"Okay." She wiped her eyes, regaining her composure. "Susan's attitude shouldn't surprise me. She never knew how to be a real friend. After all these years, I hoped she would have mellowed."

"Let's try to enjoy the time we're here. And if we don't—we'll be home in a couple of days anyway. We can stand just about anything for a couple of days, can't we?"

Maggie nodded and I felt her tension ease, replaced by curiosity. "Why did you ask Susan about murder?"

"This place is giving off screwy vibes," I admitted.

"It happened a long time ago, right?" She sounded hopeful.

"I don't know."

For a moment she looked worried, then her expression brightened. "I'm not going to think about it. Remember what happened at the antique store?"

Did I ever. Troubled by visions of death, I'd gone back to the store two or three times. Finally, the owner told me the history behind the chalice, a prop in a long-running production of Hamlet. The actors must've been truly gifted for those dark feelings to be so strong.

I looked at my watch. "We'd better get started. But first, let's grab some cookies from the dining room."

"Jeff?" Her voice stopped me. "I love you a lot."

I leaned over to kiss her again. "I love you, too." I hugged her and she held me tightly. "It'll work out, Maggs. It will," I assured her.

Then why didn't I believe it?

TWO

I decided to take advantage of the late afternoon light—especially since I didn't know what the weather might be like the rest of the weekend. I wanted a shot of the main entrance, but to get it we had to do some spruce-up gardening.

Nadine showed us where to find the pruning shears, a broom and bushel basket. I trimmed hedges while Maggie dead-headed the annuals. She also swept the walk and allowed me to brush away the spider webs on the shingled exterior, a job she wasn't keen on doing. Once the entrance looked inviting, I set up the tripod and snapped away, looking much more professional than I felt.

Cars came and went. While we didn't actually meet any of the other guests, we nodded a hello to the curious few who passed on their way in or out of the place.

It was nearly sunset by the time we packed up the equipment and crowded it into our room. By then all we were interested in was finding a place to chow down. We came across a convenience store in the village, bought a sub sandwich and a couple of Cokes, and feasted in the front seat of my car.

Maggie was quiet, radiating waves of disappointment and embarrassment. I feel like an emotional leech when I glom onto someone else's feelings, and I seldom tune into the more joyful end of the emotional spectrum.

I reached over and touched her shoulder. "Maggs, it's

not your fault."

"Yes it is. I didn't clarify with Susan what was expected. I didn't cement the deal in writing, and now we're doing yard work and eating in your car—" She let out a ragged breath.

"Hey, we're together, that's all that matters. Next time it'll be different."

She met my gaze. "Next time?"

I gave her a smile. "I have this funny feeling...."

"Next time," she murmured, warming to the idea.

After we'd finished eating, I tossed the remains into a trash barrel outside the store, got back in the car and pulled onto the highway.

"Do you think we'll have time to take a drive and just enjoy the scenery?" Maggie asked.

I shook my head. "We knew it would be a working vacation. We just didn't know how much work it would actually be."

"What will we tell the other guests?"

"The truth. We're there to take pictures for a magazine article. We'll spend time in the common rooms, and you'll get a real feel for the place. That'll make your article even better."

The motels, restaurants, and small shopping plazas petered out the further north we went. As we rounded a bend in the road, I suddenly thought of my brother, Richard. With the thought came an unsettling sense of urgency. Was it tied to that premonition of death I'd experienced earlier?

I didn't want to think about it.

A Mercedes, a Cadillac, a BMW, and a red hot Camaro lined the Sugar Maple's driveway. When the Dawson's completed renovating the other rooms, they'd need to come up with better parking arrangements. I left my aging Chevy sedan in back, noticing how shabby it looked in comparison.

Maggie went back to our room to freshen up and I headed to the lower level for coffee and a couple of cookies. I sat at one of the tables, scoping out the warm, pleasant dining room. Unlike the overdone lobby, here the antiques, cheerful wallpaper, and lamps with candle-like flicker bulbs, lent an air of comfort.

A miniature Christmas village sat on a wide table at the room's perimeter. Ceramic houses, shops, and churches flanked a plastic paved road. Working stoplights and street lamps glowed while porcelain skaters, whirling on a mirror pond, gave the pseudo town life. Susan had big bucks tied up in the display, which played on the beauty of the area, reminding guests that ski season was just around the corner. With blazing logs in the fireplace and a hot toddy in hand, the inn would indeed be a very romantic setting. Too bad when winter arrived we'd be back in snowy Buffalo, which had none of Stowe's ambiance.

I could set up the tripod just about anywhere in the room and get pleasing shots—that is if I could light it properly. Digital cameras are great in low-light situations, but what the average person considered great and a photo editor considered print quality were two different things. After the breakfast rush, and with a little help from either Susan or one of her staff, Maggie could dress the tables to give the appearance of a sumptuous feast. Maybe if we moved the village display a little to the right....

I was still pondering various photographic scenarios when Maggie arrived. She'd brought the novel she was reading, as well as a pad of paper and a felt-tipped pen.

"You must be a mind reader," I said, as she handed me the tablet.

"I figured you might want to sketch the placement of the lights."

"It sounds like you think I know what I'm doing."

"We can at least go through the motions," she teased, taking a seat across from me at the table.

An older, silver-haired woman, dressed in gray slacks and a bulky turquoise sweater, entered. Her sweater's bright color only emphasized her waxy complexion.

"Ah, good, coffee," she said, with a trace of an English accent. She poured a cup, snagged a napkin and a couple of cookies, and turned. "Would you mind?" she asked, indicating an empty chair at our table.

"No," I said.

She sat and offered me her hand. Warm and dry to the touch, the woman broadcasted a flood of conflicting emotions—excitement, trepidation, and a sense of anticipation. I took a ragged breath and forced a smile. God, I hate when that happens.

"Eileen Marshall," she said.

"Jeff Resnick," I managed. "And this is Maggie Brennan."

She shook Maggie's hand, too. "I saw you and your photography equipment outside earlier. Susan says you're doing an article on the inn."

"Yes," Maggie said.

"Where will it be published?"

"I freelance for Country Lifestyles," Maggie said, not mentioning her day job as a contract secretary at one of Buffalo's banks.

"I work in the publishing field and am always on the lookout for new talent," she said.

Maggie brightened. "Oh?"

"I worked for Hearst Publications for many years in their New York office. I'm currently a consultant and still have many contacts in Manhattan. Occasionally I help authors and photographers place their work." She took out a business card and handed it to Maggie, then took a bite of cookie. "Hmm. Very good. You'll mention these in your piece, won't you?"

"Yes," Maggie said, studied the card, and then tucked it in her book before she got up to pour a cup of decaf and grab a cookie.

"Are you here for business or pleasure?" I asked Eileen.

"Both. Still, I can use a few days holiday," she explained. She did look tired. As I studied her thin face, I got the feeling she really wasn't well at all.

"Have you met any of the other guests?" Maggie asked, taking her seat once more.

"A few," Eileen said. "I've been here before. People trickle in all evening. They seem to congregate downstairs between nine and ten. Susan and Zack leave a bottle of sherry out on the bar. It helps break the ice."

"Too bad Brenda's missing this," I said. "My sister-in-law," I explained for Eileen's benefit. "She's the sherry drinker in the family."

"I've visited many New England inns, but I have a special affection for the Sugar Maple," Eileen said. "We had a splendid time in the hot tub last spring. Very relaxing."

We?

"I guess I must've missed it during the tour," I said.

"It's out by the pool," she said.

"It sounds heavenly," Maggie said wistfully.

The conversation waned. I sipped the last of my coffee while Maggie nibbled her cookie. Footsteps descended the stairs, accompanied by laughter. Eileen looked at her watch. "Right on time. Shall we meet some of the others?"

I was content to sit on my ass and be thoroughly antisocial, but Maggie looked hopeful. "Why not," I said, and pushed back my chair.

We cut through the large, bright, utilitarian kitchen, depositing our dirty cups in the deep porcelain sink. Various sized skillets hung in orderly fashion over a center island. Plates, bowls, and glasses lined open shelves within easy reach. Antique cooking utensils decorated open spaces on the walls, including an impressive array of heavy, wooden mashers, standing like toy soldiers on a shelf over the sink. Several pictures of a large sailboat were taped to the stainless steel shelving. Its name: *Sea Nymph*. Exiting to the barroom, so called because of the large, knotty pine bar dominating one wall, we followed the voices into the next room.

An attractive woman, maybe half a decade older than Maggie, barely noticed our entrance. She wore the clothes of a twenty-something—a form fitting mini skirt and a low-cut blouse—and had the body to go with them. She held a pool cue in one hand, her eyes fixed on a much younger man, who racked the balls for a game. She looked at him with a restless hunger that her air of sophistication couldn't disguise.

"Hi," he said. Tanned and good-looking, he had an athlete's physique. His sun-streaked brown hair and even white teeth were perfect, and his vivid blue eyes were almost as striking as Maggie's. He looked like he belonged on a billboard somewhere. He was probably twenty-four—twenty-six at the most—and at least twenty years younger than his companion.

"Hello," Eileen said. "We were having coffee in the dining room when we heard you come downstairs. I'm Eileen Marshall."

The woman turned away, her face filled with sudden anger, but the younger man shook Eileen's offered hand. "Ted Palmer." He indicated the woman. "This is my friend, Laura Ross."

"How do you do," Eileen said good-naturedly.

Laura eyed her coldly, and then let her gaze fall back to the table.

I finished the introductions and Ted thrust his hand at me. I grasped it and the floodgates opened once again.

Emotions and sensations burst upon me—chief among them was boredom.

I hate when that happens. Time seems to stop and I never know how long I've stood there with my mouth open, looking foolish. I yanked my hand back and glanced at Laura. Despite the age difference, I knew these two were lovers.

Ted scrutinized Eileen's face. "Were you here Fourth of July weekend?" At Eileen's nod, he said, "I thought I remembered you."

"Laura Ross..." Maggie repeated. "Aren't you the editor of American Woman magazine?"

"Former editor."

"She's taking a well-deserved break," Ted finished for her.

"Did you arrive today?" Laura asked stiffly, her gaze riveted on Maggie.

"This afternoon."

"They're doing a magazine article on the inn," Eileen volunteered. "I'm sure we'll all be interested in reading it when it comes out."

Why did she suddenly sound so snide?

Laura ignored her. "Is this your first time here?"

"Yes. It's very nice," Maggie said.

Laura glanced around the room. "Not as exclusive as some of the other inns in the area, but there's a peacefulness here that fills your soul."

As one sensitive to such things, I could've disputed that claim, but I kept my mouth shut. Eileen merely rolled her eyes.

"It sounds like you've been here many times," Maggie said.

"I've been coming to Stowe since I was a child. I've known several of the inn's past owners. Susan and Zack have done a marvelous job renovating the place. It really is lovely." The words were perfect—it was the delivery that sounded sour.

Ted set the rack aside and grabbed a cue from the wall. "Don't let us hold you up," I said, feeling the need to escape.

"We'll see you later," Maggie said brightly.

Neither of them seemed particularly sorry to see us go.

"Let me show you the hot tub," Eileen offered, sliding back into her friendly persona, and led us through another quaint room. "This is the sun room."

And aptly named because of the bank of windows on three sides. The rustic woodwork looked and smelled spanking new. Comfortable overstuffed chairs were grouped for conversation. An old maple table, refinished and suitably distressed, held a checkerboard. Shelves filled with old books and collectibles lined another wall.

Eileen walked us out the French doors into the backyard. Spotlights were trained on the pool and the swirling waters of the oval hot tub, which looked large enough to seat six. Clean, white towels were draped over patio chairs. The whole setup looked inviting.

"Can I tempt you?" Eileen asked, looking at Maggie.

"I'm game," Maggie said.

Something in my gut held me back. Besides, getting naked in front of strangers isn't my idea of a good time. "I don't think so."

"Oh, come on, Jeff, it'll be fun," Maggie insisted.

"Maybe tomorrow night."

"Suit yourself," Eileen said, disappointed. "Perhaps tomorrow you'll want to check out the trail that circles the property. It goes past the creek and through the woods. It's a pleasant walk."

"Sounds great," Maggie said.

It was almost ten o'clock and I was tired. "What say we call it a night?" I asked Maggie.

"All right," she said, and smiled at Eileen. "See you at

breakfast."

"Good night, my dear."

We left her, and I took Maggie's hand, leading her back into the inn and up the stairs to the main floor. I wanted to head straight for our room, but Maggie paused at the landing. "More people," she whispered, and was off before I could protest.

The older woman we'd seen earlier, again sat on the plush loveseat. Across from her in a wing chair sat an overweight, balding, weary-looking man of about the same age, thumbing through an old issue of National Geographic. An old-fashioned glass filled with amber liquid—scotch I guessed—sat on the table next to him.

"Hi," Maggie said. The woman looked up from her novel but said nothing. "I'm Maggie Brennan and this is my friend, Jeff Resnick."

"Nice to meet you," the man in the wing chair said. An air of defeat seemed to hover around him. "Fred Andolina, and this is my wife, Kay."

"How do you do," Kay said stiffly. She looked at Maggie with downright suspicion. Then her gaze drifted to me and she stared, as though memorizing my face.

"It sure was a gorgeous day," Maggie said, trying to inject life into the already doomed conversation.

"Yes," the woman said, her eyes still fixed on me, making me feel downright uncomfortable.

"We're just here for the weekend—" Maggie blathered.

The woman finally looked away. "How nice," she said, an edge to her voice. Her gaze dipped back to her book. It seemed like she was nearly as unnerved as me.

Maggie seemed to have missed the little staring contest. Puzzled, she just stood there. I snagged her arm. "Come on, Maggs."

"Good night," she tried, but there was no answer from the two.

We were on a different—lower—economic level than the other guests in the place. Our clothes, our car—we— were totally outclassed. My millionaire brother, Richard, had fewer pretenses and more money than all of them put together, but his manners were better. I guess that's the difference between his old money and Susan's nouveau riche clientele.

I started up the stairs and stopped so fast that Maggie nearly ran into me. "Damn. I just remembered, I promised Brenda I'd call to let her know we got here."

"Well, one of the charms of a country inn is there're no phones in the rooms." Would my cell phone even get a signal so close to the mountains? Maggie was thinking the same thing. "If you can't get a signal, they actually have a pay phone down by the kitchen," she said.

I gave her the room key. "I'll only be a few minutes."

"Okay." She sounded depressed.

"Don't let that stuck-up bitch upset you. You're every bit as good as anyone here. We both are."

"I love you," she whispered, kissed me quickly, and started back up the stairs.

I made my way to the kitchen, and out the back door. No one was in the pool or hot tub. I pulled out my cell phone and found I'd forgotten to charge it. Had I brought the charger? I went back inside, which wasn't exactly private, but even if I drove down the road, was I likely to find another pay phone? Ted and Laura still played pool, but their voices seemed far away. I dropped in a couple of quarters and dialed.

I'd fibbed to Maggie. I hadn't promised my sister-in-law I'd call, but I felt a need to connect with my home base. Besides, the weird feelings I'd gotten from Eileen gave me an excuse to ask a medical question. Since my brother's a doctor and my sister-in-law's a nurse, it didn't matter who answered the phone.

An operator came on the line. "Collect call from Jeff,"

I said. The phone rang three times before Brenda picked up and accepted the charges.

"Hi, Brenda. Is Rich around?"

"He went to Antonetta's to pick up a pizza. What's up?"

I glanced at my watch: It was 10:10. Kind of late for a pizza—at least for them. "Can you get infected from being in a hot tub?"

"Whoa, you don't waste time with small talk."

"Sorry."

"The answer is, of course," she said, sounding flip. "There're lots of organisms that can live very nicely in that environment."

"Such as?"

"I once read about a whole cruise ship that was exposed to Legionnaire's Disease. It was airborne. They traced it to the hot tubs. If someone has chlamydia they can spread via a hot tub. I'd stay away from it if I were you."

"Okay. Thanks."

"Has somebody there got a social disease?"

"Maybe. I don't know for sure."

"Uh-huh." She didn't push for more answers. "So what's the place like?" she asked, her interest genuine.

"Okay, but not all it's cracked up to be." I told her about the inferior accommodations that we, as unpaid help, had been given. Then I told her about cleaning up the front of the house to take the photo.

"If that's the way they are, don't you dare set foot in that hot tub."

"I won't. Is everything okay at home?"

"Nothing to complain about. Is that all?" She knew me well.

"I've got a feeling something big is going to happen. I'm getting very weird impressions."

Brenda was well acquainted with the consequences

that followed my funny feelings. Her tone changed to concern. "Be careful, Jeffy." She's always called me that. "When are you coming home?" She was starting to sound like my mother.

"Monday."

"Okay," she said. "Take care of my girlfriend, now."

"I will. Say hi to Rich for me. Tell him—" I hesitated, remembered that sense of urgency I'd felt earlier when we'd passed that curve on the highway.

"Jeffy?" she prompted.

"Tell him ... to eat a slice of pizza for me."

"Okay, hon," she said, not disguising her worry. "Bye-bye."

"Bye." I hung up.

I was glad I'd called, but talking to her hadn't reassured me. Like a kid away from home for a first-time sleep over, I found I missed Richard and Brenda.

Was it them or the safety and security they represented?

I took the back route through the kitchen to the stairs that led to the living room.

What was I afraid of anyway?

That was it. I just didn't know.

THREE

The Andolinas had left the living room by the time I made it back upstairs, and I realized that Susan and the elusive Zack hadn't made an appearance all evening. It looked like I was never going to meet our host, which suited me fine. But then the door to the Dawson's residence opened and they headed straight for me. I made like I hadn't seen them and took another step, but Susan's voice stopped me.

"Jeff, this is my husband, Zack."

I stepped down. Just looking at the guy gave me the creeps. Tall and lanky, he had a shock of pure white, perfectly trimmed hair that formed a halo around his thin, smooth face. His sly expression reminded me of a used car salesman. He extended his hand, his smile as phony as a three dollar bill. "Glad to meet you, Jeff."

Courtesy demanded I shake hands and, as anticipated, I got another unwanted blast of emotion. Anger, tinged with desperation, boiled from him. An argument—over money. A matter of survival. The intensity startled me, and I quickly pulled back my hand, stuffing it in my jeans pocket.

"Susan says there's a problem with the photography." There was no mistaking the challenge in Zack's voice.

"No problem. Except for time. We'll set up in the dining room after breakfast tomorrow. Then we'll get some shots of the common areas."

"I spoke with Ms. Marshall," Susan said. "You can take pictures of her room tomorrow morning while she conducts business off the premises. I'll have Nadine make up her room first and you can get started right after breakfast." For all the sweetness in her voice, her eyes seemed sharp as a raven's.

"Fine."

"Is your room okay?" Zack asked, to taunt or to placate?

"Not really. Do any of the other unfinished rooms have a working shower?"

He shook his head. "Sorry. Plumbing's next on the agenda. But let me know if you have any other problems."

As Maggie and I were just a means to an end for them—free publicity—they could have put a little more effort into assuring our comfort. What did Maggie feel she owed this woman?

"It's been a long day," I said.

"Even longer for us. We've been working since dawn," Zack said.

Maggie and I were on the road long before sun up. Didn't he realize how far we'd driven? Hadn't Susan told him about the yard work we'd done? Hadn't he even noticed?

I squelched my anger. "Good night," I said, and turned back for the stairs. I wanted to close my eyes and lose myself to eight blessed hours of unconsciousness. Something told me it wouldn't happen that easily.

The door to our room was ajar. I closed and locked it behind me—a useless gesture, as the flimsy lock could probably be opened with a toothpick. Maggie was on the bed, lying on top of the spread, reading her book. Clad in her filmy satin nightgown, she looked far more charming than any of the surroundings, making me wish I didn't feel so tired.

Maggie turned the page of her novel, not bothering to look up. "Are you sure you don't want to use the hot tub? It's a great way to relax."

I leaned against the door. "I don't want to smell like chlorine. Especially since we don't have a shower."

"Oh ... I guess you're right." She sounded disappointed.

I was tempted to blame her for everything that had gone wrong. But how could I when she was just as much a victim of the place?

"I met our host."

She looked up, my tone warning her of my mood. "You don't sound impressed."

"Let's just say he and Susan deserve each other."

She closed her book, tensing for a fight. But that's not what I wanted.

"There's some serious anger going on between them, only I can't tell where it's directed," I said. "I hope you don't mind, but I don't want to spend a lot of time with either of them."

"I'm sorry."

I pushed away from the door and sat on the edge of the hard bed, kicking my shoes off. "Don't keep apologizing." It came out sounding a lot sharper than I'd meant. She glanced away, her eyes filling with tears.

"I'm sorry, Maggs. Please don't cry. There's so much emotion spilling out of every corner of this place, it makes me feel sick."

She wiped a hand across her eyes. "It doesn't take a psychic to know we're not really wanted here."

I winced at her use of the 'p' word.

"Hey—" I pulled her close. "I want you. I think you're the prettiest, most desirable, nicest person here."

She blinked back tears as mirth brightened her eyes. "You're only saying that because it's true."

I pulled back. Her funny, little-girl smile made me

laugh. "No more apologies. We'll make the best of it. We'll go home, and next weekend we'll go on vacation in my loft. I'll cook you wonderful dinners—" Her eyes rolled at that boast. "—and pamper you, and we'll take long showers together in my fully functional bathroom."

Her smile broadened. I kissed the tip of her nose and rose from the bed, peeled off my shirt, and headed for the bathroom.

"It's not fair," she called. "You've got a shortcut to knowing if you should trust or even like people."

"I can't read everybody. I can't always read you. I can't read Richard at all. Just sometimes I know some things about some people. Unfortunately, I seem to know a lot of things about a lot of the people here."

She padded to the bathroom door, watching me as I finished undressing. "If you know so much, tell me just one thing about one person."

I turned to the mirror over the sink. "No."

"Why not?"

"It'll not only change the way you think about that person, but the way you act toward him or her, too. And you can't do that. You have to give people their privacy."

"Why?"

"Because it's just good manners." I wasn't getting through to her. I squirted toothpaste on my toothbrush. "I don't feel comfortable blabbing what I know about people. It's not stuff they'd want you to know. It's like Big Brother watching. Nobody should have to worry about that."

I began to brush my teeth, but I could see she wasn't appeased. I spit and caught sight of her reflection in the mirror. "Just what do you know about Laura Ross?" I asked.

"Only her name. Not that I'm a fan of that magazine. It's a bit pretentious for me."

"Pretentious? With a name like American Woman?"

"More like the American Woman Snob. It's not something *this* American woman can relate to." Her eyes were wide, and I could see my diversion wasn't successful. "Come on, Jeff. Tell me something about one of the other guests," she pleaded as I put my toothbrush back into my travel kit. "Please, Jeff?" She sounded like a little kid.

I tried not to meet her gaze, because Maggie's blue eyes can bore right through to my soul, I weaken and almost always regret it.

"Jeff?"

I looked at her and let out a weary sigh. "Okay. Eileen Marshall isn't here for just a business trip. She came here to meet her married lover."

"Mr. Andolina?" she guessed. They were roughly the same age.

I shook my head.

She turned away. "What a bitch, trying to steal someone's husband." Maggie's marriage had been destroyed by an interloper, only her husband had been attracted to another man—not a woman.

"See, I told you it would change the way you think about her. A couple of minutes ago you thought she was a charming woman, and probably hoped she'd help you sell your writing."

"That was before I found out she's trying to destroy someone's marriage."

"Maggie, you don't know that."

"Why else would you come to the same inn as your lover and his wife if you didn't want to break up the marriage?"

"I don't know. And you don't know. If Eileen's lover was a cheat, he was a cheat before he got here."

"Who? Who is it?"

"I don't know, and I don't want to know. Besides, Eileen's lover may have nothing to do with anyone at the inn. It could be someone who lives in the area."

"Well, if I knew, I'd tell the wife. She deserves to know."

"It's not fair to judge people without knowing all the facts."

"Now you sound like Richard."

"Thanks for the compliment." I switched off the bathroom light. "Can we just go to bed?"

"To sleep?" she asked, disappointed, but she was still radiating anger as she folded down the bedspread.

"If you don't mind."

Maggie wouldn't look at me. She turned off the overhead light, got into bed and pulled the sheet up to her shoulder, her back toward me. I crawled in and stared at the darkened ceiling, counting to ten. Rolling onto my side, I put my arm around her and we lay together like spoons. Her anger had cooled, and her hand snaked down to clasp my arm. "'Night, Jeff."

"Good night, love."

Time dragged.

Maggie's body relaxed as she drifted off to sleep. Tired as I was, my mind refused to shut down. I found myself analyzing all the odd emotions I'd encountered from the people I'd met that day.

And I wondered which one of them was going to die.

FOUR

"Hot water," I groaned, staring at the ceiling the next morning. I literally had to pull myself out of that bed, which would've been right at home in a medieval torture chamber. The fact that I couldn't linger under a shower to ease the ache in my back and shoulders didn't improve my mood.

Maggie straightened painfully, her lips tight. She didn't complain, although I could tell she was hurting as much as me.

We took turns at the bathroom sink. I heard water running in the other bathrooms on the floor below us, and swallowed a pang of jealousy. With the liberal use of deodorant, I was sure we wouldn't offend any of the other guests. Maggie had a hard time rinsing the shampoo from her hair. We only had two small towels and I was determined to get more, even if I had to strangle Susan.

By the time we ventured down to the dining room, two other couples were already there. We hadn't met them the night before, but I waved a perfunctory hello to the young couple closest to the entrance. They looked as out-of-place as Maggie and me. Their clothes said they couldn't afford it, and they looked too young to appreciate the experience. The well-tanned, muscular guy had a huge plate of food before him, shoveling eggs into his mouth, while his blonde companion applied ruby polish to her nails. An empty muffin cup sat on a napkin before her.

The other couple, probably ten years older than the first, seemed engrossed in each other—perhaps they were there on a romantic get-away as Susan's brochure suggested. The pretty, longhaired brunette gazed into her companion's eyes, enraptured.

Maggie and I headed for the coffee pots. Pouring our own, we settled at one of the empty tables. "Now what?" I asked, looking toward the kitchen. "Do they serve us like in a restaurant?"

"Some inns and larger B and Bs have a buffet," Maggie offered.

Revived by the aroma of bacon and sausage, I knew food had to be nearby.

A beefy kid in his early twenties, with sandy-colored hair and dark eyes, came out of the kitchen and placed a pitcher of orange juice on the sideboard next to the coffee pots. A tattoo of a large pink rose, pierced by a dagger dripping blood, decorated his bulging bicep.

He noticed us and strolled over. "Hi, I'm Adam."

"Nice tattoo," I said.

The kid actually blushed and yanked his sleeve down. "Not really. I'm saving to get it removed. Laser treatments aren't cheap, though." He cleared his throat. "Our buffet has scrambled eggs, bacon, sausage, home fries, fresh fruit, strudel, and three kinds of muffins. Zack's making blueberry pancakes or omelets. What'll you have?"

"I'll take the blueberry pancakes."

"May I have a Western omelet?" Maggie asked.

"Sure thing. While you're waiting, you can check out the buffet." He pointed toward the kitchen. "Follow me."

The kitchen radiated warmth and hospitality. Whatever hostility I'd sensed from Zack the night before was either suppressed or gone. Stationed at the big commercial stove, he wore a ratty old sailor's cap while flipping pancakes and nursing omelets along. He kept staring at yet another picture of the *Sea Nymph* that was taped to the stove hood, while across the way Nadine, the young woman we'd spoken to on our arrival, washed dishes. Adam gave Zack our order and resumed chopping vegetables at the counter.

Maggie and I each took a plate and perused the stainless steel warming trays on the center island. Just as Adam said, there was enough food to feed an army. And as Susan had promised the day before, we wouldn't go hungry at breakfast. If I ate enough, maybe I could save on a lunch tab.

Maggie chose carefully—a carrot muffin, two sausages and a single pat of butter. Since I wasn't getting paid for my labor, and still suffered from that rock disguised as a bed, I loaded my plate with bacon and a piece of strudel, determined Zack and Susan would pay for our services, if only in food. My eyes were bigger than my stomach, however, and I was stuffed by the time Zack brought my pancakes and Maggie's omelet to the table.

The daytime Zack was different from the hard-nosed businessman I'd met the night before. He stopped at the other tables, chatting with the guests, refilling coffee cups. Jovial, he was the positive yang to Susan's dour yin. Confusing, but I decided to concentrate on the pancakes before me instead of our host. Even though I could only eat half of what was on my plate, by the time Adam cleared the table I was so full I could barely move. Maggie's smile of contentment gave me warm fuzzy feelings.

"We have to get to work, love," I said. "Susan said we could take pictures of Eileen's room this morning. Then we can do the dining room."

"Do you think she's already gone for the day?"

"Let's find out."

We headed for the living room and the reception area. Susan sat in front of her computer, half glasses poised on her nose, looking older than she had the day before.

"Hi," Maggie said. "When's a good time for us to take pictures of Eileen's room?"

Susan looked up at us over her glasses. "About eleven o'clock. Ms. Marshall has already left for her meeting. Once breakfast is over, Nadine will make up the room and you can set up."

I glanced at my watch: it was already 9:30. Oh well, that gave us a little time to check out the countryside. "Sounds good. After that, I'd like to shoot the dining room. Can Zack save muffins or anything else to approximate breakfast?"

"No problem," Susan said, sounding almost affable. With a little work, maybe she'd be a decent human being. I pushed my luck.

"Great. By the way, could we have more than two towels? Even though we don't have a working shower, we need—"

"Yes," she said curtly, and turned back to her computer. So much for being a decent human being.

More or less satisfied, I turned to Maggie. "How about a short tour of the town?"

"I'd love it."

I went back to the room, grabbed the camera, and off we went.

We were about a mile from the inn when I slowed the car and took special note of the countryside. Something about it bothered me. Maggie looked around, puzzled. A car horn blasted behind us, so I stepped on the gas.

"Did I miss something?" she asked.

I was still in a fog. "What?"

"Why'd you slow down?"

"I don't know. There's something about—"

"Uh-oh, you're not getting one of those funny feelings of yours, are you?" She knew that meant trouble.

"No. It's just—" I groped for a plausible lie. "I was

wondering why Susan and Zack didn't buy a place closer to the village?"

"That's easy. Money. The farther from the village you are, the less the price. Also the less you can charge your guests. But if you think about it, in the winter they're actually closer to Mt. Mansfield. If you're a skier it all works out; and maybe they can squeeze more out of those guests."

I nodded, concentrating on the road, but I could feel her eyes on me—studying me—until she finally looked away. I knew my lie hadn't fooled her, but she chose not to mention it.

Stowe's a quaint little New England town, but more commercial than some of the smaller villages. With an almost European feel, its Victorian houses turned into storefronts, and shops with creaky wooden floors, exude old-fashioned country charm. The town survives on tourism in the summer and skiing in the winter, but there's no denying the surrounding scenery is beautiful no matter what the season.

Although most of the shops were just opening, the streets were already filled with tourists. We found a parking space in the municipal lot.

Strolling down the sidewalk, we paused in front of a clothing shop, its carved doorway painted to look like gold leaf. Although the summer wasn't quite over, the energetically posed mannequins in the window were already wearing $300 ski sweaters, looking like they might abandon the village and hit the slopes at any moment. Despite my lack of enthusiasm, Maggie dragged me inside to admire the designer wear.

"Isn't there a bookstore we can go to? Something at least marginally interesting?"

She grabbed an Aran sweater from a table and held it against my chest. "You'd look terrific in this. It goes so well with your eyes."

The tag caught my attention. "Yeah, and it would take me at least two paychecks just to buy it."

With a martyr's sigh, she folded the sweater and replaced it on the table, then looked around the place.

"Can I help you?" a young woman asked. College student—or one of the marginally employed locals, I guessed.

"No, thanks. Just looking," Maggie said.

She nodded, and started to refold the sweater Maggie had just put down on the counter.

Maggie wandered down the aisle, and then pointed toward the back of the store. Ted Palmer was admiring himself in a three-sided mirror while Laura Ross looked on critically. He studied his reflection from all angles, pulling on the sleeve of a green sport coat.

"Come on," Maggie whispered. She grabbed my hand and tugged me after her, darting amongst the clothing racks. Crouching low, we duck-walked along the aisle until we could hear their conversation.

"Maggie, this is stupid."

"No, it's fun!" She motioned for me to keep still.

"I don't know," Laura said. "Maybe you should try the blue one on again."

"Or I could just take both," Ted said.

"Do you believe him?" Maggie mouthed.

"No. And what's more, I don't care. I feel ridiculous. Can we get out of here?"

"May I help you?"

A pair of polished Florshiems appeared next to me and I looked up at a tall, elegantly dressed gentleman.

"Uh, I dropped something," I said, while Maggie smiled sweetly at him. I straightened, cleared my throat, and helped Maggie to stand.

"Is there something I can show you?" the salesman persisted.

I risked a glance over my shoulder and saw Laura looking at me as though I'd just mooned the joint. "Uh, no. In fact, we were just leaving."

I grabbed a giggling Maggie by the arm and steered her toward the entrance.

"Do you mind telling me what that was all about?" I asked once we were out on the crowded sidewalk.

She frowned. "I'm sorry. It's just ... the inn is filled with such stuffed shirts, I needed to cut loose. Are you mad at me?"

I gave her what I hoped was a stern look. She struggled to keep a straight face, but I was the first to crack. "Yes, but it isn't the first time and it won't be the last."

"Spying on the rich folks?" came a voice at the doorway. It was the young woman who'd greeted us when we'd first arrived.

Maggie's cheeks flushed. "Were we that obvious?"

She laughed. "I'm afraid so."

"They're staying at the same place we are," Maggie volunteered.

I nodded toward the lovebirds. "Do they come here often?"

"She dropped a couple grand the other day. Hadn't seen them before that."

"Won't you get in trouble telling us this?" Maggie asked.

She shrugged. "I'm out of here on Monday. Back to school."

"Kathy?" came a male voice from inside the store.

"Gotta go." She schooled her features before heading into the store.

"Two grand," I mused.

"When you've got it, flaunt it," Maggie suggested.

I looked down the street. "Anywhere else you want to go?"

Her gaze traveled across the road to a store placard

that read *Everything Cows.* "How about there?"

Ten minutes later, our shopping expedition was over. Maggie bought black-spotted cow salt-and-pepper shakers as a souvenir of our Vermont trip.

"What'll we do about dinner tonight?"

Maggie clutched her gift bag and shaded her eyes, looking toward a restaurant up the street. "I don't want to eat for a week. How about that place?"

We inspected the menu, and the menus of every other restaurant along the street, trying to narrow down the choices. We came to no conclusions and decided we'd better start back for the inn.

It was close to eleven by the time we hit the road. About a mile from the inn, I again got that sick feeling in the pit of my stomach. I tried to take in as much of the scenery as possible, but could see nothing but trees, meadows, and more trees. Nothing out of the ordinary.

I wanted to believe that odd feeling in my gut was heartburn, but I knew better.

FIVE

"There you are," Susan said, her mouth pursed as we slunk past her like a couple of truants. "Ms. Marshall's room is all ready for you."

She ushered us directly to Eileen's room, which had been restored to move-in order, with her possessions neatly stacked in the closet.

The spacious, attractive corner room had windows on the outside walls. Two double four-poster beds lined an inside wall. Maggie admired all the knickknacks, the coordinating wallcoverings, bedspreads, curtains, and new carpet. A cozy little sitting nook, with a loveseat and cocktail table, beckoned. Most attractive to me was the huge bathroom with a working double shower. Compared to the hole in the wall we'd been assigned, it seemed like we'd stepped into heaven.

We hauled the equipment downstairs and I spent the next two hours setting up. Maggie seemed to be underfoot the whole time. I could've assembled the rig a lot faster if she hadn't been there. But while I fiddled with the umbrellas, she played photo stylist, arranging and rearranging the furniture and bric-a-brac until she achieved feng shui—a thoroughly harmonious composition. I thought she'd been reading too many decorator magazines, but the room did look more inviting for her efforts.

If I'd been a more experienced photographer, I'd have had a laptop on hand to give me a better idea of the results I could expect. A variety of lenses would've been nice, too, but we already had too much money tied up in this little escapade to justify spending another nickel. I took a number of shots from every possible angle and hoped for the best.

Between changing sheets and taking stints on the vacuum cleaner in the other guest rooms, Susan popped in to check our progress. She let us know we were making a much bigger deal out of the job than was necessary.

Actually, the whole process went faster than I would have guessed. If we had to take photos of more of the bedrooms on Monday, perhaps we could leave the inn about one—but that meant we wouldn't get home until early Tuesday morning. Since neither of us had to work Tuesday, it made more sense to stay another night. That is if Susan and Zack were willing. We'd have to negotiate.

While I packed the equipment, Maggie restored Eileen's room to normal, which seemed boring in contrast. Then we carried the equipment downstairs and set up in the dining room.

Compared with the bedroom, the once-homey dining room seemed as welcoming as a cave. I turned on every light in the place, plus my strobes, and still had doubts the photos would come out. Thank goodness for Photoshop. Nadine, the not-so-helpful employee we'd met the day before, had an interest in interior design. She stayed after her regular hours—unpaid, as Susan was quick to remind her—to help Maggie set tables and arrange the food. Susan watched our every move, and I wondered if she thought we'd try to walk off with some of her precious knickknacks.

About mid-way through the set up, I discovered that I had my own audience. Ted, sans his new jacket, parked himself well out of range, studying the whole procedure. It wasn't until Maggie and Nadine fussed with an alternate table setting that he ventured nearer the camera.

"You really know your stuff," he said.

"I wish I did, but I'm taking a good stab at it."

He took in the rented equipment. "Aren't you a pro?"

"Nope. I'm a bartender. We're doing this as a favor for Susan and Zack."

"You mean you're not even getting paid?" he asked, incredulous.

"No."

He frowned. "You don't look like a bartender."

"What's a bartender look like?"

His frown deepened. I decided to cut him some slack. "I was an insurance investigator for a lot of years. But with corporate downsizing and all—" I didn't want to get into all the grim details.

"Yeah. My old man's a big shot at one of the airlines. He's had to let a lot of people go over the years."

"Oh, yeah?"

"I worked for him for a while after college. He kept me on, but he let others go who had twenty or thirty years with the company. People with families, mortgages...." For a moment he seemed to stare at nothing, in what was probably a rare moment of introspection. Was it guilt I read on his face? "I quit," he said. "I mean, why stay at a place where they're ultimately going to trash you?"

"It's those mortgages and families and car payments," I suggested.

He tugged the sleeve of his cashmere sweater. "Yeah, but I found the good life without the pitfalls."

"Laura takes care of you?"

"So far. These older broads are great, aren't they?" he said, nodding toward Maggie across the room.

Now Maggie may be four years older than me, but she's not a broad. "Hey, that's my lady you're talking about."

Ted backed off. "That's cool. I just mean they're grateful for anything they get in the sack—"

"Yeah," I cut him off.

Suddenly the connections on the power packs fascinated me. Ted took the hint and moved a discrete distance, although he continued to watch. Meanwhile, I pondered his reaction. Did Maggie look that much older than me?

My next visitor was the nail-polishing young woman I recognized from breakfast. "Hi," she said, sauntering into the dining room, clad in a black thong bikini, leather sandals, with a beach towel draped over one arm.

"Hi, yourself."

"Do you need a model? I have had some experience. I was almost in a lingerie layout once, but at the last minute they chose another girl. I've been seriously thinking of going to modeling school, though."

"How nice."

I suppose she was pretty, and maybe all of twenty three. Her bleached blond hair had only the barest hint of dark roots. Women with her identical tiny waist and almost nonexistent breasts were always plastered across the sales flyers that came in the newspaper.

"I'm Alyssa Nelson." She offered her hand.

I shook it. Bony—and no impressions. Good. "Jeff Resnick. Nice to meet you."

She leaned her equally bony behind against one of the tables. "I'm here with my boyfriend. I won a contest on the radio. Four nights and five days at the Sugar Maple Inn."

"Where are you from?"

"Long Island. Yeah, it's nice here. But I wish they had heart-shaped tubs. My mom says it's not a major place unless they have heart-shaped tubs."

I would've settled for any kind of a tub. "What do you do on Long Island?" I asked, more out of courtesy than interest.

"I work in a jewelry store. But like I said, I've been seriously thinking of going to modeling school. Doug—that's my boyfriend—he says I could make some good money, and maybe we could travel."

"Where is Doug?" I asked, glancing around.

"By the pool. I just wanted to see if you could use me in any of your shots."

"Sorry, but we're featuring furniture."

"Too bad." She waved a finger at me, her expression filled with hope. "But if you change your mind—"

"I'll let you know." I was still smiling as she walked away. I turned, surprised to find Maggie standing behind me, fists planted on her nicely rounded hips.

"Kind of young for you, isn't she?" Maggie doesn't usually feel threatened by other women, but she tends to be sensitive about our modest age difference.

"Yes, she is. And too skinny for my taste, too. I like my women with a little meat on their bones." I grabbed her by the waist, pulled her close, and kissed her.

"Oh, you," she said and batted my nose. "Let's finish up."

It was after five when I packed the last of the equipment. All that remained was for me to lug it up two flights and then I could take it easy for the rest of the day.

"What will you do tomorrow?" Susan asked, suddenly hovering once again.

"The morning light should be good in the sun room. Or we could do the living room."

"Or both," she suggested.

I sighed wearily. "Or both."

"Great." With that said, she flounced off in the direction of the stairs, presumably to go back to her office to count her earnings, or perhaps berate a member of her staff. Ah, the life of the entrepreneur. Here it was Friday of a long holiday weekend, and already I longed to go back to my boring every-day life in Buffalo.

I noticed when it came time for actual physical labor, my audience of Ted and Nadine had disappeared. It was up to Maggie and me to trudge up all those stairs to stow the equipment. Three trips—and a healthy sweat—later, I plugged the power packs in the room's only outlet, recharging them for the next day's shoot, then flopped on the bed to stare at the ceiling. I longed for a shower.

"Can we go home now?" I begged Maggie.

"Not yet, I'm afraid." She joined me on the bed. "Just one more day, and we can relax all day Sunday. That'll be nice, won't it?"

"It'll have to be." I yanked at my shirt and sniffed. "I'd even be willing to take a bath right now, and all we have is that dinky sink. Boy that friend of yours is a slave driver."

"She's not really a friend," Maggie reminded me. "She was my chem lab partner—the most popular girl in my high school class. And I was—"

"Not?"

She radiated embarrassment. I put my arm around her shoulder and drew her close. "Don't feel bad, love. I was in the same boat. Why don't you tell me what's really bothering you."

She pulled back and stared at the floor. "Back in high school, we toilet-papered the principal's office as our senior prank. Afterwards, they did a locker inspection and found an empty cardboard core in mine."

"Did you do it?"

"Me and about twenty other kids. Susan lied to give me an alibi. If she hadn't, they wouldn't have let me go to the graduation ceremony. My parents would've killed me."

"Did Susan help with the prank?"

"She planned it." Maggie sighed. "You'd think at my age I'd be over all those high school insecurities. I desperately wanted to be popular, like Susan, and have all the boys trailing after me."

"Instead you turned out terrific and she's a bitch. Why compare yourself?"

"Because maybe I'm as bad as she is." She lowered her gaze again. "When Susan dangled this free weekend in front of me—in exchange for the magazine article—she reminded me of my debt to her. But I knew I could sell the article. Getting a picture-spread in even a magazine with crappy distribution would still be great for my resume. It might even help me sell my book on decorating. Only being here hasn't worked out like I thought."

I leaned over to kiss her. "You're being too hard on yourself. You're the best thing that ever happened to me."

She shook her head as though puzzled, but I soaked up her feelings of gratitude and affection. "Did I ever tell you how much I love you?" she said.

"Not in the past few hours." Then she was in my arms. One kiss led to another, and soon my fatigue vanished.

Two hours later we emerged from our room, groomed, dressed and ready to find one of the village's less expensive restaurants.

We passed that deserted stretch of road between the inn and the village and that feeling of foreboding returned with a vengeance. Once or twice was coincidence—three times was a warning, something I couldn't afford to overlook. I knew if I didn't consciously think about it, some idea—or reason—for that feeling would come to me. And I knew Maggie wasn't going to like it.

I'd gotten pretty adept at keeping these flashes of insight from her, but I'd have to introduce the subject during dinner. I had to make a decision about what to do before we went back to the inn.

We pulled into the parking lot of a little Tex-Mex restaurant and headed in. Tastefully decorated with serapes and sombreros on the walls, a saddle draped over a rail, and a mini cactus on every table, it was blessedly unlike most franchise Mexican restaurants.

The place was busy and we waited in the entryway for almost ten minutes before being seated. I looked longingly at the bar and the Corona bottles with fresh lime slices poking out the top. With our tight finances, we'd have to be content with either Maggie's bottle of gin back in the room or the complimentary sherry Zack and Susan offered.

Once seated, we studied the menus for a few minutes before ordering. Maggie waited until the waitress left before she leaned forward and spoke. "Okay, what's bothering you?"

I met her gaze. "I thought I'd hidden it pretty well."

"You can't keep much from me, buster. No, spill it."

I pursed my lips in momentary indecision. "I'm going to call Richard. I want him to come here."

Her eyes narrowed. "What for? We're going home in three days."

"I'm not so sure about that. If we have to wait until Monday to photograph the rest of the bedrooms—"

She ignored my explanation. "Why does Richard have to come to Stowe?"

I shrugged and took a sip of water.

"What will you tell him?"

"I don't know. I never know how to explain these things. But I trust these feelings. I can't ignore them."

"What feelings?"

"I just feel anxious. Like he needs to be here."

"Does this have to do with the murder you asked Susan about?"

"I'm not sure."

"What if he won't come?" Her voice was sharp.

"Then we should leave. Tonight."

"But what about the article? What about the pictures?" She sounded panicked.

"I know. This is one hell of an opportunity for both of us. If the photos turn out, it'll be a great portfolio piece."

Her frown turned into a tentative smile. "Then you're serious about photography?"

"It's more of a career than tending bar. This job is a first step, but photography's a long-term goal. Right now, I feel that Richard needs to be here."

She looked thoughtful. "Are you sure you're not just feeling insecure? You were independent for a long time, and you've had to rely on Richard a lot this past year. He's been almost like a parent to you."

"Don't think I haven't considered it."

I thought I'd bounce back a lot quicker from the mugging six months before. A residual effect of the fractured skull was crippling headaches that often plagued me. I hadn't had a really bad one in over a week, which was a record for me. But I'd also noticed that when my haphazard insights kicked in, the headaches followed with a vengeance.

Maggie touched my hand and dug into her purse for her cell phone setting it on the table. "Eat up. Then go call him."

I nodded, thankful she'd accepted the idea so gracefully.

"Besides, it'll be great to go shopping with Brenda. We could hit the outlets in Rutland while Richard and you do whatever it is you—"

"No. He can't bring Brenda."

"Why not?"

I couldn't explain why I wanted Richard to come—let alone why he should leave Brenda at home. "I ... it wouldn't be good for her."

She looked around the room before speaking. "Are you saying she wouldn't fit in because she's black?"

"No, nothing like that. I just get the feeling she

should stay in Buffalo. You know, keep the home fires burning. Something like that."

Maggie frowned, the disappointment in her eyes inescapable. Luckily the waitress arrived with our food. We ate in silence.

Maggie was still working on her entree when I excused myself and headed for the restaurant's entryway. I dialed and glanced at my watch: 7:30. Richard answered on the second ring.

"Hey, Maggie, what's up?"

"It's me. I forgot to bring my charger, so I'm using Maggie's phone. And not much is up. How're you?"

"Fine." A long pause ensued. "Jeff, what's wrong?"

The moment of truth.

"Rich, can you come to Stowe."

"Why?"

"I'm not sure. I need you to be here. Tomorrow. And I need you to stay for a couple of days."

Another long pause.

"Jeff, you know I volunteer at the clinic on Tuesdays and Wednesdays. They'd have a hard time finding a replacement on such short notice."

"Rich, please come."

The silence lingered for at least ten seconds.

"I can't. I just can't."

I stood there, stunned. Despite Maggie's warning, I hadn't believed he'd actually say no.

"Look, Jeff, I can't turn my life upside down every time you get one of those funny feelings of yours," Richard continued.

I tried to hide my disappointment. "You're right."

A plump woman in a tight black mini dress stood just within earshot, She had her cell phone ready, too. I turned away.

"I'm sure whatever it is that's bothering you will settle itself in a day or two," he said.

"You're probably right." Oh, yeah? Then why did I feel doomed?

The woman moved to stand before me, shifting her weight from foot to foot. Why didn't she just go outside? She glared at me, so I did.

"Look, Maggie's waiting for me, I'd better get back to her. I'll see you on Monday night. Bye." I slapped the phone shut, stabbed the power button to turn it off, and shoved it into my pocket.

I let out a frustrated breath and gazed around the packed parking lot. The twilight deepened. Headlights flashed on the highway. The world would soon come to an end. At least, the world as I knew it. I'd asked a lot of Richard over the past few months, maybe too much, because now, when it really counted, he'd let me down.

That wasn't true. He just didn't understand what this meant to me. How could he? He didn't have that sick feeling in his gut.

By the time I got back to the table, the waitress had cleared the dishes and Maggie was eating some local Ben-And-Jerry's ice cream. She proffered her spoon. "Want a taste?"

I took my seat and shook my head.

"Is he coming?"

"No."

"Oh." She sounded surprised. Subdued, she ate another spoon of ice cream. "You weren't serious about us leaving Stowe, were you?"

"I don't know what to think."

"Well, whatever's bothering you, we'll just have to handle it together. Right?"

I smiled and reached over to squeeze her hand. "Yeah."

But I had a feeling we were already in over our heads.

SIX

We lingered over our coffee. Not that there was an abundance of conversation. Maggie respects my quiet interludes. The waitress, however, hovered anxiously until we finally vacated the table and headed back to the inn.

Maggie drove. I couldn't analyze what I was picking up while behind the wheel, and I didn't want to get us into an accident, either. When we passed that spot in the road, I intended to surrender myself entirely to the feeling, vision—whatever it was—that nagged my psyche.

Maggie braked. I tensed as we approached that familiar stretch of road. The headlights cut a path ahead of us, revealing only the double-yellow line in the highway. Too many shadows obscured the landscape, yet something registered in my mind's eye.

"Colorado!"

"Colorado?" Maggie echoed, eyes still on the road.

"That spot in the road has something to do with Colorado."

"The Rocky Mountains versus the Green Mountains?" Maggie suggested.

"Maybe. It's not even a picture in my mind—just a vague feeling. Damn, it's frustrating only getting one piece of the puzzle at a time."

Maggie pulled into the inn's driveway, parking behind the black BMW with Québec license plates. She took the keys out of the ignition and handed them to me. "You're going to make yourself crazy. Then you'll get one of your sick headaches and neither of us will have any fun. Some vacation."

"Sorry. I won't mention it again."

She frowned. "Don't be like that. You torture yourself with these things and usually they don't amount to anything. Why put yourself through it?"

"I'll try not to think about it. Okay?"

Grudgingly, "Okay." She tried to be more cheerful. "What do you want to do next? Read? Play a game of pool?"

"I haven't played since the night I was mugged."

"Did you win?"

"Yeah," I said thoughtfully, not remembering much else about that evening.

I must've had a weird look on my face, because she reached out to touched my shoulder. "We don't have to play if it brings back painful memories."

"It won't bother me." I smiled, and then wagged a finger at her. "Just don't come after me with a baseball bat if you lose." Hey, I could joke about something that had nearly cost me my life a scant six months before. "Come on, I'll teach you to play Eight Ball."

She followed me inside. No sooner had we opened the door than a voice called out. "Jeff?" It was Zack. "There's a telephone message for you."

I met him halfway across the room, took the yellow post-it note from him. "Thanks." He retreated for the office as I glanced at the slip of paper.

"Well?" Maggie asked.

"It says 'call home.'"

"Richard?"

I nodded.

"I'm going to dump my purse in the room. I'll meet you downstairs, okay?"

She went upstairs while I went out on the back patio to make my call. It took a long time before the Maggie's phone found a signal and I could dial. Richard answered on the first ring. "I didn't expect a message from you," I began.

"And I wasn't expecting a weekend vacation, either," he said sourly.

"Then you'll come?"

"Let's just say if I don't, I'll have a miserable weekend at home."

I couldn't help the broad, idiot grin that spread across my face, or the feeling of triumph that coursed through me. Good old Brenda was always on my side.

"I managed to find someone to cover for me at the clinic, so I guess I'll be there tomorrow." He sounded ... resigned?

"Thanks, Rich. I knew I could count on you." I gave him the directions on how to get to the inn once he got into town. The logistics of actually getting to Stowe were going to be his problem. "Maybe we shouldn't let people know we're related," I suggested.

"Is all this intrigue really necessary?"

"It could work to our advantage."

He sighed. "Whatever you say."

"Thanks," I said, feeling calmer.

"Listen, don't expect me until evening. Will I be able to get a room at the inn?"

"Well, they're booked solid right now."

"Great. Where am I supposed to stay? You do know it's a holiday weekend."

"I know. But I don't think you should worry about it."

"Is this another one of your psychic messages?"

"Yes," I said hurriedly. In retrospect, I should've analyzed that piece of insight a little closer.

"Anything else?"

"Leave Brenda home."

"Oh, she's going to love that. Why?" When I didn't answer immediately, he spoke again. "Is there something you're not telling me?"

"No. It's just ... why risk it?"

"Risk it?" The impatience left his voice—replaced by concern. "Jeff, maybe you and Maggie should just come home."

"It's already too late. Whatever's going to happen ... I think we're supposed to be a part of it."

"Jeff, I don't like the sound of this."

"I don't either." If I had to describe what impending doom felt like, this would be it. I cleared my throat. "See you tomorrow night, right?"

"Yes."

"Thanks, Rich. You're the best."

"Good night, Jeff."

I slapped the phone shut, feeling more relaxed than I had in hours.

Wandering into the barroom, I found Maggie sitting at the old upright piano, flipping through a stack of brittle, yellowed sheet music.

"Do you play?" I asked.

"I used to. But *We'll Kick the Kaiser* doesn't do much for me." She picked out middle C, tapped it and winced. "Sounds like it hasn't been tuned in decades." She changed the subject. "Is he coming?"

"Brenda convinced him."

"That's one you owe her."

"More like a hundred."

She nodded toward the pool table. "Shall we?"

Laura and Ted sat at a table at the end of the game room playing backgammon. "Hi," Maggie said, but the mismatched lovers barely acknowledged our presence.

The snub burned me. For all she tried, it was apparent Maggie's natural friendliness just wasn't appreciated by most of the other guests at the inn—their loss.

Ignoring them, I racked up the table. "The object of the game is to knock the balls into the pocket."

"I got that part," she said, chalking the end of her cue like I'm sure she'd seen hundreds of times on TV, never knowing why.

"The table's divided into quadrants. You place the cue ball—that's this white one—behind the imaginary line that's right about here."

Her stony stare perfectly conveyed her annoyance.

"Why don't we just take turns knocking them into the pockets?" I suggested.

She brightened. "I'll take the striped ones."

"Ladies first." I came up behind her, positioning my arms around her, guiding her movements with the cue stick. "This is called the break shot."

Bemused, she looked at me over her shoulder. "I think I can handle that."

I backed off and she bent over the table, took careful aim and hit the cue ball. It slammed into the fifteen ball with a satisfying smack. The nine ball went into the left corner pocket.

Her eyes shone with pleasure. "How was that?"

"Just fine."

I grabbed a cue stick from the rack—not too badly warped—and stood on the left side of the table while Maggie considered her options. I had a clear view of both the barroom and the game room, and heard, before I saw, Eileen trudging down the stairs. Dressed in a heavy, white terry-cloth robe and matching terry thongs, she clutched a bottle of scotch under one arm and held a tall plastic tumbler in the other hand. Unsteady on her feet, I guessed she'd started her own personal happy hour before joining the rest of the guests. She went straight to the bar, filled the glass with ice, and then poured the scotch.

Kay Andolina sat in a wing chair by the cold fireplace

on the opposite end of the room. "Can I offer you a drink?" Eileen asked her, her words slurred.

"No, thank you!"

"Rats! I missed," Maggie said. "Your turn."

I turned my attention back to the table. It took less than a minute for me to pick off all the solid balls, and go after Maggie's, too.

She blinked, disappointed. "Maybe you're in the wrong job. You could be the next Minnesota Fats."

"Except I'm from Buffalo, and I'd have to gain a hundred pounds." She studied the table, looking crestfallen. I paused in racking up for another game. "Sorry, Maggs. If you'll play again, I'll give you a second chance if you miss."

"If we were more evenly matched I'd refuse. Since I haven't got a chance of winning, I accept your offer." Her tone of superiority was all for show. Maggie's not the competitive type.

I let her break again, my gaze drifting back to the other room. Kay Andolina stood near the bar, only a foot from Eileen, her face flushed with anger. "How dare you," she said, her voice low and menacing. For a moment, I thought she might slap her.

Eileen tried to stifle a laugh. I'd missed whatever insult she'd just delivered. This didn't seem like the friendly woman we'd met the night before.

Kay stalked up the steps and Eileen collected her bottle and glass before ambling into the game room. You didn't need to be psychic to feel Maggie's ire rise. Her ex-husband had cheated on her, and all the unresolved anger she claimed she'd conquered suddenly surfaced, threatening to erupt.

"Join me in a drink?" Eileen asked the room at large.

"No, thanks," I said. Ted looked up from the backgammon board, but Laura seemed oblivious to her presence.

"A bunch of teetotalers, eh?"

Laura continued to stare at the game board before her. "Some of us don't succumb to our vices."

Eileen blinked, then laughed. "Oh come now, my dear, everyone does. You more than most."

At last Laura's gaze rose to meet the Englishwoman's, her glare filled with absolute hatred. I got a strong sense of déjà vu. These two knew each other well. A decades-old tension hung between them. But how had they ended up in Stowe at the same place and time for a seemingly care-free weekend vacation?

Without a word, Laura rose. She brushed past me, hurrying up the stairs with Ted following a step or two behind. "Laura, wait!"

Eileen laughed. "I seem to be clearing a path wherever I go. I hope I shan't offend you too, my dear."

Furious, Maggie slammed her cue stick into the wooden rack on the wall and stalked into the barroom.

Eileen's eyebrows rose.

I shrugged. "PMS."

She took a long pull on her drink. "I'm on my way to the hot tub. Would you care to join me?"

"Don't you think you've had enough? You wouldn't want to cook yourself."

Eileen smiled. "Quite right, my boy." She stepped uncomfortably close and patted my cheek, her hot breath reeking of scotch. "Quite right." Then she turned on her heel. "You know where to find me should anyone come looking. And I'm sure someone will."

I watched her stagger toward the Jacuzzi. Her jocularity was all for show; her shoulders sagged in defeat. More than just defeat—desolation.

Maggie stood in front of the bar, clutching a half-empty glass of sherry. Bright spots of pink stained her cheeks. "Isn't it a little warm for sherry?" I asked.

"I didn't feel like going upstairs for the gin."

I took the glass from her hand, set it on the bar and led her to the loveseat across the way. "Don't let her upset you. You'll just get a sick headache and then neither of us will have any fun."

It took a moment for my words to sink in; she'd said the same thing to me earlier. A smile cracked her solemn features. "Okay, you win."

I heard footsteps cross the living room above. Moments later Susan came down the stairs, looked around the barroom and frowned. "Is Ms. Marshall around?"

"I think she's in the hot tub," Maggie volunteered.

Susan looked chagrined, picked up a clean glass and poured herself a large sherry from the decanter on the bar. I got the feeling this wasn't something she normally did—God forbid she should let her hair down in front of the guests. Ah, but we weren't paying guests, I reminded myself. I settled back in my seat, grabbed a magazine off the end table and flipped pages, trying to ignore Susan as thoroughly as she ignored me.

"Mrs. Andolina is not happy with her," Susan continued.

"So we heard."

Susan took another sip. "As long as she isn't drinking, Eileen's the perfect guest. But after she's had a few—"

Maggie joined our hostess at the bar. "I don't envy you dealing with such things."

I buried my nose deeper into the magazine, trying not to listen.

"Don't get me wrong, I love running the inn. But sometimes I have a bad day. Today is one of them."

We must have run into her when she was having a string of them, I thought as I put the magazine down and wandered back into the game room. Racking up the table, I picked up a cue and sank balls while the women talked.

"It's an odd mix of guests this weekend," Susan continued. "There's not a lot of interaction going on. But at least we have good help."

"Didn't you say Nadine was new?"

"Yes, but she's working out. Thank goodness we've had Adam all season."

As I moved to the side of the pool table, Susan perched on the piano bench, slipped off her left shoe and massaged her foot. "We hired him last spring to help Zack with the renovations. He asked to stay on when we opened again in May. He plans to go to college next semester for hotel management. He'd be good at it. But then he'll be gone and we'll have to start interviewing all over again."

"Sounds like it's hard to keep good help," Maggie said.

"It is. Especially in a seasonal business like this. I can't blame them for finding other jobs when we're closed, but it's damned inconvenient."

I racked up for another game, aware of the lag in their conversation.

"I've been admiring that mirror on the stairway," Maggie said.

"Do you want to buy it?"

I glanced up as Maggie blinked in surprise. "Well—"

"Just about everything in the inn is for sale. It's my surplus."

"Surplus?"

"I rent space in one of the antique co-ops in Waitsfield. It's not a great moneymaker, but it helps make ends meet during the months we're closed."

"I've thought about doing the same thing, but I never had the capital to get started."

"In spring, I go on buying sprees for weeks at a time. Usually in Pennsylvania and Ohio. After the autumn leaves are done and the tourists leave, we'll be closed for six weeks and I'll split my time between here and the co-op. We hope to renovate the rest of the rooms in time for ski season. That should make a big difference to our balance sheet. Come April, I'll go on another buying trip."

"Sounds like you've got all the bases covered."

Susan finished her drink, slipped her shoe back on. "I'd better warn Ms. Marshall about her mouth." She pursed her lips, as though taking on the bitch persona. She didn't have to stretch far to find it. "Good night," she said to Maggie, once again ignoring my presence. She took the dirty glasses to the kitchen. Moments later we heard the screen door bang.

I looked up over my cue stick to see Maggie watching me from the doorway. "Don't even think about it."

"About what?"

"Starting an antiques business."

"I don't have the money. But maybe I can talk Brenda into going in on it with me."

"Don't ask her for a nickel. I'm serious."

"Oh, you won't let me have any fun." She poked her tongue out at me, then wandered closer, and fanned her face with her hand. "That sherry made me feel flushed. Want to go for a swim?"

I concentrated on making my shot. The cue ball slammed into the eight ball. "We'll smell like chlorine."

"I don't care. It's hot. Please?"

The cue stick went back on the wall rack. "All right. Maybe we can steal some of those big towels they leave out."

We went back to our room and changed. Maggie's about a size twelve, which I consider just about right. I thought she'd look terrific in a two-piece swimsuit, but like most American women, Maggie believes anyone who isn't a size zero—herself especially—is too fat. Besides, she has a surgery scar she doesn't like parading around. So, she donned a conservative, black, one-piece swimsuit and her beach cover-up, which I'm sure had never been worn on any beach. She went ahead of me down the stairs and out through the gardens to the pool.

Spotlights on the inn's exterior lit the barbecue and pool area. Angry shouts split the night. I held Maggie back. Susan and Eileen were going at it down by the hot tub.

"Oh God, she's still there," Maggie grated.

"So what. Ignore her. We came here to swim, remember?"

Susan's voice rose. "I don't care how much you paid! I want you out of here tomorrow morning. Do you understand?"

Sudden quiet ensued.

I peeked around the edge of the barbecue as Susan stalked off toward the sunroom. We waited a few more moments before I took Maggie's hand and we crept into the open.

Steam curled from the hot tub into the cool night air. Eileen sat with her back toward us, the scotch bottle and tumbler within easy reach.

For once, Maggie took my advice. She ignored the Englishwoman and kicked off her slippers, claiming a large, fluffy towel draped over the back of one of the white, wrought-iron chairs. Then she took off her cover-up, walked to the edge of the pool's deep end, and dove in. Perfection. She surfaced and swam to the shallow end.

I applauded her graceful form. "I had no idea you were such an athlete."

"I used to be on the girl's swim team in high school. How about you?"

"No," I said in mock seriousness, "I never made the girl's swim team. But I passed intermediate swimming in my freshman year. Failed it the other three times." I dipped a toe into the water. "God, that's cold."

"You have to get wet all at once."

I backed off to sit in one of the chairs. "I'll pass."

"Chicken." She pushed off the edge of the pool, doing the backstroke. Once at the opposite end of the pool, she effortlessly turned and did a butterfly stroke. I liked to watch her swim. I liked to watch her do just about anything.

Maggie's splashing didn't garner much attention from our fellow bather. Eileen kept her back to us, morosely sipping her scotch. I felt a pinch and swatted a mosquito on my arm.

The breeze rose, bringing with it the unmistakable odor of marijuana. I heard a woman's laughter—Alyssa?—coming from the edge of the yard where I'd seen Adirondack chairs overlooking the creek. At least two of the nonsmoking inn's patrons hadn't kicked the habit.

I shivered in the cool night air and my thoughts drifted to Colorado, wondering how it related to my brother and that lonely stretch of road.

Lost in thought, I was totally unprepared for the cold water that splashed me. "Hey!"

"You look like you're in a daze," Maggie said playfully.

I toweled off my arm and leg. "So?"

She tread water in the middle of the deep end. "Come on in, the water's fine."

"It's freezing."

"It's heated!"

"To what? Sixty-eight? Sorry, I like my pool water warm as bath water."

"Then join me," came the voice from the hot tub. Did Eileen sound just a little desperate?

Maggie glared at me. I shrugged for her benefit. "Uh, thanks, but—" I faked a yawn. "All this mountain air has gotten to me. Are you ready to call it a night, Maggie?"

In answer, she swam over to the shallow end and walked up the steps. I handed her a towel, and she dried off. I grabbed another couple of towels to take to the room, waiting for Maggie to don her cover-up and slippers.

"Good night, Eileen," I said as we headed back for the

inn.

She ignored me, apparently tired of being rebuffed. Barefooted, I padded across the patio and opened the screen door to the kitchen for Maggie.

"Grab some glasses and ice and we'll have a night-cap," she said.

"Good idea." I handed her the towels and she continued up the stairs for our room.

The downstairs common areas seemed deserted. I went behind the bar, annoyed to find the ice bucket empty, cursing whoever left it that way. Grabbing it, I headed back for the kitchen. A single fluorescent fixture switched on over the center island was the room's only light. Except for dirty coffee cups and wine glasses in the large porcelain sink, the room was immaculate. A hulking, commercial refrigerator stood defiantly against the north wall. The freezer was full of blocks of frozen sausage, blueberries, and other assorted goodies for the breakfast buffet. I filled the bucket from a half-empty ten pound bag of ice and closed the heavy door.

Something niggled at my brain, but nothing looked out of place. My eyes were drawn back to the sink, or rather what was in it. I resisted the urge to pick up the cups and glasses. If I touched them, I might get some unpleasant flash of insight, and I was too tired to learn some new, no doubt unsavory, fact on one or more of the guests.

"The hell with you all," I muttered, and headed back for the barroom. I grabbed two of the tall glasses, filled them with ice, and went straight to our room, determined I wouldn't think about those dirty dishes in the sink.

SEVEN

Idreamed I was falling—mouth open in a silent scream—tumbling, end over end into a black abyss. Hot air whooshed past me, whipping my clothes, searing my soul. And I knew when I hit bottom it would be the end.

I awoke, muscles quivering, sweating, and panting. Faint light brightened the uncurtained window. Maggie slept on her side, facing the opposite wall, her breathing slow and even.

Still groggy, it took me a full ten seconds to figure out I was safe, but the feeling of panic wouldn't quit.

I was all right ... but someone else wasn't.

My back protested as I hauled myself out of that awful bed. I grabbed my watch: 6:15. Tossing on my clothes, I stuffed bare feet into my Reeboks and closed the door behind me. I nearly stumbled on the stairs in my haste, some inner force guiding me toward the back of the house.

Adam was alone in the kitchen, setting up the warming trays for the buffet. "Good morning. You're too early for breakfast, but I've got a pot of coffee brewing." His smile looked forced. My expression must have warned him that something was up. "What's wrong?"

"I thought I heard a noise outside. I'm not familiar with the grounds. Will you come out with me?" I'd lied. I knew exactly what I'd find, and I wanted a witness.

Adam looked at me with suspicion, studying me.

Then, reluctantly, "Okay."

He unlocked the door to the back garden and we stepped outside. Mist clung to the mountaintops, the damp, chill air penetrating my cotton shirt. I wished I'd put on a jacket. I looked around to get my bearings, and then knew where we had to look.

Across the patio, a magnificent stand of cosmos blocked the view from the house to the pool. "Over there," I said, leading the way.

We pushed past the flowers and onto the empty concrete deck. A smattering of leaves floated on the surface of the pool, and next to them Eileen Marshall bobbed face down in the hot tub.

Adam ran toward her, skidding to a halt. "Do you know CPR?"

"Don't touch her!"

"But maybe it's not too late!"

I let out a shuddering breath. "She was there when we went in last night. She must have been dead for hours."

Except for the hum of an air conditioner somewhere behind us, it was eerily silent. Adam kept staring at the dead woman, his face twisted with distress.

"Come on," I said. "We'd better call 911."

"Damn," Adam grated. "Susan's going to have a shit fit when she hears about this."

Susan was pissed. Lips drawn into a thin line, she surveyed the hot tub's victim. By the time the first Stowe PD patrol car showed up some ten minutes later, a rather breathless Zack had also arrived. His expression was unreadable, but Susan seemed more angry than upset that Eileen had died on her property. Typically, she viewed the woman's death from strictly a commercial perspective: how was this going to affect her business?

"Her name is Eileen Marshall," Susan volunteered to the young officer.

"Who found her?"

"We did," Adam answered, and nodded toward me.

"What happened?" the officer asked me.

I read his nametag: Dan Morris. "She was pretty drunk last night. Maybe she fell asleep," I offered, although I'd known from the moment I saw Eileen floating that she'd been murdered, but I wasn't eager to volunteer that information and become the prime suspect, either.

"I suppose she could have had a heart attack. We posted a sign warning people with medical conditions not to use the hot tub, but there's not much we can do to stop them," Susan said.

"We'll wait for the ME to decide the cause of death," the officer said.

I glanced back at the inn. Some of the other guests had awakened and were rubbernecking and speculating on the scene before them.

Susan spoke to Zack. "I'm sure we both don't need to be out here. You'd better go in and supervise breakfast. I can answer any questions the police have."

"Are you sure, honey?"

"Yes," she snapped—her standard mode of speech. Oblivious, Zack nodded and headed for the house.

"Can I go in now, too?" Adam asked.

"No, we'll need you here for a while yet," the officer said and ushered us away from the site—standard crime-scene protocol. I guess I wasn't the only one thinking this might not be an accident.

Adam slumped into one of the patio chairs. "It'll be okay," I assured him.

He shrugged, unconvinced.

"Sir," the cop said, and motioned to me.

Another standard procedure: separate the witnesses so they don't contaminate each other's stories. This cop was good.

"You said the victim was drunk last night," Morris

said.

"I'm a bartender. She was definitely over the legal limit."

"What was her state of mind?"

"Argumentative. She said some caustic things to several of the other guests." I told him Eileen had insulted Mrs. Andolina, what she'd said to Laura Ross the night before, and her loud discussion with Susan.

"What time did you last see her?"

I frowned. "We left the pool about ten forty-five, maybe eleven o'clock."

"We?"

"Me and my girlfriend, Maggie Brennan."

He wrote down her name. "And you say the victim had a bottle of whiskey?"

"Scotch. Grand Macnish, in a plastic bottle. She was drinking out of a plastic tumbler. Pool rules, no glass."

The cop looked around. "There's no sign of it. Was anyone else around?"

"Two other guests may have seen her. Doug and Alyssa. They were out by the creek," I said, leaving out my suspicions on how they'd spent their evening.

Within minutes, two plainclothes detectives had arrived, along with the chief of police. The yellow crime tape came out and the investigation began in earnest.

I was impressed with the care the small town cops gave the scene—especially since at first glance the area looked totally innocent. As a former insurance investigator, I was used to looking over possible crime scenes. Being there brought back a kind of macabre nostalgia.

When the crime photographer arrived, I admit a degree of professional curiosity. Though they kept me pretty far back, I watched as he took photos from every conceivable angle, including flat on the cement deck for a shot of the body at ground level. They paid particular attention to the concrete deck, and I wondered if I'd missed traces of blood.

After the initial photos were taken, and the county medical examiner arrived, they hauled Eileen's bloated, naked body from the tub, laying her on the concrete deck. In death she looked younger than she had the night before. A discolored, crescent-shaped cut and bruise marred the left side of her forehead. The photographer took close-ups of her face, as well as the edges of the hot tub; there were no other signs of trauma on the body. The bruise didn't match the edge of the tub. But something else was wrong. Eileen's abdomen should've been discolored by pooled blood. Could she have bled to death? The police had the same idea, for next they took water samples, then completely dismantled the hot tub's filtering system.

I turned away, embarrassed for the dead woman. The last thing she would have wanted was strangers gawking at her wrinkled, naked body.

With all the questions and photos, it was hours before the Eileen Marshall's body was removed by the medical examiner. By then I'd told my story to four or five officers of different ranks, making sure to tell it exactly the same every time. Sgt. Beach seemed to be in charge. He wasn't a local. His voice bore the trace of a mid-western accent—maybe Iowa. He wasn't much older than me, and maybe five-ten in height.

Meanwhile, Morris and the other officers interviewed the rest of the guests. They even went through the inn's trash looking for the missing scotch bottle. And while there wasn't talk about them coming back with a warrant to search each room, it seemed like the next step. At one point Susan disappeared with two of the cops, and the photographer, to chronicle and then pack Eileen's belongings.

When the ME's wagon pulled away, Sgt. Beach gathered all the guests in the dining room. "Folks, I know this is going to be an inconvenience to some of you, but until we determine how Ms. Marshall died, I ask that everyone stay in the area. If you move to different accommodations, please let the police department know. We'll be in touch."

The Andolinas looked grim as they left the dining room, presumably for their room. Alyssa and her beau seemed shell-shocked, and wandered out back, probably to look over the death site.

I was starved, and it was almost eleven when I finally sat down to eat. A tense-looking Maggie waited for me, and pulled her chair close to mine. The meal was a somber affair. The camaraderie evident in the kitchen the day before was gone. None of the guests were particularly hungry, as evidenced by the food still heaped in the warming trays. Even though they were booked for another week, we overhead the young Canadian couple debating whether they should cancel and go home. I put odds that the wife would win and as soon as the police cleared them they'd be on their way home to Québec as fast as their BMW could take them. Personally, I didn't blame them.

Maggie sipped her coffee and picked apart a carrot muffin. "How do you think it happened?"

"Not here," I said under my breath.

She nodded and pushed her plate aside. I finished my breakfast in silence.

About the time the dust from the preliminary investigation had settled, Susan came looking for us. Her eyes were haunted. "You'll still take the pictures and finish the article, won't you?" Her voice just broke a whisper.

"We'll finish the job," I said.

"Thank you." Real humility colored her voice. "We've worked so hard, I hope this doesn't ruin our business." She turned and slowly walked toward the stairs.

I downed the rest of my orange juice, pushed back

from the table, and we headed for our room.

"Well?" Maggie asked, as soon as I'd shut the door.

"Eileen was murdered."

Her pale face and worried eyes reflected her fear. "That means somebody here at the inn killed her. Why? Do you think they'll come after any one else?"

I took her in my arms and brushed a kiss along her forehead. "Now why would they do that?"

"I don't know. I'm scared. I've never seen a murdered person before."

"It's scary," I admitted.

"Is that how you felt when Shelley was killed?"

My wife and I had separated six months before the police came to my Manhattan apartment to tell me she'd been killed, execution style, in what they figured was a drug deal gone sour. Shelley's cocaine habit had caused our breakup.

"It was disbelief, more than anything else. The woman I married was not the same woman they found dead in a bathroom at Grand Central Station."

"What did that sweet old woman do to make some-one—" She stopped, no doubt remembering what I'd told her, her own anger toward Eileen, and how the woman had treated the other guests the night before. "Did you tell the police what you know?" Maggie asked.

"They'll do a background check. Maybe her friends can tell them who her lover was."

"So you won't?"

"I don't know who it is."

Maggie looked worried. "You knew this was going to happen, didn't you?"

"I felt something was going to happen—that some-one was going to die. I didn't know it would be murder. Now I feel foolish asking Richard to come all the way up here."

"What will you tell him when he gets here tonight?"

"I don't know." The truth was, I didn't want to think about it. "Come on, let's go downstairs and finish the photography. Then we can relax. Besides, it'll keep our minds off of all this other stuff."

The setup went much slower, probably because it had become a chore instead of a lark. Eileen's death had cast a pall over the inn. Most of the guests had gotten in their cars and taken off; those who didn't went to hide in their rooms. Zack and Susan seemed to be in seclusion as well, and, after what transpired the night before, I didn't care if I saw any of them ever again.

The work dragged. Once, while Maggie rearranged the props, I looked out the window and saw a couple of cops walking the grounds, presumably looking for evidence. It made me uneasy.

I found it hard to concentrate, constantly rehashing the conflicting emotions and events I'd experienced since arriving at the inn. At least two—possibly three—people might've had reasons to murder the woman: Eileen's lover, the lover's wife, or maybe Eileen had been black-mailing Laura Ross and she had done the evil deed. Eileen seemed to have intimate knowledge of her past or present. And what did any of that have to do with that empty stretch of road and Colorado?

We took a mid-afternoon break. I was hungry and had the beginnings of one of my bad headaches. Despite the disruption in routine, the glass jar by the coffee maker had been refilled with fresh-baked cookies. Maggie and I were the only ones around to enjoy them. I took my medication and crossed my fingers, hoping to counter-act the worst of the pain in my skull.

The empty dining room echoed like a cavern, rein-forcing my feeling of isolation. Maggie stared morosely into her decaf. "I want to go home."

I reached over and touched her hand. "It's not fun

anymore, is it?" She shook her head. "What about the article?"

"I haven't even started it. Right now I just don't care."

"Maybe later you should sit down and write some really great fiction about this place. Pretend we were guests and had a wonderful time."

"It would take a Pulitzer prize winner for that," she scoffed.

"It'll get your mind off things. Think of it as a stepping stone. This article could lead to something better. We can turn this negative experience into a positive one." God, I felt like a cheerleader, and a hypocritical one at that.

Maggie braved a smile. "Okay. I'll start after we finish in the living room."

We drank our coffee and swiped another couple of cookies for later, then trekked all the gear up the stairs for what I hoped would be the last time. My back, already sore from that uncomfortable bed, was starting to feel the strain.

As I'd anticipated, Maggie got lost in the work. She suggested we start a fire in the fireplace to make the room seem cozier. Susan agreed and sent Adam to bring in wood.

About the same time, a battered Chevy van pulled up outside and a petite young woman got out. Dressed in jeans, sneakers and a baggy gray jacket, she had short-cropped hair, and silver-framed glasses.

"Ashley Samuels," she said, flashing her identification card. "I'm with the Burlington Free Press."

Susan looked wary. "Susan Dawson. I own the Sugar Maple."

"Can someone tell me about the murder last night—"

"Accident," Susan nearly shouted.

"Sorry. I got the impression she was—"

"You got the wrong impression," Susan corrected her.

The reporter consulted her notes. "A Jeffrey R. Resnick and an Adam T. Henderson found the body in the hot tub."

"I'm Jeff Resnick."

She reporter gave me a quick once over. "Do you mind answering some questions?"

Susan glared daggers at me, and Maggie's expression said *don't rock the boat*.

"I ... heard a noise. On my way to investigate, I ran into Adam. We went out back and found Ms. Marshall."

The reporter glanced at her notes. "Eileen Jane Marshall? Was she another guest?"

"That's right."

"The cops said she was probably drunk."

I nodded.

Ashley took in the photographic equipment. "Doing a layout or something?"

"We hope to," Maggie answered.

Adam came in with an armload of wood, and I introduced him. Ashley asked him the same questions. He shot a look at Susan, as though looking for her permission before he, too, answered. She grudgingly nodded and he corroborated my story.

Ashley closed her notebook, stowing it in her large purse. "Do you mind if I have a look at the crime scene?"

"Accident," Susan reiterated. She forced a smile. "I'll show you."

While Susan tended to the public relations dilemma, Adam finished making the fire. "Let me know if you want more wood," he said, and took off.

The cheerful blaze quickly raised the temperature to an unbearable level, despite the fact we'd opened every window. I readjusted the lights, sweating freely by the time I started snapping photos.

I glanced out the window and saw Susan walk the reporter back to her van. Silently fuming, she watched until the van was well down the road before she returned to the inn and headed for her office without saying a word to us.

By then I wasn't feeling overly ambitious. I was almost finished snapping shots when we heard another car pull up the gravel drive outside. I motioned to Maggie and we glanced out the window.

A big, old, white Buick Roadmaster station wagon rolled to a stop. The driver's door opened and my half-brother Richard stepped out, making a visual recon of the inn. Dressed in light colored slacks and a white golf shirt with green piping, he looked like a typical, well-heeled vacationer. Older than me by twelve years, and taller by about six inches, his presence radiated trust—something even I'm not immune to.

Maggie's suggestion that I was too dependent on my brother was right on the money. But that's what families are for—at least Richard thought so. And he'd been right about one thing, a burden was a lot easier to shoulder when you had family to depend on. Since we hadn't been close for many years, it now felt good to count on him as my best friend.

Richard opened the screen door and entered the living room. "Good afternoon. I'm looking for a place to stay and hoped there might be a room available."

I struggled to keep a straight face. "If you ring the bell on the office door over there, I'm sure someone will be along in a moment to help you, sir."

"Thank you."

He passed by me, giving the photographic equipment a quick once over. Since he'd loaned me the money to rent it, I figured he was probably just checking up on his investment.

Richard rang the bell and in moments Susan opened the Dutch door. "Can I help you?"

"I'm looking for a place to stay. Do you have a room?"

"As a matter of fact, one of our guests checked out suddenly this morning," she said. That was putting it mildly. "It's our deluxe suite. There're two double beds. The cost is $425 a night. A full breakfast is included in the price. It's available for two nights."

"I'm not sure how long I'll be staying. At least until Monday morning."

"That will be fine," she said. "I'm afraid we're a little short-handed this afternoon. Can you wait half an hour?"

"That's fine," he said.

"Your name, sir?"

"Alpert. Dr. Richard Alpert."

I had to jab Maggie in the ribs to stop her from giggling. Susan introduced herself as the owner, and Richard signed all the necessary paperwork, letting her swipe his American Express card through a scanner.

"Let me give you a tour of the premises," Susan said.

"I'd be glad to give the doctor the tour if you want to get his room ready," Maggie volunteered.

Susan smiled sweetly. I'm sure she would've preferred Maggie get the room ready. "Thank you. Dr. Alpert, this is Maggie Brennan. She's writing an article about the inn and is knowledgeable about all our amenities."

Richard turned to Maggie, smiling broadly. "I'm sure I'll be in good hands."

Susan nodded and disappeared around the corner before Maggie lost it entirely.

"Having fun?" Richard asked.

Maggie's smile quickly faded. "No." She looked to me to explain.

"You got the room because the woman who was in it was murdered sometime last night."

"Oh, great." He gazed at us, suddenly looking very tired. "Just what have you gotten me into?"

EIGHT

We planned to meet later at a restaurant, where we could talk in relative privacy. Maggie and I finished taking the pictures, packed the equipment and changed before heading out. We left first, hoping none of the other guests would frequent the same eatery.

I still got that anxious feeling when we passed that bend in the road. I thought once Richard arrived it wouldn't bother me so much. Instead, the urgency seemed to have intensified. I tried to ignore it.

We arrived at The Ranch House, snagged a table and ordered drinks while we waited for Richard. Preoccupied with trying to puzzle out my emotional response to that empty stretch of highway, I was not good company. Maggie looked relieved when my brother strolled in ten minutes later, and we ordered a second round of drinks.

"How was the nap?" Maggie asked.

"That bed is almost as comfortable as my own at home."

"Lucky you," I said. "I swear we're sleeping on planks."

The drinks came in record time and we asked the waitress to give us a few more minutes before we ordered.

"Did you have a hard time getting here?" I asked Richard.

He took a sip of his Manhattan to fortify himself. "Last night, after we talked, I called the airline and booked myself on an eight o'clock flight to Albany. Then I tried to charter a flight to Stowe. But you can't fly directly to Stowe, you have to go to Morristown. Only I couldn't get a car there, so the rental people got on the computer and found one in Rutland, meaning I had to change the charter.

"Now I'm not usually a nervous flyer, but that Cessna vibrated like it was about to fall apart. After I got to Rutland, the rental car I was supposed to pick up had been given to someone else. I had to wait two hours for them to dig up the old station wagon. Then it took another two hours to drive here." He sighed. "It's been a very long day."

"A real comedy of errors, huh?" I said, trying not to smile while imagining all six two of Richard squashed into a miniature plane. His expression was grim, but telltale amusement lit his eyes.

The waitress returned and we had to figure out what we wanted. After she'd gone, Richard said, "So tell me everything that's happened and what I'm doing here."

I gave him my impressions of the people we'd met, even the things I'd kept from Maggie, figuring they both had a right to know just as much as I did.

While I spoke, Richard jotted the names of the players on his cocktail napkin. He underlined one of them. "Do you suspect Laura?"

"She qualifies. I can only guess the depth of her anger or embarrassment. I've got a feeling that whatever Eileen knew about her might have something to do with her little paramour. But Eileen also insulted Kay Andolina, although I missed whatever it was she said. Because of that, she argued with Susan Dawson. Susan was seething, but I got the feeling her anger was deeper than this one incident warranted. She ordered Eileen to leave in the morning, which didn't go down well."

"This is all very convoluted," Richard said, consulting

his notes.

"Don't forget the bend in the road," Maggie said.

I told Richard about those disquieting feelings I got.

"You said someone hit Eileen. Could they have ditched the standard blunt object in the field by the road?" he asked.

I thought about it. "Maybe. It might not hurt to look."

Richard drained his glass. "Then what?"

"We wait to see what the police come up with."

"And what part am I supposed to play in all this?"

"I'm not sure," I admitted.

He shrugged. "Then I guess I'll just hang around and see what happens. Too bad I don't have any company."

"You ever shoot pool?" I asked.

"Not since college."

"Maybe we can play a few games when we get back. Maggie hasn't got a clue."

"Hey," she protested.

I winked at her, but spoke to Richard. "Or maybe you could mingle with the other guests. We seem to be at a disadvantage, being hired help and all."

"Some of the guests are a little ...." Maggie's words trailed off.

"Rude," I finished for her. "But you've got the right clothes and a lot more polish than me. They'll probably accept you right off."

"Snobs, eh?"

Maggie nodded ruefully.

The waitress arrived with a tray laden with food and that was the end of our murder discussion. We reverted to tourists, comfortable in each other's company and enjoyed the good meal.

Maggie and I arrived back at the inn about nine. We agreed Richard should show up later, and since he'd forgotten his shaving cream, he asked directions to a store.

A patrol car and the two plainclothes detectives were waiting for us when we pulled up at the inn. My stomach tightened as I parked, then got out of the car. Sgt. Beach approached.

"Mr. Resnick, Mrs. Dawson says you have pictures taken in the victim's room yesterday."

"That's right."

"We'd like a look at them."

"How can that possibly help? All Eileen's stuff was jammed in the closet. There was nothing that belonged to her in any of the shots, and we rearranged the furniture and the objects in the room and brought in more from the common areas."

"May we please have the pictures?"

"They're on a memory card. Will I get it back?"

"The pictures, please."

He wasn't about to negotiate. He didn't have a warrant, or he'd have already confiscated the camera. It would probably be better to give it up voluntarily than draw unwanted attention. "It's in the camera bag, up in my room."

"We'd be happy to accompany you to get it."

They weren't going to take any chances that I'd destroy it. But why? What did they think it contained?

I shrugged. "Suit yourself."

"Should I come?" Maggie asked.

"The room isn't big enough to hold four people. I'll meet you in the barroom in a few minutes. Come on," I told the cops, who dutifully followed me inside the inn and up the stairs.

My camera bag was exactly where I'd left it on top of one of the equipment trunks. I fumbled with the side of the camera and extracted the memory card. "Can you at least let me know how they come out?"

Beach took the card without a word and turned to leave.

"Uh, a receipt please."

Beach came up with a notebook and glowered as he scribbled a receipt, thrust it at me, and left the room.

I watched from the window as the two detectives got into their car and drove off. Something didn't feel right about them taking the memory card, but then nothing felt right since the moment we'd arrived.

Maggie's writing tablet sat on her suitcase and I decided to take it to her. Working on her article might distract her. I found her in the barroom, sitting on the loveseat, flipping through an old decorating magazine.

"Doing research?"

"Why not? I'm in desperate need of inspiration."

"Here." I handed her the tablet. "Mind if I shoot some balls?"

She wrinkled her nose. "That sounds so risqué."

"Only if you have a dirty mind." I bent down, kissed her, and then headed for the game room.

The Canadian couple was already there, occupying another loveseat. A bottle of wine and a couple of half-full glasses sat on the coffee table in front of them. I nodded a hello and the man gave a brief wave while the woman smiled shyly, her eyes shadowed with worry.

I racked up the balls and started sinking shots.

I missed playing pool. When I'd been unemployed the year before, I found it a good way to pick up a few extra bucks. I racked up for another game, and it wasn't long before I was engrossed. Then I practiced trick shots. If only my high school geometry teacher had used a pool table as a visual aide, he might've had a class of Einsteins instead of bored-to-death teenagers.

While I amused myself, Richard ambled into the room, walking straight past me and heading for the bookshelves on the far side. He scanned the titles for a moment. The Canadian couple looked up and he smiled at the woman, who was paging through a magazine, its cover printed in French.

"Québécois?" Richard asked.

She looked at him over the top of her magazine. "Oui."

Then Richard launched into a flood of French and the woman visibly brightened. Moments later, the couple invited him to join them and they sat together in animated conversation.

I didn't even know my brother spoke French. But the fact that he did might be to my advantage; maybe he could worm some information out of the couple. Not that I thought they knew anything about Eileen's death, but they'd been here at least a day before us and might've seen something that could prove useful.

There I was, making this situation into a case. Why is it so hard for me to keep my nose out of things that really don't concern me? As soon as the police cleared me, we could leave. But even though we'd finished the photography, some part of me didn't want to go, not without knowing the truth about what happened to dear old Eileen. And I knew my funny feelings about her death would continue whether I stayed in Vermont or went home.

I'd just set up a complicated shot when I heard footsteps on the stairs. Laura and Ted turned the corner and stopped dead in the doorway, looking expectantly at the table. I took my shot and all the balls streaked across the table, everything but the cue ball going into three different pockets.

"Wow," Ted said, "you're a jack of all trades."

"I learned some tricks from a pro a few years back." I handed him the cue stick. "It's all yours."

"Thanks," he said, and started racking up for a game. Laura ignored me once again, blasting me with a wave suspicion. Her stuck-up bitch persona annoyed me, but there was more to it. Did she think I'd killed Eileen?

Still pondering that thought, I wandered into the barroom. The full sherry decanter was again waiting on the bar, along with a sweating pitcher of iced tea. I poured a glass of tea and sat beside Maggie on the loveseat. Her yellow tablet had some sentences scribbled on it, but most had been crossed out.

"Having a hard time getting started?" I asked, and took a sip.

"The muse has not struck. I wish I had a laptop computer."

"How would that help?"

"I find it easier to compose on a keyboard."

"Try the piano," I suggested.

Her eyes narrowed and she frowned. "Very funny."

Laura came into the room, poured herself a glass of sherry, and left without acknowledging our presence.

"Why don't you start by mentioning the friendly atmosphere here at the Sugar Maple. How the guests are just brimming with good cheer and the love of their fellow man."

"Some love. One of them killed Eileen."

"So, lie."

Her smile was fleeting. "You know your funny feelings?"

I nodded.

"I have one. Only it's what Brenda would call bad vibes. I feel like something's going to happen, only I don't know what."

"There's a lot of tension here. Everyone's afraid. And they're radiating that fear."

"You can feel it?" she asked.

"Yeah. It's really wiping me out." I glanced at my watch; it was almost ten o'clock. "I'm going to hit the sack early. Do you mind?"

She looked panicked. "But I'll be down here all alone."

I nodded toward the game room. "Rich is here. You'll

be okay."

"Well ... all right. I'll keep trying to get something down on paper. I won't be long."

I leaned over and kissed her. "Night, love."

"Good night."

As I headed up the stairs, I realized the scattered conversations downstairs would make an excellent cover for a little nosiness on my part. Since no one was in the living room, I crept close to Zack's and Susan's door and heard a television. I did a mental head count; the Andolinas had also been absent from the crowd downstairs. Were they still at dinner? I glanced out the window overlooking the drive. The Cadillac was parked outside; they had to be in their room. I'd bet it wasn't as claustrophobically small as ours. The Camaro was gone. Alyssa and her boyfriend, Doug, were probably at one of the village nightspots; they didn't seem like the stay-at-home types.

On a whim, I decided to do a little reconnoitering and padded down the corridor, listening in front of each of the doors. I heard muffled voices in the room next to Richard's, but it was hard to make out what they were saying; probably the Andolinas steeped in conversation.

I straightened, feeling absolutely stupid. I was tired and really wasn't up to any further investigation, so I turned around and crept back down the hall, hoping the floor boards wouldn't creak beneath me.

The staircase was dark. I flipped the wall switch on and off to no avail.

Great. The damn bulb had burned out.

I started up the steps, inwardly cursing Zack and Susan, stuffed my hand in my jeans pocket and grasped the key to our room. As I topped the stairs, something struck me mid-chest, shoving me backwards. I fell, cartwheeling down the darkened stairwell and smacked my head against the floor.

Then everything went black.

NINE

Celestial noises—like the tinkling of wind chimes—and a melodious voice seemed to murmur in my ear, but I couldn't understand the words. They faded, replaced by an irritating buzz of overlapping voices—sound without meaning. A ferocious pounding whacked the back of my skull, and I cracked open my eyes to see a fuzzy Richard and Maggie overhead, with a throng of curious, troubled faces crowded around behind them. I blinked and the focus sharpened.

"Are you okay, kid?" Richard's voice sounded like it came from an echo chamber.

I was flat on my back, at the bottom of the stairs, with a small pillow tucked behind my head. I blinked at him, unsure how to answer—surprised I had the presence of mind to keep his cover intact.

"Jeff?" he tried again.

I swallowed, took a shaky breath, and noted the concern in my brother's face. "Yeah."

He held up two fingers. "How many?"

"Two."

"What happened?" Maggie asked, her face pale, scared.

"I ... fell." I struggled to sit and my stomach lurched as the world tilted crazily.

Richard pushed me back to the floor. "Take it easy for a few minutes." He turned to the others. "He'll be all right. Let's give him some air, okay?"

"Lucky there was a doctor around," Laura said, shaking her head, and she and Ted retreated to the living room with Susan in tow.

"I'll get another bulb," Zack said, his eyes worried; seeing me, lying on the floor, meant a possible lawsuit.

Footsteps headed back downstairs and a door down the hall closed, then only Richard and Maggie were left.

"How's the head?" Richard asked.

"It hurts."

"You've got a lump the size of an egg."

"Can I get up now? This is really embarrassing."

"Wait until Zack gets that light bulb in, okay?"

I sank back with a sigh.

"Is he going to be all right?" Maggie asked Richard.

"Yes," we said in unison.

Moments later Zack was back, and soon after the hall and stairwell basked in the glow of 100 watts. Richard helped me sit. "Do you think you can make it up the stairs?"

"Of course."

Despite my bravado, my legs were rubbery as they pulled me to my feet. I had to lean on Richard to make it up the stairs. Maggie opened the door to our room and Richard led me to the bed, where I collapsed.

He pulled up the straight-backed chair and sat down. "Okay, what really happened?" he asked, once Maggie had closed the door.

"The light at the top of the stairs was out. Someone was up there and gave me a shove that sent me flying."

"Who?"

"It was too dark—I couldn't see."

"Are you sure you were pushed?" Richard asked.

I nodded and winced. "How long was I out?"

"Maybe a minute. We heard one hell of a crash and everyone came running."

"Did you see anyone?"

"Mrs. Andolina was bending over you when we got there. I didn't see anyone else," Maggie said.

I rubbed the back of my head, my pulse reverberating through my skull. "Could you get a couple of my pills and some water, Maggie?"

"No," Richard said. "That stuff is for migraines. I'll give you some Tylenol."

"You brought your little black bag along?"

"Lucky for you I did."

I exhaled a long breath, trying to collect my thoughts. "Did you learn anything from the Canucks?"

"Only that they're frightened. It's put a real damper on their honeymoon. They've only been married a week. We had a nice conversation about Old Québec. Michele's studio is in the heart of the old city. Sounds wonderful. I've got to take Brenda there some day."

I lifted my head and looked around. Nothing in the room seemed to have been disturbed. "Was the door locked?" I asked Maggie.

"Yes. You had the key in your hand when we found you. I took it," she said, and showed me she still held it.

"Are you sure you were pushed?" Richard asked again.

"Yes, dammit! I must've interrupted them—him, her—before they could do whatever it was they wanted to do in our room." I sank back on the pillow, frustrated. "Oh, my head."

"You don't seem concussed, but if you have any problems—double vision, nausea, anything unusual—call me." He shook a finger of warning at me. "I'm serious."

"Okay."

He rose from the chair. "Hang on. I'll go get the Tylenol." He finally noticed the room. "Boy, this place really is small." Then he was off.

Maggie sat on the bed beside me. She took my hand, radiating fear. "I want to go home."

I squeezed her fingers. "We can't. Not until the police say so."

"Whoever did this could have killed you."

"Everyone was accounted for...." I thought about it for a moment. "Well, I'm not really sure about Susan and Zack, or the blonde bimbo and her boyfriend, but—"

"You can't suspect Zack and Susan."

"I suspect everyone except you and Richard." She frowned. "How well do you know the Dawsons, anyway?"

"Not well," Maggie admitted. "This is Susan's second marriage. She met Zack in Mystic, Connecticut, a couple of years ago. He used to own a landscaping business and was living on his sailboat. I guess they fell in love. He sold it and his business and they bought the inn a little over a year ago."

"And you haven't even seen or heard from her in at least ten years, right?" She wouldn't meet my gaze. "Susan's carrying a secret about Eileen that even Zack doesn't know."

Maggie looked up at me. "How do you know?" Her frown deepened. "Why do I even bother to ask?"

The silence that followed weighed heavy between us. I squeezed her hand again, hoping she'd feel reassured. Stupid really, since someone had deliberately hurt me, proving just how ineffective I was as her protector.

Richard knocked on the door, pushing it open. Maggie rose, went into the bathroom and got me a glass of water. I downed the pills he gave me.

"Get some rest," Richard ordered. He looked at Maggie. "Come get me if he's too stupid or macho to admit he's having problems."

"I will," she promised.

"See you at breakfast, right?"

"Thanks, Rich." I gave him a wan smile. Words couldn't express my gratitude for him being here. And I still didn't really know why I needed him.

He gave us a smile, and then closed the door behind him. I watched Maggie lock it.

"Why do I feel like the worst is yet to come?" she asked.

"I don't want to scare you, love, but I've felt the same way all day."

"Damn, I wish we'd never come here. Damn it all!" Teary-eyed, she hurried to the bathroom and shut the door.

I sank into the mattress. Someone had been up here, either in our room or contemplating entering it. Here, where none of the other registered guests would go—not unless they had something to hide ... or to plant. Maybe Richard and I should have checked all the empty rooms on the second floor.

Could someone still be hiding there—listening to us?

Who?

Why?

Maggie said Kay Andolina had been the first to find me. Could Susan or Zack have pushed me, then come downstairs by another route? I didn't even know if the inn had a back stair. I'd have to check it out in the morning. At that moment, I wanted to do nothing more than escape in sleep, because in sleep I was oblivious—of blame, of fear. And much as I wanted to deny it, I was beginning to feel afraid.

And I didn't like it. Not one damn bit.

TEN

I was up early the next morning. Thin gray light came in the window at the far end of the inn's empty second floor hall. Shoeless, I padded down its length and found no back staircase. I'd been waiting since before dawn to investigate the other rooms on the floor. All were sealed with the same flimsy locks on our door, but that didn't stop me. With a little finesse, Maggie's hairpin let me inside the first room.

As Susan had said, the rooms were in various stages of renovation. Two had no plumbing fixtures; none had carpet, exposing wide pine plank floors—and all of them were bigger than the cell Maggie and I shared.

I opened a window overlooking the back of the property, stuck my head outside and saw metal escape ladders from all three back rooms. None of them were extended. It would have been impossible not to hear the rattle of metal if the person who'd pushed me down the stairs had used one of them to escape. The hot tub and pool were visible from this vantage point. If any of the guests had seen Eileen floating face down two nights before, they hadn't said so.

The room next to ours was the biggest, and might well be the best in the inn when finished. Zack and Susan planned to install a gas fire, as a brochure for one was taped to the wall. A layer of drywall dust covered the floor. Footprints marred it, but it was impossible to tell the number of people who'd stomped around or how long ago they'd been made. My attacker could have stood in that room and simply waited until we went to sleep before escaping by way of the main staircase. I closed my eyes, concentrating, hoping to soak in the residual aura from the last person who'd been in the room.

I got nothing.

Signs of life from the floor below made me check my watch and realize I'd been gone for almost an hour. I headed back to our room.

Maggie was awake, sitting on the edge of the bed, brushing her hair dry. "Where did you go?"

"Just to check out the other rooms on this floor."

"And?"

I shrugged. "Nothing."

"Good. I don't need any more surprises. What are we doing today? I mean, can we go someplace? I need to get away from here."

"How about ice cream at Ben and Jerry's?"

Her smile was dazzling. "Sounds wonderful."

I sat beside her on the bed and kissed her. Then I kissed her again. And again. And we started the day all over again ... together.

We made it to the dining room about halfway through the breakfast rush. Richard had beaten us there, and was seated with the Andolinas. An empty plate sat before him, along with a half-filled coffee cup. Kay Andolina was in her glory in the midst of an anecdote, telling it with great delight. Richard's glazed expression was one I recognized from other occasions: bored to death. I felt a little sorry for him, but that didn't keep me from smiling at his predicament.

We grabbed coffee and parked at a table nearby. The atmosphere wasn't so grim this morning. Zack, Nadine, and Adam were in the kitchen once again bantering back and forth. I decided against an entree, but went through the buffet and grabbed scrambled eggs and sausages. Maggie stuck with her favorite Western omelet and toast.

We'd almost finished eating by the time the Andolinas got up, leaving Richard with his cold coffee. He sat alone for a few minutes, staring out the window before getting up. He paused briefly at the table where the Canadian couple sat, spoke to them, again in French, and must have made a wonderful joke because they broke out in delighted laughter. I was working on my third cup of coffee when he finally made it to our table.

"My, we're popular with the other guests."

He ignored my comment. "You're looking better. How do you feel?"

"I've got a bit of headache, but it's the kind I'm used to having."

"Did you take your medication?"

"Of course. It's already fading."

"Good. Then maybe you'll feel like exploring the area."

"Sounds like a plan. Meet me out in the garden in ten minutes and we'll talk."

"Okay."

He wandered off and I sipped my coffee.

The Canadian couple finished their breakfasts and got up. I was surprised when they stopped to speak to us.

"How are you today?" the woman asked in only slightly accented English. She brushed a strand of her long, brown hair behind her left ear, her expression concerned.

"Much better, thank you."

"I am Michele DuBois and this is my husband, Jean."

I introduced Maggie and myself.

"I was so worried when you had your accident last night. Frightening things have been happening here." She studied my face for a moment, perplexed. "Do you know, you seem to resemble the coctor."

I nearly choked on my coffee. "I do?"

"Oui. It's impossible, no? But your noses are very similar. I am an artist. I paint for a living. My specialty is portraits."

Jean gently nudged her arm. "We must go."

She smiled. "Good day."

After they'd gone, I found Maggie studying me. "I don't think you look like Richard."

"He got our mother's blue eyes, I got my father's brown eyes."

She shrugged and pushed back her chair. "I'm going to the room. Want me to bring you anything?"

"Yeah, my camera bag. If we're going out, I may as well take some pictures." That is if I can buy another memory card.

"Okay. Meet you at the car in fifteen minutes." She headed for the stairs and I left my empty plate and cup on the table and made for the door to the gardens.

Although the temperature was in the mid-sixties, the trees were already beginning to show the change of season. The highest branches were tinged with yellow and orange. Zack and Susan had dug a fishpond near the inn's namesake sugar maple, and I wandered across the enormous yard, stopping by the miniature lake. Seeing my shadow, the fish gathered before me, impatiently waiting for food.

"Sorry, boys, it ain't feeding time." I sat down on the bench provided and watched the fish swim in lazy circles.

A lot of care had gone into the gardens in the back, but like the front of the inn there were signs of neglect. Maggie said Zack used to own a landscaping business, so he must've had the green thumb. I couldn't imagine Susan getting dirt under her long nails.

"Penny for your thoughts," came Richard's voice from

behind.

I turned. "I don't think I can make change."

He held a slice of bread, broke off a corner and tossed it into the pond. The fish went wild, like hungry piranha.

"Are you supposed to do that?"

"Probably not." He threw in another piece. "What's on tap today?"

"Maggie's freaked. She wants to go home. Hell, I want to go home. But I have this feeling something's going to break today. If it does, maybe we can leave tomorrow. In the meantime, let's do some touristy stuff, get her mind off all this."

"Sounds like fun." Plop! went another piece of bread.

"We can rendezvous at the municipal parking lot in the village."

"Okay." Plop!

I started off, and then thought of something else. "What did you say as you left the dining room to make the DuBois' laugh?"

"Last night Michele told me people always try to get her to do drawings or paintings for free. I told her people always ask me for free medical advice. At breakfast Mrs. Andolina entertained me with the history of her uterus."

I couldn't help but smile. "What's Michele's husband do for a living?"

"He's an editor at a magazine in Quèbec."

My smile waned. "Interesting. Laura Ross is a former editor; Eileen Marshall agented for magazines, and Jean DuBois currently edits a magazine."

"And Maggie's written for magazines. It's only coincidence, Jeff. I can't see those two young people involved in anything sinister."

"I suppose. Maggie and I haven't had any luck penetrating Laura's steel veneer. Do you think you could talk to her this evening?"

"I'll try."

I studied him. "It's got to be the mustache."

"I beg your pardon?"

"Why else would women casually unburden themselves to you?"

"People always tell doctors things they'd never tell their spouses. You have no idea how many sexual fantasies have been confided to me at cocktail parties."

"You're joking."

"Whether I want to hear them or not."

I left him to feed the fish, wondering how he rated all the fun.

Maggie waited for me in the car, reading her novel. She'd changed into the blue sundress that went so well with her eyes, with a white sweater draped over her shoulders. I got in and started the engine. She replaced her bookmark and closed the cover as I pulled onto the highway.

"Rich is going to meet us in town."

She nodded.

It was time to broach a potentially sore subject. "Do you mind if I pull over and look at that place along the road?" No other explanation was necessary.

"Of course not. Maybe you should take a picture."

The idea gave me the willies. "Can't—no memory card. Yet."

We drove in silence until we reached that desolate spot in the road. The narrow shoulder bordered a gully, which sloped into a wooded area. Birds chirped in the evergreens, the branches swayed gently in the breeze. It was peaceful, idyllic, and yet it scared the hell out of me. I could almost understand the connection with Colorado. Almost, but not quite. I felt more than saw it, but it was there.

Maggie got out the car, joining me. She wound her arm around mine, standing close, and leaned her head on my shoulder. "Wouldn't this be a romantic spot to build a log cabin?"

"It's too close to the road. You'd hear traffic all night."

"There's not much traffic." To dispel that, a truck roared by, heading north. "Jeff, you look so worried. What is it about this place that bothers you?"

"I don't know. That's what worries me."

"Could something bad have happened here in the past and you're picking up on it?"

"I don't know."

"Is it the same as what you felt in the inn?"

"No." That much I was sure. This place had an aura of … what? Pain … loss?

"If we were going to build here, I'd do some research. Maybe a tragedy occurred. Or maybe someone was hanged here a hundred years ago and that person still haunts the site." Her expression was wistful.

"Pure conjecture. You have a writer's overactive imagination."

"I know, but isn't it fun?" She smiled, but it quickly faded. "Do you think the police will let us go home tomorrow?"

"I sure hope so."

"I've got to be back at work on Wednesday morning. I can't afford to lose this job."

"You won't lose it."

"There's talk they might make me permanent. That would be wonderful. I hate living hand to mouth. If it weren't for renting out the bottom of my duplex, I don't know how I would have survived the summer."

"They'll hire you soon."

"Really?"

She had that look of hope I knew so well. Maggie and Brenda seem to question everything I say, as though I have a direct pipeline to the future. Just because I sometimes have flashes of insight, they think I know more than I do. This time I played along; she'd already had her contract extended once.

"Of course."

A string of traffic zoomed by. "Come on," Maggie said, tugging my hand. "Or Richard will get to town before us."

She got into the car and I crossed to the driver's door, taking one last look at the innocent surroundings, wishing I could pin down why I felt so apprehensive about the place—knowing I'd eventually find out, and dreading it.

ELEVEN

I was able to get another memory card at one of the shops along Stowe's main drag, and went back to the car to wait for Richard. Eventually the white Buick station wagon pulled alongside my parked car. "Where we going?" Richard called through the open window.

"To Ben and Jerry's for ice cream. Want to drive?" I said.

"Why not. I've got nothing better to do."

We transferred our stuff to the station wagon and locked the Chevy. Richard drove out of the lot and we were on our way.

Ben and Jerry's ice cream factory and amusement center was going full tilt at 10:30 on a Sunday, holiday-weekend morning. People were already lined up for the factory tours and the ice cream stand was crowded with people waiting to consume a thousand plus calories. We bought tickets for the 11:15 tour and killed time at the cow viewing area, where Richard and Maggie mugged for the camera. Next we headed for the gift shop to drop a few more bucks.

The tour wasn't as thorough as I'd hoped. Because of the holiday, the packaging line was shut down. But we got a free sample of Cherry Garcia and spent time reading the funky letters that decorated the corridors from celebrities and ordinary Joes like us.

Maggie was dying for more English Toffee crunch, so

afterwards we lined up and bought cones. Strolling down the asphalt walkway, I heard a voice call out.

"Wait! Please wait!"

I turned. Kay Andolina hurried toward us. She got within ten feet of me before she stopped dead. "Oh, I'm sorry. I thought you were—"

"Who?"

The anticipation in her eyes turned to confusion and disappointment. She looked from Richard to me as though searching our faces for some elusive answer. At last she looked away, embarrassed.

I hadn't counted on running into any of our fellow guests. I didn't want anyone to know about my relationship with Richard—and here we'd been caught in a very public place.

Maggie's smile was friendly. "Small world, isn't it?"

Kay frowned, her gaze hardening.

"Have you taken the tour?" Richard asked.

She shook her head. "Fred's getting tickets now."

"Nice as it is, we just had to get away from the inn," Maggie said.

"Yes," Kay agreed. "We'd been looking forward to a peaceful weekend in the mountains. Now, with Ms. Marshall's death, it's more like a nightmare."

Children romped by us. A dog barked somewhere behind me and an elderly couple jostled past. The building's painted murals seemed too bright. Time wavered and something flashed before my mind's eye. Actually more of an impression—of something Kay Andolina had seen.

"She argued with Laura Ross," I blurted. "The day before we got there. Wednesday, right?"

Kay looked at me strangely. "How did you know?"

"What did they fight about?"

"It was none of my business," she said.

"Jeff!" Maggie dabbed at my hand with a paper napkin. Ice cream dripped down my fingers, the cone was crushed in my fist.

Fred appeared, handing his wife a ticket stub. "Hello," he greeted us. In contrast to Kay, he seemed relieved to see some familiar faces. "We have to hurry, dear, the tour starts in a few minutes." He took his wife's hand, leading her away.

I didn't watch them go. My attention was focused on the mess that had been my ice cream cone.

Richard cleared his throat. "Why don't we sit down," he said, turned me by the shoulder and pointed me in the direction of an empty picnic table.

I tossed the cone into a nearby trash barrel and wiped the drips from my fingers as we sat on the bench. Maggie produced a bottle of hand sanitizer and squirted some onto my waiting palm.

"So what did you get?" Richard asked, all business. He'd deduced what had just happened to me.

I thought about it as I rubbed my hands together, working in the gel. "I'm not sure. It's all vague—just that she'd been disturbed by the argument. But that proves Eileen knew Laura before she came to the inn."

"I'm sure of it. Didn't Ted ask if she'd been to the inn over Fourth of July?"

I nodded.

"But then why did she introduce herself to Laura in front of us?" Maggie asked.

"Maybe she was undercover—like me," Richard said.

"Well, thanks to the Andolinas, your cover's been blown."

"Not necessarily. They didn't even seem to notice. Which reminds me, at breakfast I asked if she saw anyone on the stairs after you had your little accident last night."

"Did she?"

"No."

Nobody said anything for long minutes. Maggie and

Richard finished their cones, their attention focused on anything but me.

Finally, Maggie dug into her purse once again and came up with a travel guide. "Let's see what else is in the area," she said, flipping pages.

"Since we're in Vermont, let's find a covered bridge," Richard said.

Maggie consulted a map of the area. "Looks like there's one about ten or twelve miles down the road called The Great Eddy Bridge. Jeff?"

I was still thinking about Eileen's and Laura's argument, but her voice shook me from my reverie. "I'm game. Let's go."

Just as the guidebook promised, the village of Waitsfield did indeed have a charming covered bridge that had survived the flooding of the Mad River in 2011. I hauled out the camera and played tourist, but Maggie was more interested in checking out the Christmas and Teddy Bears store nearby.

"This bridge was built in 1833," Richard said, reading the brass placard on the side of the bridge. "And apparently lucky it didn't crash into the river like some of the other bridges during the aftermath of Hurricane Irene."

The hand-hewn timbers were ten inches square, and I marveled at the workmanship. I shot pictures from every conceivable angle and wondered if any would be good enough to sell as calendar shots, amazed at my sudden confidence in my ability. Still, I enjoyed it, glad for the distraction. Having Richard along was an added bonus.

I snapped one more shot and replaced the lens cap. "Do you realize, this is the first family vacation we've ever been on."

"So it is." He frowned, his brow wrinkling. "You know, there are a lot of things I regret not doing when you were a kid. It never occurred to me to take you on a vacation."

I'd lived with Richard and his grandparents for four long years after the death of our mother. It was not a fun time. Still in his hospital residency, Richard was seldom home and I was left to fend for myself with the elderly Alperts—who didn't care for my company, either.

"You were always working. Besides, I'd never been on a vacation. I wouldn't have known what to do."

Richard looked thunderstruck. "You never went on vacation?"

"Mom could barely pay the rent. Vacations were an unobtainable luxury."

"Jesus," he muttered.

"Don't sweat it. It's not important."

"But it should have been."

"I finally went on a vacation when I was nineteen." I smiled at the memory. "A buddy and I had a week's leave and bummed passage on a C-130 to San Francisco. I had the time of my life. We must've visited every bar on the wharf. Met a lot of ladies—and I use that term loosely. I was damn lucky not to get the clap."

"Ah, the good old days," Richard said, but his voice held no amusement.

"I've been a model citizen ever since," I bragged.

"What? Oh, sorry. I feel crummy when you tell me how things were for you growing up. I should've been there for you."

"Hey, you're here now." I had a feeling that was a lot more important. "Besides, you didn't have much choice. Look, I didn't mean to put a guilt trip on you. Let's just enjoy the day, okay? Besides, if you really feel bad, you can buy my forgiveness with a drink at dinner."

"That I can do."

We started off toward the Christmas shop. "So where'd you learn French?" I asked.

"I had a French governess. Grandmother thought it

was chic. And I spent a year studying in France before I started medical school. You sowed your wild oats in the army—I sowed mine in Paris."

"And had more fun, too."

His smile was enigmatic. "Probably."

An old Victorian mansion housed The Christmas Shop. We entered the Yuletide wonderland, its crown molding festooned with red and green twinkling lights while a forest of artificial Christmas trees lined the walls, their branches bowing under the weight of hundreds of ornaments. Christmas carols played softly in the background making the holiday atmosphere complete.

"We'll never drag Maggie out of here," I muttered.

"I want to look around anyway. If I don't come home with some kind of gift, I'll be in the dog house with Brenda."

"Suit yourself."

We split up, Richard entering the room on the right while I followed the path into the next room. Maggie stood before the sales counter, conversing with the clerk, a cheerful looking woman of indeterminate age. Heavyset, with streaks of silver in her hair, the woman's eyes seemed to twinkle behind her gold-framed glasses. She could've passed for Santa's wife, but the tag pinned to her Christmas-red apron read Barb.

" I looks like you bought out the store," I said, indicating the large floral gift bag Maggie held like a trophy.

"Jeff, this is Barbara Jenkins. She has a booth at the same antique co-op as Susan."

"It's a small world," I commented as we shook hands.

"I was telling Barb that I've known Susan since high school."

"Poor Susan," Barbara clucked.

"Poor?" I asked. Money squeezed, maybe, but certainly not without assets.

"She works so hard and she's so unhappy." Barb

shook her head in sympathy. "If only Zack would show a little more interest in the place."

"Lazy, huh?"

"Not that Susan's said. But he's away so much she seems to get stuck with most of the responsibility. We haven't seen much of her at the co-op lately."

"Their marriage is kind of rocky?" I guessed.

"She thinks he might be having an affair," Barb whispered. "Of course, you won't mention this to her, will you?"

"Oh, no," Maggie promised.

"She's having trouble financially, too," I put in, hoping to pump Barb for more information.

"She was looking for an investor, and asked me if I'd consider being her partner. But I don't want to get in the middle. I mean should there be a divorce."

"Their relationship is that rocky?" Maggie asked.

"Money can be the dividing factor when a marriage goes sour. Zack had a successful business back in Connecticut, and Susan talked him into selling it to buy the inn. Then she spent an awful lot to upgrade the place. They're still in the red and Zack resents it. I keep telling her it might take another two or three years before they see much of a profit, but Susan's impatient."

Richard wandered up, balancing a large teddy bear and several fragile-looking ornaments. "What do you think, Maggie? Will Brenda like these?"

"Oh, yes."

Barb became very businesslike and rang up Richard's purchases, then carefully wrapped them in holly-patterned tissue paper. Maggie made the mistake of admiring an unusual crèche and it was another twenty minutes before we could break loose from Barb's well-meaning lecture on the subject.

"I got the most beautiful blown-glass ornaments," Maggie said as we headed for the car. "Wait 'til you see them."

"Oh, boy," I deadpanned.

"I'd like to see them," Richard said kindly.

"No wonder you get to hear so many women's sexual fantasies."

It took half the trip back to Stowe to explain it to Maggie.

We decided against an early dinner and Richard dropped us at the municipal parking lot to pick up the Chevy. I saw the patrol car across the street when we first pulled up, but didn't give it much thought as I unlocked the car. Though the sun had retreated behind a bank of clouds, a blast of hot air greeted me when I opened the driver's door. I rolled down the window before getting in. Too bad the air conditioning had died during the former owner's tenure.

"Can we go to the grocery store?" Maggie asked. "I want to get another bottle of tonic."

"Sure."

I started the car, pulled out of the lot and noticed the patrol car slowly roll out behind me. Driving to the store, my eyes constantly darted to the rearview mirror. We parked and I waited while Maggie went inside. The cop car took a space at the other end of the lot.

Maggie smiled as she exited the store and got in the car. "I got some Vermont cheddar and a box of crackers, too. We can have a nice happy hour before we go to dinner."

I pulled back onto the highway, looking to see if my shadow followed.

It did.

"I don't want to disappoint you, love, but I don't think we're going to get a happy hour tonight."

"Why not?"

"Because we're being followed by a police car."

Maggie's carefree expression changed to concern. She craned her neck to look behind us.

"Don't panic. They might have had us staked out for a very good reason."

"Like what?"

"They probably just want to ask us a few more questions about Eileen's death. There's nothing to worry about," I reassured her.

I obeyed all the traffic laws. My shadow stuck to us like glue.

I pulled into the Sugar Maple's drive and saw two more police cars. Richard waited by the Buick, his expression grim. I'd had a feeling something was going to break in the case. I just didn't know the break was going to be me.

Richard hurried to my car. "Scuttlebutt is the ME has ruled Eileen Marshall was murdered," he said tightly. "They've searched the place and found an empty scotch bottle in your room. Don't say anything until I get you a lawyer."

"Rich, I didn't do anything. I only found the body. I didn't kill her."

Sgt. Beach shot out the front door, heading straight for us. I turned to Maggie. "They'll split us up. Don't tell them anything. Let me do the talking?" She nodded, her eyes mirroring her growing fear.

I got out of the car and leaned against it, my hands plainly visible. I was probably being overly cautious, but I didn't want to give the cops a reason to get rough with me.

"Sir, we have some questions we'd like to ask," Beach said.

"Ask away."

"Sir, we'd like to ask you these questions at the village police station. We'd like you to come along, too, ma'am."

"I don't have a lawyer," Maggie said uncertainly.

"You don't need one, ma'am."

My gaze darted to Richard. His eyes flashed, but he kept silent, unsure if he should leap to my defense. I shook my head slightly and he looked away.

"Sure, we'll go with you."

The sergeant escorted us to his patrol car. We climbed into the back seat and the door closed behind us.

There were no handles on the doors, which made me feel like a trapped animal.

Maggie plastered herself against me, clutching my hand like a lifeline. I gave her a smile. "It's okay, Maggs. Everything will be okay."

To say she looked skeptical was a definite understatement. I only hoped my assurances weren't blatant lies.

TWELVE

As predicted, upon arriving at the brick police station, they immediately separated Maggie and me, taking me to an interrogation room. Police Chief John McFadden himself and Sgt. Mark Beach did the honors. More than once they stressed it was just an informal meeting. I wasn't being charged with anything. Still, the word "yet" seemed to hang in the air.

McFadden sat across from me at a gray steel-and-Formica table, while Beach hovered nearby. The metal chair was cold, the room drab. I folded my hands on the table, trying to look the epitome of composure. I didn't succeed.

"I take it the medical examiner ruled Eileen Marshall's death a homicide." I didn't bother to phrase it as a question.

"No determination has yet been made. It's officially classed as undetermined," McFadden answered. Not according to Richard. "We're very interested in you since you were apparently the last person to see the victim alive, and you also found the body."

"That guy Adam *and* I found the body."

"You said Ms. Marshall was drinking scotch. That was corroborated by other guests at the inn. We found an empty plastic scotch bottle in your room. It was identified by several guests as the bottle Ms. Marshall had on Friday evening."

"Where was it found?" I asked.

"In one of the photographic trunks in your room. Wiped clean, no fingerprints. We'd like to know how it got there," Beach said.

"It had to be a plant."

"Why do you think that?" McFadden said. If he was trying not to be patronizing, he was failing miserably.

"Because somebody pushed me down a flight of stairs last night."

"We heard you fell," Beach said.

"I was pushed. Either I interrupted someone planting the evidence, or I messed up their escape."

"Or it could've been a clever ploy to divert suspicion."

I looked at Beach in disbelief. "Ask the doctor who checked me out. He can tell you I was knocked out—totally unconscious—from the fall. I have a lump on the back of my head to prove it."

"So maybe you're a good actor."

I took a breath to steady my nerves. They were trying to get to me, and in only a few short minutes they'd succeeded. Maybe I did need a lawyer.

"Am I going to be charged with murder?"

"Not at this time."

Great. Were they going to hold off until tomorrow?

"Let's go over your story again," Beach said.

We did.

In detail.

Twice.

When I'd finished, McFadden was glaring at me. "Your story hasn't changed in all the tellings. Like you rehearsed it."

"I've done my best to keep it the same."

McFadden's intense gaze betrayed his growing anger.

"Listen, Chief, I used to be an insurance investigator. I know what I saw, and I know how to tell my story in exactly the way the police need to hear it."

"Which leads me to believe you're lying."

"What reason do I have to lie? What motive would I have to kill a complete stranger?"

"You tell me. "

I exhaled loudly, desperate to keep my own rising anger in check. I spoke slowly, distinctly. "I don't have any reason to lie. Until three days ago, I didn't even know Eileen Marshall. I didn't know any of the people at the inn. I came to Stowe to take pictures of the inn for a magazine article. That's all."

"Then why did we find that scotch bottle in your room?"

"Obviously someone put it there to frame me. The locks on those guest room doors are as sophisticated as latches. You can open them with a hairpin."

"How would you know that?" McFadden asked.

I didn't answer.

McFadden shifted in his seat. "What's going on with you and this Dr. Alpert—the one who says you were knocked out last night."

"Can't you tell?"

His eyes narrowed in suspicion. "Look, if you want to be a wiseass, you can rot in a cell in St. Johnsbury for obstruction of justice. It's your choice."

I bristled at his tone. Cops are notoriously humorless. It was in my best interest not to make him angry.

"Now," he continued, "we happen to know you spent a good deal of time with this so-called doctor today. You were seen in Waterbury by two of the other guests. What's your connection to him?"

I hesitated. There was no point keeping this truth to myself.

"We're brothers. Half-brothers. And he really is a doctor."

"What's he doing here?"

"I asked him to come."

"I thought you were here with your girlfriend."

"I am."

"So what's he doing here?"

"He's here because I asked him to come," I repeated.

The cop spoke slowly, as though I was dim-witted. "*Why* did you ask him to come to Stowe?"

I answered in kind. "Because I wanted him to be here."

He exhaled loudly. "So, your brother drops everything, travels from where—Buffalo?—just because you asked him to?"

I nodded.

McFadden's patience snapped. "Listen, Resnick, you know more than you're telling me. "

I would've been more than happy to agree, but I was already in enough trouble.

"Are you going to tell me what you know?" he demanded.

I could ... but they weren't going to believe me. What I needed was instant credibility.

"Maybe. But I'm not saying a word until—"

"I don't make deals.

"You haven't heard it yet." The edge to my voice took some of the steam out of him.

"What do you want?"

"Call Detective Carl Hayden of the Orchard Park, New York, Police Department."

"Why?"

"Just ask him about me."

"And?"

"Then I might tell you everything I know." I couldn't keep the belligerence out of my voice.

McFadden's glare could blister paint. "What's the number?"

"Call directory assistance. The area code is 716."

He dialed, wrote down the number then punched it

in. Of course Detective Hayden wasn't there—it was, after all, a holiday weekend. McFadden gave them the number and asked them to pass on a message, agreeing to accept a collect call.

Beach went in search of coffee, and McFadden and I were left to stare at each other in uncomfortable silence. I wondered how much slack he'd cut me. An hour—less?—before he threw me in a cell. Lucky for me, Detective Hayden called back within five minutes. I owed him one for that.

The Chief introduced himself. "I have a man in custody who's either a suspect or a material witness in a murder investigation. Name's Jeffrey Resnick, of LeBrun Road in—"

McFadden listened for a few moments, then turned his skeptical gaze on me. "He's a what?"

I shrugged, sat back in my chair, listening to the one-sided dialogue. Beach returned half way through the conversation with only two cups. He set one in front of McFadden and sipped the other.

"And how about Richard Alpert? Uh-huh. You're sure?" McFadden paused, listening for a couple of minutes. I could just about hear the voice on the other end of the line, but I couldn't make out what was being said.

"Yes. I see. Thank you. Good-bye." He replaced the receiver, keeping his laser-like glare fixed on me.

"So, you're a psychic."

Beach spewed his coffee.

"That's what Detective Hayden calls it. I call it knowing some things about some people ... sometimes." No way did I want to label myself all-knowing.

"Just what do you know?"

"About this murder?" I thought about it for a moment, wondering how I could begin to explain it. "Sometimes I know things. Sometimes something trivial will trigger a flash of insight. Something like shaking hands when meeting someone."

They weren't buying it. I cleared my throat and decided to just tell them everything. If it already confirmed what they knew, so much the better.

"I shook hands with Eileen Marshall and I knew she was sick—probably deathly ill. She came to Stowe to see her married lover. I don't know why. I kind of thought there'd be a confrontation."

"Is that it?" he said, his tone indicating I was wasting his time.

"Something is going on between Ted Palmer and Laura Ross. Eileen knew what it was."

"Going on how?"

"You'd have to ask Laura. But whatever their connection is, Eileen Marshall knew about it and may have been in a position to use it against her."

"So who's Marshall's lover?"

"I'm not sure. It could be Fred Andolina, or Zack Dawson, or anyone in Stowe—or even you. I don't know."

"What made you look outside the inn to find Ms. Marshall?"

"I woke up that morning and had a feeling that something was very wrong. I knew someone was dead."

"How did you know?"

"I don't know. I just did."

Beach did a slow circuit around the table. "You say you get this insight by shaking hands?"

I nodded. "Sometimes. Then I'll just know things."

He thrust his hand in my face. "Try me."

"It doesn't work like that. I can't turn it on and off like a faucet."

"Try me," he challenged again.

My fists clamped shut. I hate this kind of crap. What I feared most was looking utterly stupid. Yet I could feel the air around him begin to charge with emotion.

Reluctantly I reached out and clasped his hand, hanging on. I looked him in the eye for a long moment. His brow furrowed and I could feel him draw inward, away from me. I took a sharp breath as his hand clenched convulsively around mine. An image from long ago flashed through my mind. I yanked back my hand, stared at the table for long seconds.

"Well?" he demanded. He sounded less confident than he had moments before. Whatever passed between us, he'd felt it, too.

I took my time before answering. The burst of strong emotion I'd experienced was a little overwhelming.

"Your sister ... is dead. She ... drowned. The two of you were just kids, fishing on a dock. You weren't supposed to be there." I thought about it for a moment, trying to remember exactly what I'd seen. "She ... had on a blue dress. Her shoes were—"

"Shut up!"

Waves of anger and embarrassment radiated from him like heat from a fire. Eileen Marshall's drowning had reignited Beach's grief, shame, and guilt over his sister's death. My words had reinforced it.

McFadden stared at his subordinate in disbelief.

I let out a shaky breath, trying to distance myself from his distress. "Sorry. But you asked."

He leaned in close, his eyes only inches from mine, his breath hot on my face. "I don't trust you."

I backed away. "Hey, the feeling's mutual."

McFadden cleared his throat. "Mark." He motioned the sergeant to follow him to the door. They spoke in hushed tones for several moments, looked back at me, and then abruptly left.

I sat in self-conscious silence, noticing the mirror on the wall. Was it two way? I really didn't care. I rubbed at my eyes, realizing I had the beginnings of another one of my headaches. The one I'd gotten the night before had never really left me, and invoking this psychic ability only seemed to aggravate it. I grabbed my prescription bottle from my pocket, doled out a pill and let it dissolve under my tongue, wondering how long they'd hold us here.

I'd told Maggie not to say anything to the cops, but what gentle means of persuasion would they use on her? How soon would she crack?

Folding my arms on the table, I rested my head on them. Was there a way to manipulate McFadden, get him to see another viewpoint? Had they established the time of death? The inn provided guests with towels for the pool. Did they leave them out all night? Was the Jacuzzi heated day and night? Were the lights trained on the pool on a timer or did they have to be turned off manually?

Maybe McFadden didn't really suspect me at all. Could this little exercise be a ploy to give the real killer a false sense of security? Anything was possible in a murder investigation.

My eyes squeezed tighter, and I felt a pang of pity for Eileen. Her lover had chosen not to make himself known. She'd lived with the prospect of a fatal disease, and she'd died naked and alone, possibly at the hand of one she'd loved.

I wished Maggie were with me. I wondered what mental acrobatics Richard was putting himself through. Lucky Brenda was home in Buffalo, oblivious to our predicament. She was a kindred spirit. Sometimes she could feel the same things I did. She called it second sight—but her gift wasn't as pronounced as mine. I reached out for her over the miles, but I was too far away.

Six months before I'd been living in Manhattan, truly alone. Since the mugging, my life revolved around those three people—I depended on them. Without them, my world would be pretty empty.

A shudder passed through me, and I felt my tenuous connection with them threatened. I covered my eyes, unsure if that swell of emotion was my own or a remnant from Beach's shaken psyche.

I lost track of time. After a long while, the door opened and the lights brightened. Sgt. Beach entered and tapped me on the shoulder. "You can go now. Ms. Brennan is waiting for you."

I glanced at my watch. It was after seven. "Can someone give us a lift back to the inn?"

"Yeah."

I followed him to the reception area. Maggie rushed to hug me.

"C'mon, Maggs, let's get the hell out of here." I put my arm around her shoulder and we followed a policewoman to a squad car, got in the back and traveled in strained silence.

A frightened, dry-eyed Maggie clung to me like a second skin. I couldn't guess what they'd put her through, and held her protectively in my arms.

Damn them. Damn them all.

THIRTEEN

Dark gray clouds thickened over the mountains and large drops of rain streaked the squad car's windows. Outside the muted landscape looked as bleak as I felt.

Finally the officer pulled up the Sugar Maple's drive. We had to wait for her to get out and open the back door from the outside. We said nothing and ran for the inn's covered porch. Richard had been waiting for us behind the screen door. He burst out and, without a word, embraced us.

"Let's have a drink," I said. "We've got some gin."

"I'll get the ice. Shall we meet back in my room?" he offered.

I retrieved the tonic, the cheese and crackers, and the camera from the Chevy, and left Maggie in Richard's care while I went upstairs to get the gin bottle.

The police had wrecked our room. The suitcases were dumped, our clothes and personal belongings were scattered in disorderly heaps. The bed was in pieces, the mattress and box springs leaned against the wall, while the sheets, blanket, and the bedspread were piled next to it. The rented camera equipment was strewn across the floor and I hoped to God none of it was broken.

I found the gin bottle amidst the clutter in the bathroom. Grabbing it, I closed the door on the mess, too heartsick to deal with it.

Richard let me into his room, which looked orderly

and sane compared to where I'd just been. He took the bottle from me and played bartender while I flopped down on the loveseat next to Maggie. A minute later he handed each of us a stiff drink.

"You both look shell shocked."

"I feel shell-shocked," I said. "Did they question you?"

"Not about the murder. Obviously I didn't arrive until after Ms. Marshall was dead."

"They know about you, Rich. I had to tell them we're brothers."

He shrugged, helplessly. "I did, too."

"I didn't tell them," Maggie blurted. Her voice cracked, her eyes brimming with sudden tears. "I did as you said—I didn't tell them a *damn* thing."

She blasted me with pent-up frustration and betrayal. For a moment I was stunned—by her revelation and her reaction. She'd endured God only knew what kind of verbal abuse from the local law, and had been the most resilient of the three of us. I reached for her hand and she yanked it from me, turning away. Richard stared at the floor, plainly embarrassed to be intruding on her emotional distress.

"Maggie, I'm sorry. I—"

She raised a hand to stop my feeble apology. When she finally turned back to face me, she'd regained her composure. "I'm just glad it's over."

"What did they say to you?" Richard asked.

She glared at me. "They tried to get me to say you killed Eileen. They didn't seem to care about the truth, they just wanted me to say it."

I turned to Richard. "What did they ask you?"

"First—where I live. As soon as I said Buffalo, the officer consulted his notes. He asked me my address, then wanted to know my relationship with you."

"Some real slick detective work on his part," I grumbled.

"Did you get a feel for what they know or don't know?" he asked me.

"I'm pretty sure McFadden believes I didn't do it, but he doesn't know who did, either."

Richard took a pull on his drink. "After the cops left, I found an old phone book behind the bar downstairs, went out on the patio, and I tried calling every lawyer listed. Thanks to the holiday weekend, I couldn't get hold of anyone. In desperation, I called my lawyer in Buffalo. He said he'd find someone to represent us by nine tomorrow. I told him I'd call back in the morning."

"Thanks."

I sipped my gin. The headache was still with me, and it wasn't wise for me to be drinking. Right then I preferred gin to my headache medication, even if I'd regret it later.

"So," Richard asked, "what happened?"

"Interrogations aren't fun. I needed someone in my corner, so they put in a call to Detective Hayden back home. He told them about my talent, and they put me to a test."

"Did you pass?"

"In spades. I think I freaked the sergeant. I nearly freaked myself." I told them about the vision. "After that, they left me alone. A while later, they let us go. But you know, I'm still shaking."

He raised his glass in salute. "Hear, hear."

"I'm hungry," Maggie said. It sounded so out of context—so incredibly normal.

"We've got the cheese and crackers," I suggested.

She shook her head. "Let's go someplace where there's lots of people and noise and comfort food, like soup and maybe a couple of rolls."

"Wouldn't you rather have a hot fudge sundae?" Richard asked.

"Maybe that, too," she sheepishly admitted.

I smoothed the hair around her face. "I'll bet the restaurant we went to last night could handle that."

"Are you up to driving yourself?" Richard asked. "After we eat, I'm going to hit the drugstore again."

"No problem. Come on, pretty lady. Your dinner awaits."

"I'll catch up with you at the restaurant. I want to change clothes and get cleaned up, too," Richard said.

"Okay. See you there."

He closed the door on us and we headed down the hall.

Kay Andolina sat in one of the wingback chairs in the lobby. She looked up from her book, craning her neck to see us as we headed for the front door. She shook her head in disapproval, as though the police must've made a mistake by letting us go.

I ignored the old witch, too weary to care what anyone—with the exception of Richard and Maggie—thought of me.

The rain came down in sheets. Maggie covered her head with her arms as we ran for the car. I was thankful I hadn't locked it. Once inside, Maggie tried to fluff her flattened hair. She looked absolutely ridiculous. I couldn't help but laugh.

"Hey," she protested as I leaned over to kiss her.

"You make me happy," I told her.

"You make me happy, too. But I'm hungry. Let's go!"

"Okay, okay."

I started the car, feeling better than I had in hours. We buckled up and I pulled onto the road.

I like to drive without distractions, but prolonged silence unnerves Maggie. She turned on the radio, playing with the scan button, trying to find a station. My attention was focused on the road when suddenly bright headlights appeared uncomfortably close behind us. Richard doesn't drive like a maniac, and the blinding lights were too high up to be the Buick. Right on my ass, they obliterated everything else in the rearview mirror.

Then it bumped us.

"Hey," Maggie cried, bracing herself against the dash.

I gripped the wheel, pressed the gas pedal closer to the floor and sped up, but the vehicle leapt forward and tapped my bumper again.

A car whipped by in the oncoming lane. The vehicle behind me made to pass, or so I thought. Instead its driver rammed me in the side.

"Who's doing this?" Maggie wailed.

I recognized the make as it smashed into us again—a Chevy Blazer 4x4. I held the steering wheel in a death grip, but the wet pavement and the force of the blow sent us skidding. Then we hit that spot in the road that I knew so well. Suddenly we were airborne, shooting like a projectile off the asphalt and into infinite space.

The Chevy hit the ground nostrils first, and then somersaulted ass over end. Papers and maps flew wildly around us. The Chevy righted itself before smashing into the earth, momentum gouging a trench as it carried us along the bottom of the embankment. A utility pole loomed. Maggie's screams seemed endless until the squeal of tearing metal and shattering glass obliterated them.

FOURTEEN

My senses returned one at a time. Sound registered first—a hissing noise. The radiator?

The car listed at almost a forty-five degree angle. I hung from my seat belt and shoulder harness like a snagged parachutist. It had kept me from going through the windshield, but my neck and chest were on fire, and my insides felt jumbled, like they'd gone through a Cuisinart. The interior of the car was dark, but the beam of the left headlight cut a narrow shaft through the darkness outside.

"Maggie?" I croaked.

There was no movement from the seat beside me. I grasped her elbow. She didn't react.

"Maggie!"

The driver's door was wrenched open, the dome light flashing on. "Jeff? Jeff, are you all right?"

I moved my head and winced. "Rich?"

"Are you okay? Is anything broken?"

"Get me out of here." I struggled with the seat belt but it wouldn't release.

"Hold on. Let me make sure you're all right before—"

"I'm okay—Maggie's hurt!"

He grabbed me by the waistband of my jeans, reached around me and wrestled with the seat belt latch, then hauled me out before I could fall onto Maggie. He leaned me against the rear door, held up two fingers. "How many?"

"You asked me that last night. It's still two!"

"Okay!" He went in after Maggie.

The dome lamp shed scant light. I watched him gently pull back the hair from her face. Blood stained the crazed glass on the passenger side window.

"Got a flashlight?" he asked.

While I fumbled under the driver's seat, Richard reached into his jacket pocket and pulled out a pair of latex gloves. Carrying them was a habit he'd gotten into after attending to an injured man some three months before. The threat of HIV still hung over him. It was something we didn't talk about.

Hands shaking, I gave Richard the flashlight. He moved back inside the car and peeled back one of Maggie's eyelids and shined the light.

"Maggie? Maggie, it's Richard. Can you hear me?"

She showed no reaction.

"She's got a pulse and she's breathing." Richard unbuckled her seat belt, checking her over for broken bones, careful how he touched her head. "So far nothing seems to be out of place."

Richard reached for her right leg and swore. The flashlight's beam ran across the twisted door. "We've got a lot of blood here, but she doesn't seem impaled." He set the flashlight on the dash.

"Where're the seat controls."

"In the front somewhere."

He fumbled with the seat in the dim light.

The odor of gasoline grew stronger. Except for sparking wires dangling from the pole above us—telephone or power?—I couldn't see a damn thing in the darkness.

"Rich, the gas tank's ruptured."

"As long as there's no fire, we should be all right. The rain will help dissipate it." He pulled the lever and the seat jerked back an inch or so—no more. He gave up, crouching over Maggie and swearing. I strained to see what he was doing when suddenly he sat back, fumbling with the belt at his waist.

"What're you doing?"

"There's too much blood. We've got to stop it."

My insides churned. "Shouldn't we get her out of the car first?"

"There's no time."

I watched helplessly as he stuck a hand under her thigh, brought the belt up, shoved the loose end through the buckle and pulled it taut—an instant tourniquet just I above the knee.

"Is there a hospital or a fire station nearby?" he asked, his voice remarkably calm.

"The fire department's in the village—next to the police station."

For a split second, his face registered indecision. Then, "No time to wait for help. We'll put her in the back of the wagon. The keys are inside. Go open the gate. Put the back seat down."

I turned, running—stumbling up the embankment and practically skidded to a halt in front of the old car. I yanked the keys from the ignition, and then slipped on the wet gravel on my way to the back. The gate flew open, but I had no clue how to get the back seat to lay flat.

"Jeff!"

Frantic, I hopped inside. Searching the seat's top and sides, I finally found the catch and folded it flat.

"Jeff!"

I slid on my backside down the muddy hillside to the hulk of my car. The Chevy had shifted. Above it a power line writhed like a snake, with sparks dancing from it.

My God—the ruptured gas tank!

Cradling her head and neck, Richard backed out, pulling Maggie's dead weight across the shifter, then stopped, struggled out of the car, reached back in, and then dragged her some more.

"Help me! Careful of her leg."

Richard took most of her weight, frantically trying to support her neck as we half-dragged, half-carried her up the rain-slick embankment. A whoosh broke the night as the Chevy went up in a huge, orange fireball—the force of the explosion rolling over us like the concussion from a bomb.

I stumbled and swayed.

"Jeff," Richard hollered, his voice keeping me alert. We staggered the last ten feet to the back of the wagon. "Support her head," he ordered, as he transferred her weight to me before he crawled inside the back of the car. He took her from me and carefully pulled her inside. Scrunched alongside her, Richard shoved a hand into his pocket, grabbed his clean handkerchief, caught my hand and slapped it against Maggie's mangled calf.

"Hold this."

When he removed the belt, her warm blood gushed into the cotton.

"What're you doing?" "Moving the tourniquet farther down her leg." He struggled out of his jacket, tucked it around her head like padding, then reached for her throat to take her pulse.

"She's in deep shock. We've got to get her some help—now!" He looked up at me. "Can you drive?"

"Yeah," I answered automatically.

He pushed my hand aside, taking the sodden handkerchief. "Do it!"

I slammed the gate, jumped into the car, jabbed the key into the ignition and started it, then fumbled with the controls on the dash until I turned on the dome light.

The flames from my car reached into the dark night as I shoved the Buick into gear and took off, gravel flying, heading for the center of town.

We flew down the road, past hotels with no-vacancy signs and deserted strip malls with all the stores closed. Traffic was sparse. I ran a red light, turned the corner and gunned it until I saw the fire station lit up like a beacon in the night. A police cruiser sat under the sodium vapor lamp. I pulled in, braked and honked the horn.

"I'm going in," I told Richard, then I jumped out of the car and ran.

The lady cop who'd driven Maggie and me back to the inn sat perched on the edge of a desk, drinking coffee with a uniformed fireman. Her face went blank as I skidded to a halt in front of them.

"We were in an accident! My girlfriend's hurt bad." They spilled their coffee as their cups hit the table with a thunk.

The cop shoved me back outside. "They're on a call," she said, her sweeping hand taking in the empty station as we ran.

"My brother's a doctor—he's with her."

The cop ducked into the still-open driver's side of the wagon. "What've you got?"

"Lower extremity—possible torn artery, and a head injury. "

"Jesus," she breathed.

"Can you give us an escort to a hospital?"

"The nearest one's in Morrisville—about nine miles north of here."

"Have they got a c-collar or gauze inside? I need a pressure bandage!"

I yanked the keys out of the ignition once more, ran to the back of the wagon and opened the gate.

The firefighter pushed past me, bogged down with a big tackle-box-like first-aid kit, a backboard, and a couple of blankets.

Richard grabbed a blanket, shoving it under Maggie's injured leg.

I stood back, feeling useless.

The fireman donned surgical gloves before he opened the back door. He secured the collar around Maggie's neck while Richard set up the dressing on her leg.

I couldn't take in their shorthand conversation, spoken in medical jargon. The rain and the chill air seeped straight into my bones. I peered through the rain-dotted window. Maggie's pale, slack face looked bloodless under the eerie yellow light. Usually she's an extension of my soul—a calming influence that's a pleasure to glom onto. My connection to her was now shattered. She breathed so shallowly I was scared to death she might stop.

"What happened?" the lady cop demanded of me.

I tore my gaze from Maggie. "We ... were forced off the road. A black Blazer four-by-four. We got her out of the car—it blew up."

"Fire?"

I nodded.

"Where?" she demanded.

"A mile or two back up the road."

"The Mountain Road?"

"Yes."

"I'll call it in and alert the hospital we're coming in." She dashed back into the building.

Richard and the fireman maneuvered Maggie onto the backboard.

I stood there, soaked by the pouring rain, feeling stupid and useless.

The officer was back. "Whenever you're ready," she told Richard.

"Let's go!"

"Good luck," the fireman called as we took off.

The drive to Morrisville was the longest twenty minutes of my life. Richard and I didn't speak—I was too scared to ask any questions, but he spoke to Maggie, telling her she'd be okay, his voice calm and reassuring, though I doubted she could hear a word. By the time the lights of the town appeared, the muscles in my arms were quivering from my death grip on the steering wheel.

The police cruiser slowed and cut its siren. We pulled up in front of the hospital's emergency entrance. A team of people in scrubs descended on the car, their voices a tangle that was impossible to comprehend.

Richard squirmed out the back of the wagon. In a fluid motion, they transferred Maggie to a gurney and whisked her inside, with Richard still holding onto the pressure bandage.

"You can park over there," the lady cop told me.

Still on autopilot, I did as I was told, yanked the keys from the ignition and sprinted for the emergency entrance. The automatic doors whooshed open—the bright fluorescent lights stung my eyes. The cop was waiting for me.

"Do you need help, sir?" The urgency had left her voice.

"What?"

"Were you injured in the crash?"

"I ... I don't know. I don't think so."

"Sit down." She pushed me into a chair. A minute or so later she returned with a nurse.

The matronly, gray-haired woman in a white polyester pantsuit held a clipboard in one hand, and a pen in the other. "Are you a relative or friend of the patient they just brought in?"

"She's my girlfriend."

"I need to ask you some questions. Are you okay to answer?"

"I think so."

She sat beside me.

"Was it a car accident? Was she wearing a seat belt?"

I nodded and winced. "Yeah. "

She asked me about the accident before getting to

Maggie's name, age, and address. Did she have allergies? Was she taking medication? Alarmed, I found I couldn't answer even the most basic questions on her medical history.

The nurse studied my face. "You look pretty shook up. Our staff is small, but we'll check you out as soon as we can, okay?"

I nodded, grateful for her kindness. She smiled, patted my shoulder, and disappeared.

The policewoman was back at my elbow, pressing a cup of vending machine coffee into my hand. Double sugared, it tasted terrible. Shaky, I sipped it anyway.

She sat beside me, a notepad in hand. "Where exactly did the accident take place?"

It took a moment for the facts to assemble in my brain. "Route 108, about two miles north of the fire station.

"Do you think you could identify the car that hit you?" For a split second the Blazer's back end had been illuminated in the glow of my headlights. Until that moment I hadn't made the connection between the vision and reality.

"Colorado," I whispered, closed my eyes and remembered in photographic detail what I had seen. "Colorado license plate FWP-284."

"Are you sure?" she asked, sounding skeptical.

"Yes."

"Because Vermont and Colorado plates are similar—both green and white."

I shook my aching head. "There were snowy mountains. It said Colorado."

"And you say the truck deliberately hit you?"

"It was a Blazer. Too bad my car went up in flames—you'd have seen the black paint on the driver's side."

She asked me where we'd been headed, if I knew a reason why someone would do this, and I don't know what else. The interrogation exhausted me. Finally, she promised she'd call a wrecker to tow what was left of my car. Someone would follow up on our case tomorrow.

Great, now we were somebody's case.

She patted my shoulder, wished me luck and left me alone.

Time dragged.

My heart pounded endlessly. Could that much adrenaline pumping through you for hours on end be detrimental?

Half an hour passed and Richard hadn't reappeared.

That was okay. If he was with Maggie, he'd make sure she got the best care ... professional courtesy and all that.

I looked down at myself. Maggie's blood stained my shirt and pants, making me look like I'd dived into the slops of a slaughterhouse. I got up and asked the woman at the reception desk where to find the men's room, then staggered off in that direction.

Leaning against the counter, I avoided looking at my reflection in the mirror. As I washed the blood from my hands, my gaze strayed. Red-rimmed eyes looked back at me. My stiff neck and chest ached like I'd gone nine rounds with a heavyweight champ. I raised my shirt. Red and purple welts—the beginnings of bruises where the seat belt had saved me—were livid.

I'd survive.

I shuffled on unsteady legs back out to the waiting room and sat as far away from everyone as I could. I couldn't concentrate to read the out-of-date magazines. I couldn't watch whatever nonsense boomed from the TV attached to the wall. I avoided the eyes of the other people waiting for word on their own loved ones or friends. My head ached and I couldn't think, and it was all I could do to keep from crying. For Maggie, for me, for this whole convoluted mess we were in.

Eons passed.

Like a tape on a loop, in my mind I replayed the image of Maggie lying so deathly pale in the back of the station wagon. Her eyes closed, her hair matted with blood.

Should I call Brenda? What would I tell her? That her best friend was hurt. That she might die.

No, I couldn't put her through that kind of worry.

I'd let Richard do it ... later, when the crisis wasn't so close at hand.

So I sat there. Trying not to think. Trying not to feel. I couldn't manage that either. Instead, I tried to numb my thoughts by staring at the floor, counting the tiles, reciting my times tables. Everything and nothing occupied my mind. I leaned back in my chair, idly rubbing the back of my sore neck. I wanted a drink, no matter how badly my head would pound for it. A nice warming glass of bourbon—

Then I remembered that nice, tall, stiff gin and tonic Richard had made when we'd gotten back from the police station earlier in the evening. Could that comforting drink have impaired my reactions enough to nearly get Maggie and me killed? If I hadn't had that goddamned drink, could I have steered out of the skid? If I'd never taken a sip, would Maggie be bumped and bruised but otherwise okay? If the lady cop had given me a Breathalyzer test, could I have passed it?

Yes, damn it! I knew my limits. I knew the legal and moral ramifications of driving drunk. And after my ordeal at the police station, it would've taken a hell of a lot more than one drink to numb my reflexes—not to mention my anger.

At the time of the accident I was stone, cold sober.

If I owned any guilt for this, it was because I hadn't listened to that feeling of warning every time I passed that spot in the road. Why hadn't I investigated an alternate route into the village? Why?

It was a long time before Richard, dressed in pale blue cotton scrubs, finally walked through the double doors into the waiting room. Instantly on my feet, I met him halfway.

He rested a hand on my shoulder. "They've got good people here. She lost a lot of blood—has a nasty muscle tear—but she's going to be okay."

I could've cried with relief; instead, I hugged him. "Thanks. I can't tell you—"

He pulled back and looked me in the eye, looking haggard. "*This* is why you needed me to come to Vermont, right?"

"I think so ... yes. I ... just—she would've died if you weren't there for her. Thanks, Rich. Thanks for saving my lady."

He brushed aside the comment and clasped my shoulder. "She's got a concussion. They're going to keep her for a few days. Are you okay?"

I rubbed the back of my neck. "I think I got whiplash. I don't care. Can I see her?"

"Just for a minute. Come on." He led me back to one of the curtained treatment rooms.

Maggie lay on a gurney with an IV in her arm; a unit of blood and some other bag filled with clear liquid hung overhead. A blanket was drawn up to her chin. I searched under it for her other hand and her eyes fluttered open.

"Were you trying to scare me to death?" I asked her.

"Are you okay?" she whispered, taking in my bloodied clothes.

"I'm fine—it's you I'm worried about."

"Richard took care of me. He held my hand the whole time. He made me feel safe." Her voice was so quiet, so strained. She squeezed my hand ever so slightly. "Will you bring me some clothes so I can get out of here?"

"Sure. I'll be here first thing tomorrow."

A nurse tapped me on the shoulder. "Sir, you'll have

to leave."

"Okay." I turned back to Maggie. "I gotta go." I kissed her. Her skin still felt cool to the touch. She wouldn't let go of my hand.

"I gotta go, Maggs," I said again, and reluctantly pulled my hand free. "I'll see you in the morning."

A tear seeped from her eye. I dabbed it with the corner of the blanket before turning my back on her, feeling like a monster for leaving her alone.

I couldn't look back.

Richard waited for me in the hall. "Come on, Dr. Wimberly's going to check you out before we go."

"I don't need—"

"No arguments." He grabbed me by the elbow and steered me to an empty treatment room.

A couple of x-rays later I, too, was dressed in clean scrubs—my bloody, bio-contaminated clothes discarded—and was released from the ER. Though bumped and bruised only, I still felt lousy.

"Do you want to stay in town tonight? If we can find a place," Richard amended.

I glanced at my watch, shocked to find it was after one. "No. I have to bring some clothes up for Maggie in the morning anyway. Do you think you can find your way back to the inn?"

"I expect so. Come on. You look beat."

We headed for the car. The rain came down hard, that steady downpour that makes flowers grow in the spring. But this was early fall; the flowers would die at the first hint of frost.

I handed Richard the keys and maneuvered myself into the passenger seat. I remembered the bloodstained rug in back and idly wondered what the rental company would charge Richard for a cleaning fee.

Moments later we were on the road, heading south back toward Stowe.

The thump, thump of the windshield wipers was hypnotic. I must've fallen asleep, for the next thing I knew Richard was nudging me awake. I blinked, taking in the inn's familiar parking area and the line of cars I recognized. Of course there was no black Blazer sitting among them.

"You ought to stand under a hot shower for a few minutes," Richard suggested.

"We don't have a shower."

"I do—and I've got two double beds. You can bunk with me tonight."

I opened the car door and just about every muscle in my body screamed as I struggled to stand. Richard had to steady me as I staggered to the front door. It was locked. Richard leaned on the bell and it wailed somewhere in the quiet, darkened inn. Nobody showed up for what seemed like ages. Finally the lights came on and a bleary-eyed Zack shuffled to the door, clad in a fluffy, white terrycloth bathrobe like the one Eileen had worn the night she was murdered.

"Do you know what time it is?"

"Somewhere around two o'clock," Richard answered easily, pushing past the startled innkeeper.

"We have rules—" Zack sputtered.

"Take a look at us. Do we look like we've been partying?" I asked.

Zack finally noticed our hospital costumes. "Good God! What happened?"

"I had a little accident." I didn't have the energy or the patience to explain it to Zack—I just wanted to crash. I started in the direction of Richard's room.

"Good night," Richard said, ever polite, and followed in my wake.

I leaned against the wall, waiting for Richard to find the key and unlock the door. He went in ahead of me and turned on the light. I stepped into the room, saw the bed and made a beeline for it.

"Oh no you don't—get in that shower," he ordered, grabbed my arm, and led me to the bathroom.

"I just want to sleep."

"You won't be able to move tomorrow if you don't."

"It'll wake the other guests."

"Well, one of them is a murderer anyway. Besides, in case it escaped your attention, little brother, that same person probably tried to kill you and almost killed Maggie tonight."

I met his angry gaze.

"I'll try to stay in the shower for twenty minutes."

Too tired to stand, I think I only lasted five.

By the time I toweled off and staggered into the bedroom, I found the bed turned down and Richard gone. A note on the pillow read: *Went downstairs to call Brenda. Back in a few minutes.*

I found two Tylenol and an empty glass on a tray sitting on the bedside table. I poured water from the carafe, downed the pills and hit the sack.

As I drifted off to sleep, I thought about what Richard said. One of the other guests was probably a murderer.

Either that, or one of the inn's owners.

FIFTEEN

"Jeff—hey, come on, wake up." I squinted up at Richard looming over me. My head ached. Every muscle in my body protested at the slightest movement. I closed my eyes, burrowing back under the covers. "Go away."

"They're shutting down the kitchen in fifteen minutes. If you don't get up now, you won't eat."

"I don't care."

"Yes, you will. Besides, Maggie will be waiting for us."

That, at last, made an impact on me.

I remembered Maggie's frightened, crystal blue eyes boring through me with such trust back in the emergency room the night before. I promised to be there for her—that I'd bring her some clothes. I'd felt like a heel at leaving her.

I managed to rouse myself, feeling hung over and sick to my stomach. The thought of greasy eggs and bacon made my stomach roil. "I can't eat."

"Yes you can. Listen, I'll go down and get you a muffin and some fruit. Get in that shower, or I'll throw you in when I get back." His voice was stern and I had no doubt he'd carry through with his threat. The door closed behind him.

Richard was right. I needed to eat; I needed to take my medication. I had to get rid of the headache or I'd find myself cowering in a dark, silent room all day, and I couldn't afford to waste that kind of time.

Straightening, and then walking, proved an ordeal. Evidently Richard had gone up to my room, for I found a clean change of clothes on the vanity in the bathroom. It took nearly ten minutes in the shower before the hot water eased the aches down to my bones. I'd hoped the cloud of steam would clear my head as well, but things were still a muddle when I emerged.

Richard waited for me in the bedroom, flipping through an old copy of Smithsonian magazine. As promised, a breakfast tray sat on the coffee table in front of the loveseat, along with a muffin, a banana, and a small carafe of coffee. Richard's prescription was simple: "Eat."

"Thanks. Thanks for getting the clothes, too."

He moved to sit on the chair adjacent to me. "The police really did a number on your room."

"My God, that's right. It'll take me an hour to straighten it out."

"It's okay. I got most of it back in order."

"What time did you get up?"

"About seven. You were dead to the world. I was the first down to breakfast, too. I apologized to Zack for coming in so late last night, and explained what happened to Maggie. Susan seemed quite concerned."

"She's probably worried the article won't get finished."

Richard frowned. He isn't half as cynical as me.

"Thanks, Rich. I don't know what I would've done if you weren't here."

"Until we got to the hospital—until I knew she was okay.... I was worried that I'd made the wrong decision, that I—"

I started working on the muffin's paper wrapper. "What are you talking about?"

"The way we got Maggie out of the car wasn't exactly by the book."

"We had to get her out. The fire—"

"I know. I was afraid she'd bleed to death, and yet I didn't know how serious her head injury was. If her neck had been broken...."

"Don't dwell on it, Rich. There was no time. We did what we had to do and she's going to be fine."

He nodded. "You're right. You're absolutely right."

Then why did he look so guilty?

I took a bite of muffin and remembered something Richard had said the night before. "What did you mean when you said Eileen's murderer tried to kill Maggie and me last night?"

He looked up, surprised. "You're the psychic. You mean you don't think these incidents are connected?"

"Yes, but—"

"First someone tries to implicate you for Eileen Marshall's murder. Next they push you down a flight a stairs, then ram your car. I'd say someone's serious about getting you out of the way. Now what did you see or know about the murder that can expose the killer?"

"I don't know."

"Well, you'd better think about it."

I poured the coffee, doctoring it with milk from a small metal creamer. I dug in my pocket for my prescription bottle, shook out a pill, and downed it with a sip of coffee. Some things just didn't add up.

"How'd you find us so fast last night, anyway?"

"I decided not to change clothes after all, just grabbed a sport jacket and headed for the restaurant. I didn't see the car that ran you off the road, but as I came round the bend I saw headlights down the embankment. I didn't know it was you until I stopped."

"Thank God you did."

"Now I want some straight answers."

I didn't like his tone.

"Jeff, you knew something wasn't right—that's why

you asked me to come to Vermont. Why didn't you come home? Why did you stay here?"

"Because ... this was Maggie's trip. I couldn't ask her to leave." Not exactly an articulate defense.

Richard stared at me, his worried frown like a judgment.

"Besides, what if I'd been wrong? What if being wrong blew Maggie's chance at another magazine article? She doesn't want to be a secretary for the rest of her life. She wants to write. How could I spoil it for her on a dumb feeling I wasn't even sure about?"

"Because you trust those feelings."

"Maybe I don't trust them as much as I think I do. As much as I should."

"Maybe none of us listens to our survival instincts like we should," he admitted. "I didn't want to believe in this psychic ability of yours, but we both know it works."

"Then maybe you'll believe me when I say that I just can't walk away from this crap. It holds me prisoner." I wasn't explaining myself well. "If I'd gone home, I would've gotten the same insights—the same feelings, and what I know would've forced me back here. Like it forced me to go to Buffalo with you after I was mugged in Manhattan."

"'There are more things in heaven and earth than are dreamed of in your philosophy,'" Richard misquoted. "Okay, no more guilt trip. But Maggie won't be up to traveling for a couple of days, which means we're stuck here. At least she'll be safe at the hospital—away from this place."

"Then you really think we're in danger?"

"Don't you?"

I nodded wearily. "I guess so." I peeled the banana and broke it in half. God, I really wasn't thinking clearly. Was it some kind of delayed reaction? "What do we do next?"

"It's your call."

"See Maggie. Tell her we're going to leave her up in Morrisville alone ... she'll love that."

"Jeff, she could've died. She needs complete rest for a couple of days. And coming back here is not conducive to the peace and quiet she needs."

"That sounds very logical. But she's Irish, like our mother, and you don't want to mess with those fightin' Irish genes."

"I'll talk to her. We'll get her a TV, make sure she's hooked up to a phone. It's not like we're abandoning her. We'll go see her this morning and later we'll have dinner with her."

I mulled it over. What he said made a lot of sense, and I was more than content to let Richard try to sell Maggie on the idea. He could probably pull it off, too.

I drained my cup and stood. "I'd better go up to the room and figure out what to take to her."

"Meanwhile, I'll take this tray back downstairs and meet you by the car." He dug in his pocket. "Here's your key."

"Thanks."

The stairs seemed steeper, and I found myself slowing as I neared the top but there was no one there.

The door to our room swung open and I saw that thanks to Richard's efforts a certain degree of order had been restored. The bed had been put back together, with the spread drawn up and smoothed over the pillows. Though Richard would never make it as a domestic, our clothes were neatly folded in piles on top of the bed.

I sorted out some things I figured Maggie would need, putting them in her overnight bag. The camera equipment was stacked neatly on top of the trunks, looking none the worse for wear. I replaced each piece in its foam packing and wondered if the cops had made the mess before or after they'd found the scotch bottle. Had they done as thorough a job on the other guests' rooms, or had I been singled out?

The thought bothered me.

Grabbing the overnight bag, I shut the door behind me and hurried downstairs, turned the corner, and headed outside.

"Jeff?"

It was Susan. No way did I want to talk to her. If it hadn't been for her, we never would've come to Stowe. I would've been home in Buffalo, my car intact. I'd be grilling hot dogs for lunch instead of heading for a hospital, in a strange town, to visit Maggie.

She came to the screen door. "Jeff, the doctor said he was going to drive you to the hospital."

"Yeah."

"Please tell Maggie how sorry I am that this happened. If there's anything she needs—"

I tried to swallow my anger at her phony display of friendship. "Sure. I'll tell her." I turned and walked away.

Richard waited for me by the Buick.

"Let's get out of here," I said. He took the bag from me and put it on the back seat. I levered myself into the passenger seat. He got in, started the engine, and pulled onto the highway.

As we neared the accident site Richard slowed the car, pulling over to the side of the road. "I thought you might want to take a look."

I made no comment as we inspected the area. No more bad vibes—not a damn thing. If not for the scorched grass and the tilted power pole, no one would ever guess what had happened there the night before.

I faced him. "Let's go."

Hospitals are the scariest places on Earth. But the neat brick building looked a lot friendlier in the light of day than it had in a downpour the night before. We paused at the reception desk to get directions to Maggie's room. Next we stopped at the tiny gift shop for a teddy bear and an African violet in a little ceramic pot before heading up to the second floor. Maggie had a private room, no doubt at Richard's request. A huge floral arrangement sat on the bedside table.

"Hey, someone beat me to it," I said in greeting, eyeing the vase filled with cheerful chrysanthemums and carnations.

"They're from Brenda and Richard. Aren't they pretty?"

Maggie sat up straighter in bed. Her stringy hair, lack of makeup, and a pasty skin tone made no difference to me. She looked absolutely beautiful.

I leaned down to kiss her. She hugged me, wrapping her fingers in the folds of my shirt—reluctant to let go. "I brought you some company," I said, and managed to escape her embrace. I put the plant on the table and handed her the sad-looking, little blue bear.

"He's so cute. I'll bet his name is Roger."

"As a matter of fact, it is."

Richard stepped forward. "How're you feeling, Maggie?"

"Better, but I've still got an awful headache. If yours are anything like this, Jeff, you have my sympathy."

I gave her a half-hearted smile.

"Did you bring my clothes?"

Richard held up the overnight bag.

"Great. I can't wait to get out of here."

"I don't think you're going anywhere, love."

Maggie's blue eyes narrowed in betrayal. "What?"

"Did the nurses say you were being released today?" Richard asked.

"No, but—"

"If you were my patient, I'd insist that you stay for a couple of days at least. You were involved in a very serious accident."

"Yeah. The car didn't survive," I told her.

"The car was totaled?" she asked.

"It blew up like an H-bomb."

She leaned back against the pillows, suddenly a lighter shade of pale. "But I don't want to stay here by myself. I want to go home—to Buffalo."

"We still haven't been cleared by the cops. But it won't be so bad. We'll get you fixed up with a TV and a phone—"

"I can't afford even that. My purse—it was in the car."

"Rich will take care of it—"

Her gaze darted to my brother, her voice hushed. "I can't ask—"

"Maggie, please let me do this."

She looked away, her hand gripping the bedside rail, her knuckles going paper white. Her sorrow, grief and embarrassment rolled over me. Unprepared, I gasped, groping for the other bed rail to steady myself.

Richard was suddenly beside me. "Jeff?"

I waved him aside, trying to take in a lung full of air. "I'm ... okay."

Maggie looked at me, wiping her nose with her free hand. "What's wrong?"

I swallowed. "Don't ... ever say ... I don't know ... how you feel." My throat felt like it was closing, making it hard to speak. "Right now ... I know exactly ... what you're feeling."

Her eyes squeezed shut and she bit her lip as the tears overflowed. The onslaught of renewed emotion constricted my chest.

Richard grabbed my elbow and hauled me up off the chair, steering me toward the door. "Go take a walk while Maggie and I talk."

My proximity to Maggie was a definite influence—with every step away from her, my breathing eased. "I'll be back."

The angst quickly dissipated as I headed down the hall to a cluster of empty chairs by the nurse's station. "Drinking fountain?" I asked.

"Down the hall, on the right," said the woman on duty.

Absorbing someone else's emotional baggage is a bummer. Maggie and me—I considered us soul mates, but I'd never had to deal with such an intense explosion of feeling from her before. In the future I'd have to learn to guard against it.

I found the fountain and took a couple of sips. The water tasted flat, metallic. I headed back for the chairs and collapsed into one. A well-read copy of the morning newspaper lay on a table. I leafed through it, bored. A three-paragraph story with no byline recapped Eileen's murder, quoting Susan. I wondered if Ashley Samuels, the reporter who'd showed up at the inn on Saturday, had written it. I tore it out, stuck it in my wallet, and set the paper aside.

Sitting back in the chair, I watched as robe-clad patients walked by, pulling their rolling IV poles. It was nearly noon. Hospital personnel pushing food carts emerged from the elevator and passed by me. I glanced at my watch. Ten minutes had passed; long enough. I got up and headed back down the hall.

Maggie's laughter never sounded so sweet. I paused in the doorway, drinking in her mood change. The little bear was secured in the crook of her arm, and a carnation from the flower arrangement was tucked behind one ear. "Welcome back," she said.

"I'll see about getting the TV and phone put in," Richard said, and got up from the chair. "I'll be back in a few minutes."

I watched him go and took the seat he'd just vacated.

"You're a whole different person than the one I left a few minutes ago. What did Richard say to you?"

"I don't know. He's just so easy to talk to."

I feigned insult. "What about me?"

"You're just easy." She reached for my hand, squeezing it with warm fingers, so unlike the night before.

"Are you really okay?" I asked.

"I hurt, but I've been worse."

"Me, too. And when you consider the alternative, I guess we were really pretty lucky. You should see my seat belt bruises."

She pulled at the collar of her hospital gown, looking down at her chest. "Bet I could match them. And boy, do they hurt." She laughed again and winced.

"We're going to bring you dinner tonight. Do you want anything special?"

"I don't care."

A rattling at the door captured our attention. "Lunchtime," said the aide. She moved the flowers aside and pushed the bed table closer, setting the brown plastic lunch tray within Maggie's easy reach before turning back for the door.

Maggie removed the warming cover and wrinkled her nose at the thin broth, can of ginger ale and cup of gelatin. "Anything's better than this."

I looked over the tray. "They can't really ruin Jell-O."

"But it's green." She sniffed the soup, scowled, and then pushed the tray table aside.

"I brought your tablet of paper and stuff in case you feel like writing. And the book you're reading is in there, too. We can get you some magazines from the gift shop if you want."

She shook her head, reached for my hand and held it, smiling at me. "I love you, Jeff."

I pulled my chair closer. "I love you, too, Maggs. In good times and bad." I kissed her fingers.

"The good times have outweighed the bad, haven't they?"

"Ever since the day I met you."

"You're just saying that because it's true."

"You're right." It was my turn to smile; it was a game we'd played many times before. I held her hand as though it were made of glass, realizing just how close I'd come to losing her.

"What'll you do about your car?"

"It's insured. And the accident certainly wasn't our fault."

"And it wasn't an accident either, was it?"

"No."

We ran out of things to say, just sitting there, staring into each other's eyes, hanging onto one another other, and feeling grateful to be alive.

Richard returned and the three of us talked about everything except the situation back at the inn. Richard cajoled Maggie to at least sip the ginger ale before the aide took the lunch tray away. After a while, Maggie's eyelids began to droop.

"You need a nap, and I have to find out about the car," I said, getting up from the chair.

"You will come back tonight, right?"

"Of course." I set her book and writing tablet on the bed table within her reach. We kissed her good-bye and started down the hall.

"Are you okay?" Richard asked once we were out of Maggie's earshot. "You had me worried there for a minute when you started hyperventilating."

"She caught me off guard. I've never tuned into her feelings like that before. I'm used to experiencing some of what she feels, but that was scary."

He shook his head ruefully. "I keep telling you, you'd make a great study project."

"And I keep telling you I don't want to be anyone's guinea pig." I rubbed my stiff neck.

"We can get you a cervical collar at the drugstore," he offered.

"No, thanks. They look stupid."

"It'll make you feel better."

"No, thanks."

"God forbid you should feel better."

"Speaking of feeling better, what did you say to turn Maggie around?"

"That you love her—that we all do. Love is a powerful force for healing the sick."

I thought he was kidding, but his dead-serious expression humbled me.

We climbed into the car and headed back toward Stowe. I tried to keep my gaze straight ahead, but with every bump and turn the muscles in my neck screamed. I might regret not taking him up on the offer of a collar.

"Should we head for the police station?" Richard asked, once we'd crossed the Stowe village line.

"We may as well. They should be able to tell me where my car was towed."

Richard braked, looking past me to the right. "Unless I miss my guess, that's it."

He pulled into a service station, stopping the car alongside the tangle of metal that had once been my trusty Chevy.

I hauled myself out of the station wagon, my legs feeling shaky at the sight of the buckled passenger door. Only a miracle had saved Maggie from dying on impact.

All the glass was gone, blown out or melted—the interior was a charred mess. The back end was crumpled like an old soda can, with not a trace of paint remaining.

Richard placed a hand on my shoulder. "Let's go."

We drove back to the inn in shattered, unnerving silence.

SIXTEEN

The answering machine at my insurance company reminded me it was a holiday and to call back Tuesday morning after 8 o'clock eastern time. So much for customer service.

I went in search of Richard, but instead found Sgt. Beach waiting for me in the inn's living room. He held a paper sack in one hand.

"More questions?" I asked.

"Yes. Sorry to hear about your accident."

"Thanks."

"I read the report. Last night a black Blazer four-by-four was stolen from one of the motels along the strip. It was found this morning with damage consistent with what you described to the officer last night."

"What about the license plates?"

He shook his head. "No plates. No fingerprints, either. How's your girlfriend?"

"She nearly bled to death. My brother, the so-called doctor, saved her life."

"Hey, I'm sorry if you feel we hassled you yesterday, but this is a murder investigation."

"So it's been ruled homicide?"

"Did you have any doubts?"

I shook my head. "No."

"We're spending most of our time trying to get background information on all the guests. That's not easy on a holiday weekend. But we're pursuing some leads. I'm here to question several of the guests again. We'll have this nailed down in the next thirty-six hours. Toward that end—" He shoved the paper sack at me. "Take a look."

I opened the bag; Eileen's scotch bottle. "What am I supposed to do with this?"

"You tell me. You're the psychic."

I sighed, looked down at my feet and winced, grabbing my sore neck. Anger, humiliation and defeat crowded around me. "Does McFadden know you brought this here?"

"I'm in charge of the investigation."

"So what do you want me to do, touch it, get my fingerprints on it so you can charge me with Eileen Marshall's murder?"

"For what it's worth, I don't think you killed her. But you know things about this case. You knew about my sister and nobody, I mean nobody in Vermont knows about that. There's no way you could've known, unless...."

"I really am psychic?" I finished for him. I backed off my hostility by half, realizing Beach was a decent guy. "I don't read minds. I tap into strong emotions and then things just come to me. Obviously your sister's death still bothers you or I would've never picked up on it."

"Yeah, well, that's what convinced me."

I looked into the sack and sighed. "There's a very good chance I won't get anything from this."

"Try." The urgency in his voice surprised me.

I sat on one of the wingback chairs, took the empty bottle out of the sack and studied it. The label was wrinkled, like it had been soaked and had dried unevenly. Traces of black fingerprint powder still clung to it. I held it in my hands, rolled it between my palms, closed my eyes, and waited for something to happen.

"Well?"

I frowned. Hazy, indistinct images began to coalesce

in my mind. "I'm not sure. I feel like it's somebody ... here. Someone who—" Then, like a camera lens focusing in, I recognized the aura of the person who'd touched the bottle. Sudden anger boiled within me. "What do you know about our little friend Adam? The guy who found the body with me?"

"Do you think he killed Eileen Marshall?"

"I don't know about that, but he's the one who planted this in my room!"

"Are you sure?"

"Look, you wanted me to get something—that's what I got."

He took it from me, putting it back in the bag. It was his turn to frown. "Let's have a chat with him."

I followed Beach to the kitchen where the budding chef was taking a baking sheet filled with chocolate chip cookies out of the oven. "Hi. Nothing better than cookies still warm from the oven."

"Nice as that sounds, that's not why we're here." Beach opened the sack and withdrew the scotch bottle. "Do you recognize this?"

Adam's expression soured. "No," he said, turning away.

"Interesting," I commented, "considering you planted it in my room."

He whirled, his tone icy. "I don't know what you're talking about."

"A polygraph test would tell us if you're lying," I said, not knowing if the Stowe cops even had such equipment.

"Come on, Adam, we know," Beach said quietly, a great bluff. The younger man looked away, his expression bitter. "Adam?" Beach prompted.

"I—I did it for Susan."

I nearly blew a gasket. "You what?"

"I was afraid she'd get in trouble. I know she argued with Ms. Marshall—told her that she had to leave. I thought the police might think she killed her. Susan's my friend. I had to do something to protect her."

"You knew the old lady was dead before I came downstairs. You found her when you went to retrieve the towels, didn't you?"

"I'm always the first one in every morning. I check to see that all the night chores are done. I noticed the towels weren't in the hamper and that the pool lights were still on. So I went outside. That's when I saw her. I didn't know what to do. I saw the booze bottle floating in the water and stupidly picked it up. Then I realized what I'd done and figured I'd get in trouble. So I hid it in the kitchen."

"That was some acting job you did when I came down," I said.

"How would *you* like to find a dead person?"

"I thought I did!"

"Cut it out," Beach ordered.

"Hell, no. Somebody tried to kill me, my lady's in the hospital, and my car was destroyed!" I turned back to Adam. "Where were you last night about eight-thirty?"

"Hey," Beach protested, "I'll ask the questions."

"*He* pushed me down the stairs—that's assault. *He* tampered with evidence. Who knows what else he's capable of doing."

"I got scared—I didn't know what to do," Adam said, sounding as frightened as he claimed.

I whirled on him. "So you attacked me?"

Reluctantly, he faced me. "I didn't mean to hurt you. I felt bad when I saw you lying there in a heap. I heard a door open and that bitchy Mrs. Andolina came running out. She took your pulse and made sure you were breathing. I figured she was a nurse or something. Then everybody else came running up from downstairs and I hid in one of the empty rooms until everything calmed down. Then ... I went home."

"What were you doing here at night? I thought you worked mornings," Beach said.

"Sometimes when I don't finish my work during the day, I come back in the evening."

"I'm sure the Dawsons will be able to confirm or deny that." Beach's intense gaze made the kid look away.

"Okay, I had to get rid of the booze bottle."

"Why did you pick me?"

"I told you. I didn't want anyone to think Susan could've killed her."

"What if she did?"

"She wouldn't," Adam insisted. "I thought if you did it, the cops would figure it out. If you didn't—you wouldn't be in any real trouble."

"Thanks a lot."

"Are you going to tell Susan?" Adam's voice was quiet as he looked over at Beach.

"It'll probably come up," Beach said.

Adam's shoulders slumped. "I'll get fired."

"That could be the least of your troubles. Obstructing justice is a crime."

Feeling no sympathy for the kid, I turned on my heel.

"Do you want to press charges?" Beach called after me.

I turned. "What's he liable to get for it?"

"He's got no record. Probably just a slap on the wrist."

"Then there's no point," I growled, and started off again.

"Are you planning to hang around today?" Beach asked.

"I'll be here until dinner time," I called over my shoulder and headed upstairs. My blood pressure was on the rise, making my head pound. I rounded the top of the stairs and nearly slammed into Richard.

"Whoa! What happened to you?"

"What do you mean?" I growled at him.

"Your face is beet-red. You look like you're about to have a stroke."

I exhaled loudly, balling my fists, ready to explode.

He grabbed me by the arm. "Come on, let's take a walk."

It took a couple of minutes before I calmed down enough to give him a coherent version of what had happened. We followed the trail behind the inn, pausing by the creek where Adirondack chairs and a table and benches had been placed for guests to enjoy the vista.

"Sit," Richard invited.

I flopped into the chair and winced at jarring my stiff neck. "How do you always stay so calm?"

"I haven't been pushed down stairs, implicated in a murder, involved in an accident that totaled my car, or nearly lost my significant other in the past twenty-four hours—definite stress inducers. Besides, I was trained not to panic in emergency situations. It comes in handy at times like these."

I watched the rushing white water. The creek was fifteen or twenty feet across, and no doubt the rain the night before had contributed to its fast-running pace.

"Adam said something interesting. When I was lying unconscious at the bottom of the stairs, Kay Andolina seemed to know what to do. He thought she might be a nurse. But you said she talked your ear off about her medical history, so that doesn't seem to wash."

"Maybe she's had some first-aid training," Richard suggested.

I got up, too restless to sit. "Maybe."

Richard took a last look at the scenic view and stood. He pointed to the trail and we started off again. "What do you get from her?"

"Nothing. Just that she's an old witch."

"No, to me she seems ... troubled."

We left the clearing, following the trail into the

woods. I thought about his assessment of the woman. To me she seemed aloof, judgmental, particularly toward Maggie, but that was purely a gut reaction. "She did open up to you, didn't she?"

Richard nodded. "She's compassionate enough to worry about birds with broken wings ... that kind of thing. Does it matter? Do you suspect her?"

I shook my head. "No."

As we strolled along the shaded path, I found my anger had cooled. The winding trail eventually led to the inn's namesake, a huge sugar maple tree. We passed under it and walked toward the fishpond, heading for the drive. An old Toyota and a battered Ford pick-up truck were parked on the grass—probably the hired help's vehicles. I'd bet Susan didn't pay either of them enough to live on.

We turned the corner and came upon the open garage. Garden tools, an industrial-sized snow blower, snow shovels, and more of Susan's surplus collectibles filled the space.

"Maggie would love to poke around in here," I said, taking in the boxes overflowing with chipped pottery, broken lamps, and old books. Mismatched chairs hung Shaker style from pegs on the wall. Something caught my attention; an old milk crate filled with license plates. I pushed my way through the stack of boxes, crouched down, and flipped through them, knowing what I'd find: Colorado FWP-284. Though rusty, it also had new scratches around the screw holes.

"What's that?" Richard said.

"The plate from the four-by-four that forced me off the road."

"Why would someone put it here? Why not just leave it on the truck?"

"The truck was stolen. I'll bet the plate came from right here in this box and was put back this morning."

"Who had access to the garage?"

"My guess is everybody at the inn. Or maybe it's here for the same reason the scotch bottle was in my room."

"A plant?"

"Exactly. And that means the killer isn't finished trying to pin the blame."

"On whom?"

I love how Richard speaks so grammatically correct. "How about Zack, or Susan—or both?"

"Or one of them could be trying to pin the blame on the other." He thought for a moment. "Who here would know how to hot-wire a car?"

"Ted Palmer or maybe that rocket scientist with the bimbo."

"I'd lay my money on Ted."

I straightened. "I've got to find out what Eileen knew about Laura Ross. I need to get into their room and rifle through her stuff."

"Isn't that just a little illegal?"

"So is framing an innocent person for murder. Besides, it's only breaking and entering if you're caught."

"The police have already searched the inn. If they'd found something incriminating, wouldn't they have confiscated it?"

"Not if they didn't know what they were looking for?"

"You've lost me."

"It's like that scotch bottle. The cops saw it as just a plastic bottle. I knew Adam had handled it. I might get a whole wealth of information just by touching Laura's things." I smiled at a new thought. "Have you got any more of those latex gloves in your little black bag?"

"It sounds like aiding and abetting to me. What's your plan?"

My smile faded. "I don't have one. But there's got to be a way to get everyone out of their rooms—and keep them out for a while."

Richard shrugged. "A cocktail party. Free food—free liquor. That usually does it."

"Oh, sure. We could just throw a cocktail party with a couple hours notice," I said.

"Why not?"

"I can't afford a pizza, let alone a party."

He sighed. "When are you going to stop worrying about money? I'll take care of it."

"This whole trip is turning out to be on you," I reminded him.

"I'm on vacation," he said. "Although I'll admit my life's a lot more interesting—and expensive—since you came back into it."

"I'll take that as a compliment. So, how do we arrange a party on the spur of the moment?"

"I bet Susan can throw one hell of a cocktail party with only an hour's notice. Besides, we're not expecting a buffet."

"What if she says no?"

"Then we call a restaurant down the road. But Susan doesn't seem like the type to shy away from making a little extra cash."

"Amen. How do we explain it to the guests?"

"I'll let Susan take the credit. I'll go talk to her now."

I watched him go inside, and then looked down at the box of license plates and back to the one in my hand. It wasn't much to go on.

Leaving the garage, I climbed the porch steps and paused to look through the bay window. Richard spoke with Susan outside her office. After a few moments she came out of her cubbyhole carrying a clipboard and they sat on the loveseat in front of the cold fireplace. Negotiations for the party were well underway. Something told me Susan would really soak Richard for it, too.

Beach's car was still parked in the drive, so I sat on the

porch swing to wait for him. I stared at the license plate in my hand, frustrated. I got no empathic vibrations from it—nothing. Maybe the person who tried to kill Maggie and me had worn gloves and never actually touched it. On its own, it was just another damned annoying piece of the puzzle.

I leaned back in the swing, letting it sway back and forth, content to stay there until Beach came out. I'd give him the plate and that would be that.

Richard showed up first.

"It's all set. I told her eight-thirty would be fine. That gives us half an hour to get back from the hospital."

"Damn. I almost forgot we promised to have dinner with Maggie." I scrutinized his face. "What's this going to cost you?"

"A lot."

"I appreciate it."

"I know." He glanced at his watch. "I'm beat. I didn't sleep well last night. I'm going to take a nap for a couple of hours. If you're smart, you'll do the same."

"Maybe. I still have things to do." I indicated the license plate.

"Suit yourself." He went back inside.

Restless, I got up from the swing and gazed at the lawn in front of the inn. The overgrown bushes near the sign by the road needed pruning. The forest on the other side of the two-lane road looked dark and foreboding on that sunny afternoon. I leaned against the porch's support post and gazed up the road. A grove of evergreens marked the property line.

Curiosity got the better of me. I headed down the steps, walked over to the road and looked up the rise, then started north. I'd gone about a hundred yards when I saw ruts cutting into the brush. A few yards in, a cleared space overlooked the Sugar Maple property, with ample room for a Blazer to turn around. Under the cover of darkness, the location would give its driver a bird's eye view of the inn's parking lot. All the driver had to do was wait for Maggie and me to leave, follow us and the rest was history.

My anger boiled as I started back for the inn to look for Sgt. Beach. I took the steps two at a time just as he opened the screen door and stepped onto the porch. "Are you looking for me?"

I shoved the plate at him. "I found this in the garage. It probably belongs to Susan Dawson, but she may not know it was used on that Blazer."

He frowned. "Of course you realize you've probably obliterated any fingerprints that were on it."

"If there was anything to soak up by touching it, I'd already know."

He nodded, conceding the point. "Let's go talk to Mrs. Dawson."

We found Susan in the kitchen, consulting an array of cookbooks—presumably to get ready for the party.

"Mrs. Dawson, Mr. Resnick said he found this license plate in your garage."

She looked at the plate, then at me. "So?"

"It was on the truck that forced me off the road last night."

"Are you accusing me?" she asked, her voice rising.

"I want to establish ownership of this license plate, ma'am," Beach said.

She sighed, angry. "It could be mine. I've got a stack of them in the garage. But I never bothered with an individual inventory. I don't keep the garage locked, so I suppose anybody could've taken it and put it back without my knowing."

Beach nodded. "We'll be in touch." He turned.

"Can I have my property back?" she demanded.

"We'll hang onto it—as evidence," he said, and continued for the stairs. Susan glared at me before turning back to her work.

I had to jog to catch up with the sergeant on the porch. "Hey, Beach, I was looking at the adjoining property. The Blazer's driver could have parked on the hill, seen us leave, then followed us last night."

He glanced up the hill. "Makes sense."

I tried to squelch a burst of renewed anger. What had I expected from him besides agreement, anyway? I changed tacks. "If they've ruled Eileen's death a homicide, then the cause of death is public record, right?" He nodded. "So what killed her?"

"Blood loss or drowning—take your pick—brought on by blunt trauma to the skull. Her alcohol level was point two nine, well over the max."

No wonder Eileen hadn't put up a fight—she was literally too drunk to know what hit her. "Did they establish a time of death?"

"Between eleven and midnight. Why?"

"Just being nosy. How about Adam? What's going to happen to him?"

"He'll have to give another statement. We'll keep our eyes on him."

"Do you still think you'll have this wrapped up by tomorrow?"

"It's possible." He brushed past me. "I'll keep you posted."

He headed for the patrol car. I watched as he started the engine, pulled onto the highway, and headed south.

Exhaustion weighed me down. Richard's suggestion of a nap sounded like a sensible idea. If I was going to break the law later on, I needed to be sharp.

SEVENTEEN

A knock on my door awakened me barely an hour later. "Come on," Richard called. "Maggie's waiting for her dinner." Still blinking, I hauled myself off the bed, slipped on my shoes and grabbed my jacket.

Thirty minutes—and a stop for take-out—later, we paused in the open doorway of Maggie's room.

With pen in hand, she was bent over her writing tablet, staring at nothing, as though the muse had just left her.

"Greetings from China," I announced.

An afternoon of rest had done wonders. A smile lit her face, and the last of the afternoon sun streaming through the window made her eyes shine. "Wow! Did you bring hot and sour soup?"

"Is the Pope Catholic?"

I gave her a quick kiss and Richard and I moved the flowers from the tray table to the window ledge. Richard won the coin toss for possession of the room's only chair. I perched on the edge of Maggie's bed and played Maitre d', passing out cardboard cartons.

"Looks like you've got a good start on the article."

She pushed it aside. "I'm more interested in food right now." She took the plastic spoon I offered her. "This is kind of fun," she said, digging in. "Only I wish Brenda was here with us."

"I wish we were at home with Brenda having this

fun," Richard added.

"I'll say. Being in the hospital is no picnic, but you guys have made it a lot better," she said. "What did you do all day?"

"Worked on the case," I answered.

"Don't call it a case," Richard pleaded.

"It may as well be. What with all the intrigue," I countered, for Maggie's benefit.

"What intrigue?" she asked, her eyes widening.

I told her it was Adam who pushed me down the stairs and planted the scotch bottle.

"What else?" she asked.

"We're giving—or rather, Richard's giving—" I amended, "a cocktail party tonight."

She pouted. "And I wasn't invited?"

"Jeff needs an excuse to snoop. I'm supposed to divert everyone's attention—all ten of them."

"I have confidence in your social skills." We moved on to the egg rolls. "I've got a feeling that we'll soon know who the killer is."

"Good. Then we'll all be safe and can go home. Do you think I'll get out of here tomorrow?" Maggie asked Richard.

"It's up to the doctor who's treating you."

I glanced at him, admiring his smooth delivery, his bedside manner working full force.

"Susan called," Maggie said. "She said she didn't think she'd get up here today, but said if I needed anything to call her."

I knew Maggie wouldn't.

"We chatted for a few minutes and you'll be very proud of me, I pumped her for information and learned some interesting tidbits. One may be the secret you mentioned the other day."

I stopped squirting duck sauce on my egg roll. "Which is?"

"She's worried about how the RSO will react when it finds out Eileen was murdered."

"The what?" Richard asked.

"Reservation service organization. Advertising is expensive. The RSO screens guests and books them for a fee. Susan's already had one cancellation because of the murder. That's why she hasn't kicked you out of your room, Richard."

"Thank you, Susan," Richard muttered.

"Let's get back to Eileen," I said.

"She wanted to come up for the long weekend, but they were fully booked, so she offered Susan money if she'd find a cancellation."

"She bribed Susan?"

Maggie nodded. "Two hundred bucks—paid in cash—plus the cost of the room. The most expensive one, too. Only she died before Susan put the credit card through."

Eileen paid for a cancellation? Something about that didn't add up. "Wait a minute, I thought we got invited here this weekend because the inn wasn't fully booked?"

She shrugged. "They weren't booked a week ago when I first talked to Susan. Since they've had trouble filling the place, she wasn't about to turn away business. Which explains why our room isn't finished. She couldn't offer it to a paying guest."

"I suppose not." I pondered the situation for a few moments. "Why was it so important for Eileen to be here on this particular weekend?"

Maggie shrugged. "I don't know, but Susan told me Eileen arranged the contest the bimbo won."

"How?" I asked.

"She said Eileen had a lot of friends in advertising. The last time she visited the inn, back in July, she suggested the weekend prize as a form of free advertising. A lot of the inn's guests come from Long Island."

"That's where Laura Ross lives. She said she'd been

coming to the inn for years. And she previously knew Eileen."

"I also got the feeling Susan didn't like Eileen and isn't sorry she's dead," Maggie continued. "She called her a conniver—said she was just a little too helpful. But she felt a kind of grudging gratitude because since that radio contest, their business has picked up."

"This is getting convoluted," Richard commented. He held up a hand, ticking off each point on his fingers. "You said Eileen came up here to see her lover. She didn't have a reservation, so she bribed one of the owners to let her have a room. She apparently came to the inn to confront her married lover. But, an old friend—possibly an enemy—Laura Ross was also a guest at the inn and Eileen knew some deep dark secret about her. She also arranged free advertising for the inn and the people who won the radio contest are here the same weekend as she was. Then, to top it off, somebody murders the woman."

"It does sound convoluted," I agreed, "and I don't have a shred of tangible proof, but I have a feeling every word of it's true."

"So this party is just a cover-up so you can search the rooms? What if some of the guests don't show up?" Maggie asked. "That Mrs. Andolina strikes me as a party pooper and a tattletale."

"I'll make a point of personally inviting her," Richard offered.

"Great." I unpacked the rest of the cartons, while Richard passed out plates and plastic cutlery.

We dug in. Considering we picked the restaurant at random, the food was surprisingly good.

"Something else puzzles me," Maggie said. "That first night, Eileen took us into the game room and we all introduced ourselves. Why didn't she want us to know she knew Laura?"

Richard shrugged. "Didn't you say Ted was there, too?

Maybe she didn't want the kid to know she knew Laura."

I hadn't considered that. "Maybe I was wrong. Maybe Eileen was *only* here to confront Laura."

"How could you confuse meeting Laura with Eileen meeting her married lover? So far as we know, Eileen wasn't gay. And Laura's still a very attractive woman, as evidenced by her much younger ... friend."

"He's a gigolo," Maggie accused.

Richard raised an eyebrow, but made no comment.

"Besides," Maggie continued, "Mrs. Andolina said she'd seen them arguing. So Eileen must have already confronted Laura."

"What if she came to the inn to confront her lover *and* see Laura."

"That would give her an awful lot of hidden agendas, wouldn't it? Pass me some of that chicken stuff, will you?" Richard said.

"If you were dying, maybe you'd want to tie up all the loose ends in a hurry."

"But she didn't really look sick, just tired," Maggie said.

"You'd have had a better handle on that, Rich."

"Just because a I'm an internist doesn't mean I can diagnose on the fly—especially for someone I'd never even met."

"Sure you could. You're great," I said and smiled.

"That testimonial not withstanding, it's a lot more complicated than that."

Maggie pushed a pea pod around on her plate. "What I don't understand is why Adam would want to hurt you, Jeff. You could've broken your neck when he pushed you down the stairs."

"He was probably just scared."

"And he probably wondered why you told everyone you fell," Richard added.

"That may have been a mistake," I conceded, and

shoveled up a forkful of rice. I thought about my conversation with Adam earlier in the day. "Something he
said today didn't ring true, but at the time I couldn't put
my finger on why. He told Beach he was afraid Susan
would be blamed for Eileen's death because Susan told
Eileen she had to leave the inn. But Adam wasn't at the
inn at the time of the argument on Friday night. Only
Maggie and I heard Susan read Eileen the riot act. So why
would Adam hide the scotch bottle the next morning and
later try to pin it on me?"

"If Adam already knew Eileen was dead, you probably pissed him off when you dragged him outside to help
you find the body. Or maybe Adam was as worried as
Susan was about the RSO finding out about the canceled
reservation," Maggie suggested. "He seems to worship the
ground she walks on."

"Maybe you ought to mention all this to Sgt. Beach,"
Richard said.

"Good idea. I don't feel any loyalty to Susan. How
about you, Maggie?"

"If the situation weren't so serious, I'd say forget it.
But a woman was murdered. When will you talk with Sgt.
Beach again?"

"I wouldn't be surprised if it was tonight."

"Do you think he'll show up at the party?" Richard
asked.

I nodded.

"One of your funny feelings?"

Again I nodded.

"Well, let's just hope he doesn't spoil the frivolity."

I couldn't tell if Richard was serious.

Maggie pushed back her Chinet plate. "That's it for
me. I'm stuffed."

I studied the remains on my plate then set my fork
aside. "Me, too."

"It's unanimous," Richard said, and collected the debris, placing the large paper sack by the door to toss later.

He returned to his chair as Maggie leaned back against the pillows on the bed. "Thanks, guys. I can't tell you what this all means to me." She reached for Richard's hand. "Thank you for everything."

He leaned across and kissed her forehead. "No thanks necessary."

The mood was definitely too maudlin. "Hey, quit kissing my woman, will you?"

"I haven't seen you do it lately."

Maggie laughed, the soapy moment past.

We stayed until the second announcement came over the public address system, reminding us that visiting hours had ended.

"I'll see you in the morning, Maggs," I said and leaned down to kiss her good night.

"I want to hear everything that happens at the party."

"You bet."

As we left her room, she picked up her writer's tablet, already going over what she'd written earlier that afternoon.

Richard and I headed for the lobby. The wall clock read 8:10. I hoped Susan would be smart enough to delay the party until we arrived.

The stale smell of Chinese food still filled the warm car, and we opened the windows to air it out. Richard slid in, dipped a hand in his jacket pocket and handed me a pair of latex gloves. "Here. For later."

I took them and shoved them into my own pocket, embarrassed.

He started the engine and headed for the exit.

"By the way, I just want to second the round of thanks."

"For dinner?" he asked.

"Yeah. And everything you're doing for Maggie. But especially the party. I've put you in an awkward position."

"Why? I'm the one who suggested it."

"Yeah, but you're such a law-and-order fanatic. That party is a cover for me to break the law."

He thought about it for a moment. "Under ordinary circumstances, I'd agree. But Maggie's in the hospital because someone wanted to kill her and you. Maybe the ends don't justify the means, but long before civil law was the Biblical saw, 'an eye for an eye.'"

I'm glad he felt that way, because I, too, wanted to nail the bastard who hurt us.

We arrived at the inn at precisely 8:30 and found the lobby deserted. All the cars were in the drive, but there was no one around. "It's understandable," Richard said. "Who wants to be the first to arrive at a party?"

"Well, I don't care if it's me."

"Then go hang out while I change clothes."

He went off to his room, and I headed downstairs.

The barroom was deserted, but I heard noises in the kitchen. I poked my head around the corner and saw Zack and Susan preparing hors d'oeuvres. Apparently Susan had decided to save money by recruiting Zack to help serve—not Nadine or Adam—the hallmark of a shrewd businesswoman.

Restless, I finally settled on the piano bench, the perfect spot to take in all the downstairs entrances. Susan came through the doorway with a tray full of hors d'oeuvres, and gave a start at seeing me.

"Looks like I'm a little early," I said.

"Don't worry, we're ready," she said with forced cheerfulness. She set the tray on the bar and headed back for the kitchen. How had she explained this little gathering to the other guests?

I clenched my fists, more nervous than I'd anticipated. Breaking and entering isn't something I do every day, and I wasn't looking forward to it.

Voices preceded the footfalls that echoed from the stairwell. "Hello, Jeffrey," Michele called, her husband Jean behind her.

"Hi."

"Do you play?" she asked, glancing at the piano behind me.

I stood. "No."

She looked around for signs of the other guests. "It seems we are early."

"I'm sure the other guests will be along soon. Can I get you a drink?" I asked, automatically heading for the well-stocked bar. Had Susan bought the liquor just for the party or did she have a stash she bought out for special occasions? No matter, Richard was paying dearly for it.

"Oui. White wine. Jean?"

"Beer."

The wine was perfectly chilled and I poured a glass for her, then cracked the cap off a bottle of Labatts. I felt like I was back at work at the Whole Nine Yards sports bar in Buffalo. Michele smiled shyly at me in thanks, then hand-in-hand she and Jean headed for the game room.

More footfalls sounded, and my brother came down the stairs. Dressed in a white polo shirt and a navy sports jacket and slacks, Richard looked every inch the well-to-do doctor on vacation. "Can I get you a drink, Dr. Alpert?"

"Scotch—on the rocks, please."

Before I could finish pouring, Zack appeared with two more trays of food before heading back to the kitchen. Richard's assessment of Susan's hostess abilities had been right on the money. Trays of canapés, shrimp piled on cracked ice, and bowls filled with mixed nuts and M&M candies were scattered around the room.

"Impressive," I said.

"I told you she'd throw one hell of a party."

Susan brought out yet another tray from the kitchen, this one filled with an assortment of cheeses and crackers. "I'm very pleased," Richard told her.

"It's amazing what you can do with puff pastry, bacon, and cream cheese," she admitted. "If you'll excuse me, I think we need more cocktail napkins."

Laura and Ted were the next to arrive. Dressed to the nines in a shimmering black mini dress, her stiletto heels showed off her shapely legs. Ted ordered for them both: a beer and a dry martini—I could've predicted it. They claimed the overstuffed loveseat in the far corner of the game room, away from the other guests, snuggling like lovebirds.

"That's half the guests," I said to Richard. "Did you ask the Andolinas?"

"Yes. They'll be down in a few minutes. You know how women are."

Suddenly mellow jazz came from unseen speakers. "Subtle," Richard commented, sipping his scotch. Seconds later, Zack rounded the corner from the kitchen. "Would you care for a drink?" Richard offered.

"Don't mind if I do. Jack Daniels—neat."

I poured the drink, handing it to him.

"Are you the official bartender?" Richard asked me.

"I guess it comes naturally," I said, absently wiping the bar top.

"I don't think it's necessary. Would you take over?" he asked Zack.

"No problem, Doctor," he said and moved to take my place.

I was already getting antsy, but had to hang around for a while longer to see if the Andolinas and the bimbo, Alyssa, and her boyfriend Doug would make an appearance. Maggie's assessment of Mrs. Andolina seemed on the money. I suspected if she saw me nosing around the guest rooms, she would tattle to Susan—or maybe even

Sgt. Beach.

"Would you like something?" Zack asked, interrupting my reverie.

I could've done with a large bourbon, neat. "No, thanks, I'm sticking to soft drinks."

"Suit yourself," he said, and helped himself to one of the shrimp.

I heard more footfalls on the stairs: the bimbo and Doug. They headed straight for the bar as well. Alyssa wore dark slacks and a peach colored, low-neck sweater. A push-up bra had enhanced what nature had given her. In contrast, Doug, in black Dockers and a leather vest, looked ready for a barroom brawl. And I thought *I'd* looked under-dressed.

Where the hell were the Andolinas?

I continued to edge away from the group, anxious for the latecomers to arrive. Parties are not my forte, but Richard seemed at ease with the casual chitchat. He'd done a lot of socializing in his former job, schmoozing government types for grant money. I wondered if any of the women at the party would confide a sexual fantasy to him. He had to be kidding about that.

I glanced at my watch, conscious of the fact that time was slipping away. Then I heard Kay Andolina's voice. I watched Richard home in on her and her husband. Once he had them engaged, I slipped out the back way, circled the house and came in through the front door.

I didn't know how much time I'd have, so I decided to concentrate on the Dawson's apartment and Laura's and Ted's room. If I was going to find anything incriminating, I felt it would be there. If not, Richard would be out of pocket for nothing.

EIGHTEEN

I slipped out of my shoes to avoid making noise. After hiding them under the loveseat, I donned Richard's latex gloves and used Maggie's trusty hairpin to open the door to the Dawson's residence.

The apartment consisted of the combination kitchen-living room, the cubbyhole office that opened into the inn's lobby, a bedroom, a bathroom and a couple of closets. Everything looked neat, tidy, and innocent. Since I didn't know what I was looking for, that made the job of finding anything meaningful that much more difficult.

I zeroed in on the bedroom. Though painted pink—with cutesy curtains and a matching spread—like the rest of the place, it seemed rather sterile. The queen-sized bed, with no headboard, was pushed against the south wall. I tested it. Much more comfortable than the slab Susan had given Maggie and me. I ran my gloved hand over the spread. Nothing. Of course not, I wasn't touching it. I peeled off the left glove and tried again, instantly picking up residual anger, like what I'd experienced when I'd met Zack that first evening. The passion between them was long gone. Every night they slept back to back, nothing more than business partners.

I stood, straightened the spread, and tried to shrug off the creepy feeling of voyeurism that clung to me. I didn't like doing this, but I liked it even less that someone had tried to kill Maggie and me some twenty-four hours before.

Next, came the dresser. The glove wouldn't go back on my sweating hand. Great. I'd have to be careful not to leave fingerprints. I balled it and shoved it into my left-hand pocket.

The top drawer held Susan's underwear; the second drawer, sweaters and blouses. Everything was neatly stacked and I made sure it looked undisturbed when I'd finished my one-handed groping. No ribbon-bound stack of love letters, nothing incriminating. I tried the other dresser and found it in the same neat condition, except it was full of Zack's clothes.

The closet was jammed. Boxes crowded the top shelf, labeled in what was probably Susan's neat handwriting. I grabbed one marked "receipts" and found receipts and tax records. Nothing of interest. My foot nudged a pair of men's shoes and a prescription bottle rolled out of one. As expected, it belonged to Zack. The doctor's name was Haskins, and the prescription had been filled in Burlington just a week before. Two refills remained. I memorized the drug name to ask Richard about later, then replaced the bottle in the shoe.

Susan's jewelry box contained mostly cheap costume stuff, along with several gold and silver chains, and a couple of old broaches. I closed the lid and ducked into the bathroom.

A small cupboard held extra rolls of toilet paper and neatly folded towels. Two plush terry robes hung from hooks on the back of the door. One white, the other pink. I touched the pink one first. Nothing. I grasped the lapel of the white one and got a vague impression of the hot tub outside, the steam rising on a cool, crisp day. It didn't make sense, but I also knew it sometimes took time for the full impact of these flashes to become meaningful.

The kitchen was sparsely decorated with more of Susan's surplus. One of the cabinets housed an extensive liquor collection, heavily favoring bourbon. I closed my eyes and held one of the opened bottles: Zack. They had arguments about that, too. Definitely a dysfunctional couple.

All in all, I'd garnered very little information. But then I really shouldn't have expected more. Susan was pretty much a closed book. And since I got no insight from touching her, it wasn't surprising her possessions held nothing for me either.

Opening the door a crack, I listened for a moment before venturing back into the inn's lobby. No one around. So far so good. The murmur of voices from the party downstairs was audible as I closed the door behind me and crept across the room.

With a few skillful twists of the hairpin, I gained access to Laura's and Ted's room. Like the rest of the inn, it was tastefully decorated with oak and wicker furniture, lots of ruffled pillows and lacy do-dads. Unlike the others I'd seen, this room had a king-sized waterbed. Two suitcases were tucked in the closet, along with two mismatched garment bags. The bathroom's vanity was decked out with a ton of cosmetics and a man's travel kit.

Laura's purse was tucked into one of the dresser drawers. I thumbed through her wallet, fat with twenty-dollar bills. Behind the wad of credit cards were several pictures of children—nieces and nephews perhaps. Replacing the photos, I made sure the drawer looked undisturbed.

Ted's belongings were less interesting. A bottle of Polo after-shave, clean underwear—nothing of sentimental value.

An old wind-up travel alarm clock, its face scratched from years of use, sat on the left side of the bed. Grasping it, I got a shadowy impression of a woman ... it had been a gift. From someone Laura admired? Could that woman have been Eileen? I wasn't sure. Using my shirttail, I wiped off my fingerprints and placed it back on the night table, hoping I'd put it in the same position as I'd found it.

Since the bed was where I'd gotten the strongest impressions in the Dawson's room, I laid back, closed my eyes. Conflicting emotions seeped into me: guilt, shame, and lascivious pleasure. I couldn't tell if the feelings were from the room's current occupants or a conglomeration of emotions from years worth of lovemaking by past guests.

The overlapping sensations left me vaguely nauseated. I crawled off, realizing my head ached, too. It took a few moments to catch my breath. As I straightened the spread so the bed looked undisturbed, I noticed a leather attaché by the side of a wicker chair. It was locked and, unlike the flimsy locks on the room doors, my trusty hairpin wasn't going to open it. I rested my hand on the top, closed my eyes and waited. Nothing. For all I knew, it could be filled with magazines or old utility receipts. Reluctantly, I replaced it and took a last look around. For all the money the party was costing Richard, I'd gotten virtually nothing useful. I glanced at my watch: the entire ordeal had taken less than fifteen minutes.

I turned for the door and tripped over a throw rug at the side of the bed. The nightstand broke my fall, but the clock hit the floor with a crash.

Adrenaline shot through me. I grabbed the clock, dropped it on the table and opened the door.

What if I'd broken it?

I turned back, picked it up, and listened.

My pulse slammed in my ears. Endless seconds passed before I heard it ticking. Hands shaking, I put it down and got the hell out of there.

I'd ripped off the remaining glove and was stuffing my feet back into my shoes when I heard footsteps coming up the stairs. I grabbed the first book I saw, planted myself in a chair, and tried not to look like I was sweating.

Susan rounded the stairwell, looked at me suspiciously. "Jeff—why aren't you downstairs?"

I looked up, as though I'd been engrossed. "I'm not really in a partying mood. Not while Maggie's in the hospital."

"Oh. Of course." Was that an actual expression of compassion that momentarily crossed her features? "I'm sure Maggie wouldn't mind," she said.

"I'll go back down in a couple of minutes." She nodded and continued to her office.

I looked at the book in my hands—an old guest book—and flipped through the pages. It began in December of the previous year. Among the names listed during New Year's weekend was Eileen Marshall. She'd mentioned visiting the inn several times, and I wondered if she'd signed it every time. Sure enough, I found her signature for the 4th of July holiday and when she'd checked in some six days previously. I skimmed through the book again. There should have have been one more entry. She'd said something about enjoying the hot tub in the spring. I couldn't find it. Something about that didn't feel right.

I shut the book and replaced it on the coffee table, disappointed my foray into crime had netted me so little information. But all the players were still assembled downstairs. Questioning them was now my best—perhaps my only—shot at finding the truth.

The food had been decimated by the time I eased back into the barroom, trying to look as though I'd never left. Filling a glass with ice, I poured myself a Coke, needing the caffeine fix for my pounding head—wishing I could have a double Jack Daniels instead.

Meanwhile, the JD drinker, Zack, was playing host, albeit with a kind of forced cheerfulness. Though conversing with the Canadians, his gaze kept drifting toward Laura, his expression not entirely friendly.

Doug sauntered up, interrupting my musings. He set an empty beer bottle on the bar. "Got any more?"

"Sure." I handed him another bottle, realizing his appearance gave me a conversation opener. "The other night you scored some weed," I said, lowering my voice. "Local connection?"

His grip tightened on the bottle. "Why'd you ask?"

I proffered my glass of soda. "I can't drink and my lady's in the hospital. I'm just looking to ease the pain. Where I can get some?"

His smile was sly. "The guy in the kitchen. Good stuff; grows it himself."

My stomach tensed: Adam. I faked a smile and clapped him on the shoulder. "Thanks, man."

"No problem." He headed back toward the game room.

In an effort to disguise my agitation, I wandered to the eats table. Not that I was the least bit hungry after our Chinese feast, but studying the leftovers gave me something to do, and an opportunity to eavesdrop.

Richard was talking with Fred Andolina when Alyssa moved to stand beside him. I popped a shrimp into my mouth, hoping I didn't look as jittery as I felt. Alyssa stared intently at my brother and, unnerved, Fred finally turned away.

"Dr. Alpert, I have a problem and I was wondering if you could help me."

Richard turned his full attention to her. "Of course."

She bit her lip, looking concerned. "I have this recurring pain—in my chest."

"Oh?"

"Yes, it's—" she took his hand, placing it on her left breast, "right here."

Richard's gaze wandered over to me with a look that said *I told you so.*

Doug erupted from the corner. "Hey!"

Richard pulled his hand away.

Doug shoved his way through the crowd, looking ready to kill. "What the hell are you doing to my girl?"

Alyssa looked embarrassed, although not for herself or Richard. "Oh, Doug, grow up. He's a doctor."

"Oh, yeah? Well, I'll bet he isn't even licensed to practice medicine in Vermont."

Maybe Doug had more upstairs than I'd given him credit for.

Richard forced a smile. "I suggest you see your own doctor to talk about this problem. I'm sure he or she will be able to advise you better than me. If you'll excuse me." He crossed the room, heading for the bar, where he filled his glass with ice and poured himself a generous scotch.

I ambled over to join him and nodded toward the bimbo, who continued to argue with her boyfriend.

Richard eyed me, still shaken by the encounter, and took a swallow of his drink. "I told you, this kind of thing happens to me all the time at cocktail parties."

"What does Brenda think about that?"

He took another long pull before answering. "How do you think I met her?"

Incredulous, I could only blink.

Finally a smile cracked his serious expression. "I'm kidding."

"Don't let Brenda or Maggie hear you kid like that."

"I suspect Alyssa's boyfriend hasn't been paying enough attention to her and she chose me as a way to get it." The two were still quarreling, and I'd bet that after leaving the party they'd make up—in bed.

Someone tapped my shoulder: Ted Palmer. "Hey, man. I wanted to tell you how sorry I am about your girl-friend getting hurt." His expression was earnest. Of all the guests, he'd been the only one to mention Maggie's near-fatal accident. Somehow, he didn't seem the type.

"Thanks."

"Is she going to be all right?"

"I think so."

"No matter what Sgt. Beach thinks, I wanted you to know I wasn't responsible."

A heaviness began to creep across my chest. "I beg your pardon."

"I mean, I made a mistake—but that was a long time ago. I don't make a habit of hot-wiring cars and causing accidents."

I struggled to keep my voice level. "You got caught joyriding?"

"Maybe I was a wild kid, but that was over ten years ago. I've never been in trouble with the law since. I swear, not even a parking ticket."

I made a mental note to ask Beach about that little incident, but put on my best poker face. "Thanks for leveling with me." I took a sip of Coke, knowing it wouldn't help steady my jagged nerves. I cleared my throat: time to go into my act. "How did you and Laura meet?"

He seemed glad to change the subject. "We were guests at a wedding reception at the local country club. I'm the tennis pro. I was a friend of the groom, Laura was a friend of the bride's mother. We were seated at the same table and things just clicked between us." He glanced at Laura across the room. "Something weird is going on with her since we came here, though. She's not the same person. One of the things that drew me to her was her confidence. This Eileen person's death really shook her."

"Were they friends?"

"They worked together a long time ago—at some magazine in New York." He shook his head. "She's usually great in bed—but now she cries herself to sleep."

"It's been a stressful weekend," I said.

"Yeah, but this started before Ms. Marshall was murdered."

I looked at Laura and suddenly realized her snobbish

behavior was only a mask to hide her fear. It rolled off her in waves. I needed an excuse to touch her to see what else I could get.

Ted's beer glass was empty. "Can I get you another?"

"I'll get it." He stepped behind the bar.

Across the room, Laura was thumbing through a book. I grabbed the half empty-tray of canapés and made a beeline for her.

"Would you care for one?" I asked, shoving the tray under her nose.

She looked up, startled. "No, thank you."

"They're very good."

"I don't care for any."

I set the tray on the cocktail table and sat beside her on the loveseat. "Great party, huh?"

She drew back, annoyed. "I suppose it would be if I didn't feel like a prisoner here."

"Well, a murder was committed. And there's a good chance one of us did it."

Laura shifted uncomfortably. "I don't want to think about it."

"It'll be okay," I told her.

"You mean about Eileen?"

"Yes."

"It never was before," she said, bitterness tingeing her voice. "She always took. She tried to ruin my life— twice—and God help me, I'm not sorry she's dead." A sudden look of panic entered here eyes. She'd said far too much.

She was about to bolt. There had to be some way I could touch her without it looking too obvious. I glanced around. A stack of old postcards sat on the table next to her. "Would you hand me those."

Stupid move. I'd witnessed her pain, ignored it, and looked like an insensitive clod. Yet she picked up the cards. I made my move—clasping her fingers as I took them from her. She snatched back her hand, glared at me.

I'd gotten nothing, but to cover my move, I flipped through the cards. "Susan has some interesting things lying around. I understand most of it's for sale, too."

"Yes. If you'll excuse me—" She stood, and went to stand next to Ted, whispering in his ear. He frowned, irritated, but followed her as she headed for the stairs. Good night, lovers. Damn. I stared after her, wondering what my next move should be.

Richard conversed with Susan at the bar. She didn't easily mingle with her guests, staying on the fringes of the crowd. Zack was better with public relations while she tended to the business end of the operation. With their conversation finished, she gave Richard a half-smile, turned and headed back into her kitchen.

My glass was nearly empty. I wandered over to the bar and topped up my Coke. Footfalls on the stairs caught my attention, and I twisted to see a slender pair of legs come into view.

"Who's that?" Richard whispered.

"A reporter. She came by on Saturday, just before you arrived." The woman approached us. "Her name's Ashley—"

"Samuels," she said by way of introduction, holding out her hand for Richard. He shook it.

"This is Dr. Richard Alpert," I said.

She raised an eyebrow, as though she'd recognized the name. "Nice to meet you." Then she turned to me, holding out her hand. I hesitated. I really didn't want to touch her, and shaking her hand might just unleash a flood of information I didn't want to know.

She grabbed my hand and a jolt went through me, the nausea briefly returning. Her expression mirrored her surprise. "Whoa! Static electricity."

I retrieved my hand. As expected, I'd gotten a number

of impressions. Although ambitious, I got the feeling she was basically an honest person. Score one for the good guys.

As if on cue, Susan reappeared. "I'm sorry, Miss Samuels, but this is a private party. I'm afraid I'm going to have to ask you to—"

"It's okay," Richard interrupted smoothly, directing all his charm toward the reporter. "We're just getting to know one another."

Susan's cheeks flushed at his mild rebuke, but she nodded curtly, and made a hasty retreat back to the kitchen.

"Is this your party?" Ashley asked, sizing up what remained of the food on the side table.

Richard shook his head. "Just a little icebreaker."

"Why now?" She moved around him, reached for one of the puff pastry canapés, and popped it into her mouth.

"It's been a little uncomfortable for all the guests these last few days," Richard said politely.

"If nothing else, it gives us one pleasant memory to take away from this god-awful weekend," I suggested.

Ashley chose another appetizer. "I did a little research on you."

"Me?" Richard asked.

"Both of you. Interesting little escapade you were involved in last winter—and again in June."

My stomach knotted.

Richard's smile evaporated. "I don't consider being shot an escapade."

"Do you get involved in murder on a regular basis, Mr. Resnick?"

"I haven't made it a hobby. How'd you find out about that?" I was referring, of course, to the murder last March back in Buffalo and the death of the guy who held my job before me. After my skull was fractured during the mugging, I'd been plagued with visions of a violent death, and felt compelled to find the killer. It wasn't something I'd enjoyed at the time, especially when the killer came after me with a gun, shot and missed—hitting Richard instead. I wasn't yet over that guilt trip. The same went for looking into Walt Kaplan's death.

Ashley smiled sweetly. "Thanks to Google, there are very few secrets left in this world."

"It's not a secret, just not something I like to go around broadcasting." I looked around the room, lowered my voice. "Let's not spread these little tales around the inn, either. Nobody here knows Richard and I are related, and we'd like to keep it that way."

Her smile was coy. She took another canapé, popped it into her mouth then licked her fingers with delight. "The Buffalo News never really said how you became involved in either of those cases. Just that you were involved." She waited expectantly, as though she actually believed I'd spill my guts.

I stared at her, hoping my calculated, vacant expression would be answer enough.

It wasn't.

"So?" she prompted.

"It's not something I care to discuss," Richard said and turned away, probably wishing he'd let Susan throw the reporter out.

Ashley still expected an answer.

"Look, that's history. I'd much rather talk about the present. Why don't you tell me what you've learned about Eileen Marshall?"

"Why would I do that?"

"Then perhaps we could trade information."

"So you are playing amateur sleuth."

"No. I just happen to be very nosy."

"A holdover from when you were an insurance investigator?"

She had dug deeply into my past.

"Maybe."

She looked smug. "What do you want to know?"

"Where was Eileen the morning before she was murdered?"

"What have you got to offer?"

Her game of cat and mouse was irritating. "Nothing, I guess." I turned away.

"Wait." She studied my face. "She was visiting a lawyer in Waterbury."

"A lawyer?"

"Yes. Unfortunately, the man refuses to divulge why Ms. Marshall was there."

I thought about it. "How did Eileen get to Stowe? Did she drive up from Long Island?"

"She flew in to Morrisville and rented a car locally. Look, I can't believe any of this is of use to you."

"It helps fill in the gaps."

She looked at me quizzically. "What gaps?"

"Like I said—I'm just nosy. Like you?"

She raised an eyebrow.

"Why else would you be a reporter?" I added.

She forced a smile.

"And you've got bigger ambitions than Burlington. What's next? Albany?"

"Boston. Then New York or Miami."

"Big-stakes towns. Take my advice—stay in Vermont. It's not as glamorous, but—"

"Safer? It wasn't for Eileen Marshall."

I shrugged. "Touché."

She took one last canapé and wiped her fingers on a cocktail napkin. "It's time for me to get back to work."

I watched as she scanned the guests, then homed in on the DuBois couple. I glanced around and saw Kay Andolina sitting alone in the farthest corner of the barroom, leafing though a magazine. It was time for me to go back to work, too.

I picked up the tray of shrimp wrapped in bacon and walked over to her. "Would you care for one?"

She looked up at me. "No, thank you, Greg."

"Jeff," I said automatically. She seemed puzzled. "I'm Jeffrey, not Greg."

Kay's eyes filled with tears and she looked away. I put the tray down on the cocktail table and sat in the chair opposite her.

"Please don't cry."

She cleared her throat, wiped her nose, and braved a smile. "I ... I understand you were in a car accident last night? I hope you're all right."

"Yes. But Maggie's still in the hospital—"

"You really should be more careful," she said, cutting me off. She didn't like Maggie. I suppose it didn't matter why, but it irked me. And yet, I got a strong impression that she felt some kind of attraction to me.

"Those mountain roads can be treacherous in the rain," she cautioned.

"Yes, they can."

She put the magazine down on the stack on the coffee table, a distracted, far-away look in her eyes.

"They said you found me when I fell down the stairs the other night. Are you a nurse?"

Her expression brightened. "Heavens, no. But I was the first-aid person at my old job."

"Where was that?"

"Burns Tool and Die in Troy, New York. I was the bookkeeper, but I volunteered for the first-aid position. I like to help people. The men weren't often careless, but occasionally someone would get his hand caught in one of the machines."

"That would be me. I'm not good with tools."

"It's lucky the angels protect you."

I blinked at her. "Angels?"

"Oh, yes. That's why you were spared in the accident."

"Spared?"

"Of course. You have work to do."

"What kind of work?"

She smiled kindly, leaned close and pressed a finger against my lips. "Listen."

Every muscle in my body tensed. "To what?"

"Listen," she repeated enigmatically.

Obviously I'd completely misjudged her: she wasn't a bitch—she was stark raving crazy. Still, she had information I wanted.

"What did Eileen Marshall say that upset you the other night?"

Her gaze dipped. "I don't like to speak ill of the dead."

"It can't hurt her now."

She thought it over, then stared into my eyes, as though she could look directly into my soul.

"She asked me.... This is very embarrassing." She looked away to compose herself. "She asked me what I thought of a woman who'd have sex with a child."

That made no sense. "Did you tell the police about it?"

"Yes," she admitted. "I felt it was my duty." Her eyes filled with tears and she pulled a tissue from a pocket and dabbed at her nose. "A woman who'd hurt a child doesn't deserve to live."

Silence seemed the best reply to that.

"I ... I didn't know Ms. Marshall well enough to judge her," she continued. "But too much drink loosens the tongue. She—she was rude to me. I suppose I overreacted. I certainly didn't mean for her to die."

I stared at her for a moment, then realized what it was she was saying. "It wasn't your fault she died."

"If I hadn't complained to Mrs. Dawson, maybe—"

"Mrs. Andolina, Eileen Marshall was murdered."

She shook her head violently. "No. It's my fault." This

time the tears overflowed.

I reached over and gently touched her shoulder. The depth of her sadness made me catch my breath. I pulled my hand back. "I didn't mean to upset you."

She wiped her eyes and cleared her throat. Then she smiled at me and patted my hand affectionately. "You never upset me, son. Never." She looked over to her husband across the way. "Fred?"

He was at her side in seconds. "Yes, dear?"

"I'm really very tired." She turned back to me, and her smile was beatific. "Thank you, Greg."

Fred's eyes darted to her, his gaze filled with surprise and pain.

Kay squeezed my hand. "Good night." She rose from her chair, took her husband's arm. They paused at the bar to express their thanks to Susan for the party, then started upstairs.

Frustrated, I sat back in my chair

Who the hell was Greg?

After the Andolinas went upstairs, Sgt. Beach made his way down. I intercepted him at the bottom of the steps. "What brings you here?"

"I just wanted to speak with several of the guests. If you'll excuse me." He turned for the game room and headed for the DuBois.

Susan picked up an empty tray and returned to the kitchen.

Richard turned to me. "Looks like things are breaking up. Did you get what you need upstairs?"

"We'll talk later." I nodded toward Beach. "What do you think he wants?"

We glanced across the room. Michele smiled at her husband and hugged him, looking relieved.

"I'd say they just got the okay to go home. Scratch two suspects," Richard said.

"Narrowing the field doesn't bother me a bit." I

turned back to the bar, topping off my cola. My head felt like it was about to split. "I have to give up shaking hands."

"Why?"

"I learn too much crap."

"Who're you talking about?"

I nodded toward the reporter. "Ashley. She's a barfer. She stays skinny by throwing up. Did you see the way she looked at the shrimp?"

He frowned, studying her.

"How much longer do we need to stay?" I asked.

"I'm ready to go now. You?"

I looked back to the sergeant. "In a minute. I want to talk to Beach first."

"Okay. This'll give me a chance to call Brenda."

"I'll meet you in your room in ten or fifteen minutes."

He nodded, looked down at his ice-filled empty glass, and then poured himself another scotch, taking it and the bottle with him.

Beach crossed to the loveseat in the corner where Doug and Alyssa sat. He spoke with them for a moment, and then they, too, looked relieved. After he'd finished, he noticed me waiting for him and started toward me.

"Can I go home, too?"

"Not just yet."

"I thought you said I wasn't a suspect."

"You're not. But you may still be a material witness. Can you stay another day or so?"

"We'll be here as long as Maggie's in the hospital." I glanced at my watch. "Do you work a twenty-four hour day?"

"It only seems like it."

"You said you'd have this solved in thirty-six hours. Does that still hold?"

"We're getting closer."

"Who're your most likely suspects?"

"I'll bet they're the same as yours."

They. That meant he had no better idea than me. There had to be a way to eliminate more of them from the running.

"Is there a chance I can get my memory card back?"

"Yeah. You were right—there was nothing worth looking at."

Was that a judgment of my photography or had they erased the thing?

Before I could ask, Beach said, "I'll see you get it back."

"Thanks. Oh, and my insurance company will want a copy of the accident report. Can you help me out?"

"No problem. I've still got paperwork to attend to. I'll be in touch."

I watched him go upstairs. I had nothing more to say to the other guests, so I downed the rest of my Coke and grabbed the last shrimp from the tray.

My work wasn't finished yet, either.

NINETEEN

Richard had finished his call and was gone by the time I looked out the kitchen door to the patio beyond. I headed upstairs and knocked on his door, glad he opened it only seconds later. Brushing past him, I headed straight for the bathroom.

"How's the headache?"

"How'd you know?"

"A, you look like shit. B, you always have a headache when you invoke this psychic stuff."

When the water ran cold, I wrung out a washcloth, then headed for the comfort of the loveseat. I already had my prescription bottle open, doled out a pill and slipped it under my tongue, and then leaned back to settle the cool cloth on my forehead.

Richard shrugged and took the other chair. "What's with the washcloth?"

"I was our mom's favorite hangover remedy. It makes your head feel better."

"If you say so. Are you keeping track of the medication you've taken?"

"Yes," I said irritably.

"You've been known to get confused when the pain's bad."

"Thanks for the reminder."

He shrugged again. "Did Beach leave?"

I nodded, kicked off my shoes and put my feet on the

cocktail table, trying to ignore Richard's look of disapproval. "He said he had paperwork to finish. The town sure gets its money's worth out of him."

"It's called dedication. The same can be said of you—and you're not even getting paid for your detective work."

"It's not detective work. It's more like plain nosiness since whoever killed Eileen also hurt Maggie and wrecked my car."

He nodded, conceding the point. "I've been meaning to ask you about the victim. You said she looked ill."

"Yeah."

"Any idea from what? Cancer? Were there any outward sign of her being terminally ill?"

I shook my head.

"From what you've described, it sounds like her condition was stable. What made you think she was dying?"

"I got the impression *she* felt her time was short."

Richard thought about it for a moment. "Is it possible she wanted to die?"

"What do you mean?"

"Could she have set herself up as a target?"

"That doesn't make sense."

"Why not? Have you ever heard of suicide?"

I sat up straighter. "You mean she was too chicken to off herself, so she set herself up for someone else to do it?"

"Every terminal patient handles the news differently. Why do you think physician-assisted suicide keeps making headlines? Some patients would rather choose the time of their death. They don't want to be an emotional or financial burden to their families. They don't want to suffer for months in agony. Perhaps she lacked the courage to do it herself and decided being killed might be a way out."

"Are you serious?"

He sank back in his chair. "I'm drained. I don't know how you do it."

"Do what?"

"Soak up other people's feelings. Like what happened with Maggie at the hospital today. It's got to drag you down."

"It does," I admitted. "And I wish everything came with total understanding. Instead it comes like a jigsaw puzzle—one piece at a time. Like searching Zack's and Susan's apartment and Laura's and Ted's room."

"What did you learn?"

"Not as much as I'd hoped. I pawed through their things, but got the most information from their beds."

"Their beds?"

I explained what I'd experienced. Then a thought occurred to me. "Which bed did you sleep in the first night you were here?"

He pointed. "That one."

"I didn't get anything from that other bed last night, and I never get anything off you. I wonder if there's left-over vibes from Eileen in your bed."

"You make it sound like cooties."

"I always feel like a voyeur when I get these funny feelings." I sobered, looking at the bed. "Do you mind?"

"Be my guest."

Tossing the washcloth into the bathroom, I moved to the bed. Perching on the edge, I laid back, closed my eyes, letting my hands rest at my sides and opened myself up to ... whatever ... willing myself to relax.

Nothing happened.

The sound of my own breathing unnerved me.

Richard shifted in his chair.

I concentrated on my memories of Eileen on her last night, but trying to force these funny feelings was a sure way not to get anything.

I needed patience.

My fingers curled into the bedspread.

A gray, hazy image seeped into my mind. "She was drinking the scotch...." My left hand moved, groping for some unseen object.

"What was she looking for?" Richard asked.

I struggled to sharpen the image, which made my head thump even more.

"Uh ... a ... writing pad. She'd been writing something."

The image grew clearer. Eileen, dressed in her white robe, sat propped up on pillows, with the scotch bottle within reach on the bedside table. She held the half-filled tumbler in her right hand. Reading glasses were perched on her nose. She held an expensive ballpoint pen in her left hand and settled the tablet on her lap and began to write.

"Everything had been going just the way she'd planned ... but then it started to sour."

"What had she planned?"

Pain flared behind my eyes, extinguishing the image. I exhaled loudly, frustrated. "It's gone." I thought about it for a moment. "It's like ... being on the verge of re-membering, but I can't quite focus on it." I folded my arms across my chest and stared at the white textured ceiling.

"Let your subconscious work at it for a while. Maybe it'll come to you."

"It's too bad you can't just hypnotize me."

"Who says I can't?"

I propped myself up on my elbows and stared at him. "You can do that?"

He shrugged. "Hypnotism is just another state of con-sciousness achieved through relaxation. I'll bet I haven't lost my touch. Are you game?"

"Sure." I leaned back on the bed, then raised my head to look up at him. "Where'd you learn this?"

"UCLA."

I raised an eyebrow, waiting for the rest of the explanation.

"Okay, so I took the course to meet the instructor."

"A woman?"

"Yes."

"And?"

He squirmed. "After that, I ... lived with her for three years."

"Before Brenda, right?"

"Of course." He cleared his throat. "Anything specific you want me to ask?"

I'd have to grill him on his past some other time. "Just whatever comes to mind. If it works, ask me about Adam pushing me down the stairs. It seems like there's something there, too, but I don't know how to capture it."

Richard sat across from me on the other bed. "Okay. Close your eyes. Leave your arms at your sides and take a deep breath."

I did as I was told.

"Breathe deeply and evenly, and with every breath you'll feel all tension within you begin to dissipate. That's it. Deep breaths."

I listened to Richard speak; his voice dropped into a gentle croon. I concentrated on the calm, soothing sound of his words and on my own breathing.

Slowly in.

Slowly out.

The intense pounding in my head began to fade as a sense of peace descended upon me.

Slow.

Deep.

Breaths.

I felt at ease. Safe. Floating—no longer one with my body, my mind open to the universe.

"Jeff?"

"Yes?" My voice sounded oddly flat. Slower. Deeper.

"You're now totally relaxed. You feel no sense of uneasiness or anxiety. You feel calm, relaxed and totally self-assured."

"Yes."

"I want you to think of Eileen. Can you see her sitting on the bed? Writing on a tablet?"

What had been a hazy image was suddenly superimposed on my consciousness in vivid detail—as though I was actually witnessing it.

There's nothing quite like a good scotch buzz, but Eileen had gone way beyond that, the liquor intensifying all her emotions. Sorrow, shame, and anger spewed from her in an uncontrolled torrent, buffeting my senses like a typhoon. I struggled to catch my breath.

"You're totally relaxed," Richard reminded me, "and any emotions you sense cannot overwhelm you. You understand them, but they do not control you. You're safe from them."

Like turning down the volume on a stereo, Eileen's emotions backed down to a tolerable level.

"That's it," Richard encouraged, "relax. Now, look at the tablet in her hands. See the pen moving across the paper. Can you tell me what she's writing?"

My point of view abruptly shifted. Suddenly I was a sponge, absorbing Eileen's essence—knowing what it was to be Eileen, taking in my surroundings through her eyes.

My gaze drifted to the tablet. Doodles decorated the page.

"Laura ... two hundred and fifty thousand dollars."

"What's the money's for?"

In a flash, Eileen's lifetime of memories flooded through me. I knew so many things I shouldn't have known: her school years, working in London and then New York, the places she'd been to, the lovers she'd known.

"Ted ... Teddy," I said, surprised. "Teddy Bear."

"What does that mean?"

My tongue seemed too big for my mouth, and my stomach tightened. "He reminds her of ... the first one."

"Her first lover?" Richard repeated.

"Yes ... no. The first ... young one."

"Young one? Who was that? When was that?"

"When isn't important ... his age was. Just a boy. Maybe ten or eleven."

"And how old was Laura?"

"Twenty-two?"

"What?" Richard said, sounding incredulous. "And Eileen knew about this?"

I nodded. "Laura worked for Eileen ... was arrested. She lost her job."

"So what was Eileen's plan? To blackmail her?"

"I nodded."

"They both ended up here over Fourth of July ... that's when Eileen started plotting?"

"Why?"

"She wanted money—a business loan she called it. But she knew she would never repay it."

"What else is written on the paper?"

"Zack ... two hundred and fifty thousand dollars."

"Was Eileen blackmailing Zack, too?"

"No."

"Was she going to give Zack the money she got from Laura?"

"Yes."

"What for?"

"To buy out Susan." The answer had come so easily, yet I really wasn't sure of its validity.

"Is that all that was on the paper?"

"No. Susan ... her name ... crossed out. Heavy ink." Dark lines, done in anger, almost obliterated her name on the phantom tablet.

"Eileen and Zack were lovers, weren't they?" Richard continued.

"Yes." Was balling Eileen a mercy fuck? She had to be fifteen, maybe twenty years older than Zack.

"Had they been lovers for a long time?" Richard went on.

"No." A warm, bittersweet memory came to me. "Eileen first came to the inn last summer. She came back three times since. Once when Susan was gone." The memory fragment I'd picked up in the Dawson's bathroom returned, enhanced to include Zack and Eileen together in the hot tub on a cool, spring day.

"Was there anything else on the paper?"

"Says ... 'Call David. September 10th.'"

"Who's David?"

"Eileen's attorney. Ashley said Eileen saw him the day she died."

"What for?"

Whatever transpired between the attorney and Eileen had not been emotionally charged. It eluded me. "I don't know."

"Did Eileen want to die?"

A ripple of sorrow shattered the calm. A shudder ran through me. "She ... thought she was going to die."

"By murder?"

Something tightened in my chest. Fear—but I wasn't sure of the source. "I don't know."

"Was she sick?"

A bitter memory of illness surfaced, what Eileen feared would be her future. "Last winter. Pneumonia." But that hadn't been her underlying problem.

"What else can you tell me about Eileen?"

Tension coiled through me, Eileen's wants and desires conflicting with my own sense of self. "She ... liked me. Wanted me the same way she wanted Zack."

"How do you feel about that?"

Eileen had been lonely. And she'd felt used. "I love Maggie. I don't cheat."

"I'm with you on that," Richard said, sounding subdued.

"She told Zack," I volunteered.

"To make him jealous?"

"Yes."

"What did Zack say?"

"'Go for it.' He wanted her money. He'd say *anything* to get the money."

"Did Eileen love Zack?"

"Oh, yeah."

"Did she believe Zack loved her?"

Another pang of Eileen's grief assaulted me. "Not love, but hoped he felt some affection ... until this week."

"What changed her mind?"

Emotional overload clouded my understanding. "I'm ... not sure."

"Okay, Jeff. You're doing fine. Stay relaxed ... stay calm. Now, do you remember your accident on the stairs the other evening?"

"Yes." I breathed easier, relieved to leave Eileen's melancholy memories and once again embrace being me.

"What happened after you left us downstairs?"

The memory flashed through me like watching a video. "I went upstairs. Listened at the doors ... Susan's apartment. Kay Andolina's room."

"Did you hear anything suspicious?"

"No."

"Then what did you do?"

The video continued in my head. "I went ... upstairs. It was dark."

"What happened when you got to the top of the stairs?"

"I saw movement. Someone hit me—pushed me. I fell ... backwards."

"What happened next?"

I'd gone tumbling—crashing to the floor. "I hit my head. Had the wind knocked out of me."

"And then—?"

"Heard noises ... no, a strange voice."

"Kay Andolina?"

"Yes."

"She checked you over."

The picture in my mind was so clear, and yet—I was looking down at myself, like an eerie, out-of-body experience. Kay, dressed in a lavender-quilted robe, knelt beside me. "She touched my face."

"What did she say?"

The words—her intonation—echoed through my head. "'Look within.'"

"Is that all?"

"Yes."

"What does it mean?"

"I don't know," I answered, confused.

"What happened next?"

"My head hurt. I opened my eyes ... you were there."

"Okay, Jeff, you're doing great. Now if I told you to look within what would you see?"

Another image drifted into my mind—craggy rocks and millions and millions of trees. With it came a hazy sense of trepidation. "Mountains."

"The Green Mountains?"

"Yes."

"What does it mean?"

"I don't know."

"Are you looking at the mountains?"

The image shifted. Low clouds—a threatening sky. "No."

"Are you on the mountain?"

Renewed tension rose within me. "Yes."

"What are you doing?"

"Climbing." Me, alone, slogging through the trees, trying to run.

"Why?"

The tension shifted to panic, growing exponentially. "Have to get away."

"From what—from whom?"

The fear grew, threatening to choke me. "I—I don't know."

"Okay, Jeff. Remain calm. That's it—breathe slowly."

Richard's quiet confidence eased the angst and caused it to dissipate.

"Now, I'm going to bring you out of the hypnotic state. When I count to three and snap my fingers you'll open your eyes and you'll feel refreshed, and you'll remember everything you've told me. You feel fine. Oh, and in the future, when you feel a headache coming on, I want you to remember how relaxed and well you feel right now, and that will help ease the pain. Do you understand?"

"Yes."

"Okay. One. You're aware of everything around you. Two. You're filled with positive energy. Three. You're fully alert and feeling fine."

He snapped his fingers and I blinked, momentarily disoriented. I looked around, grateful to find myself back in Richard's cozy room, feeling relaxed. And while a remnant of the headache lingered, I felt better than I had before we'd started, just as he'd suggested.

"How did I do?"

"You're a very receptive subject."

I struggled to sit up and took a deep breath. The clarity I'd experienced during hypnosis was already beginning to fade. Despite Richard's instructions to the contrary, under hypnosis the knowledge had still been emotionally laden. Fully conscious, it was no longer colored by Eileen's passions but mirrored my own.

"My God. Laura's some kind of pedophile."

"How do you feel about the idea of having sex with Eileen?" Richard teased.

"That doesn't appeal to me, either. I wondered why she kept inviting me into the hot tub. I had no idea I was so attractive to old ladies."

"Neither did I." He sobered. "Did I ask the right questions?"

"Definitely."

"Do you have impressions of things you didn't tell me about?"

"Lots. I need to let it percolate. All I'm sure of now is that we've got four really good candidates as murderers."

"What about that mountain stuff? What does that mean?"

"I'm not sure."

"Why would Kay Andolina say that to you?"

I remembered my conversation with her at the party. "Maybe it's because an angel looks out for me."

"A what?"

"An angel," I repeated.

He smiled. "I didn't know I'd been elevated to heavenly status."

"Very funny. She's got it in her head that she's responsible for Eileen's death because she was rude to her. She complained, and Susan was going to throw Eileen out. She kept calling me Greg, too."

Richard's amusement faded and he frowned. "I had a long conversation with her husband. That is until Alyssa came up and interrupted us." He cleared his throat, embarrassed. "Kay had a breakdown after the death of their son." He shook his head in sympathy. "She shot and killed him. His name was Greg."

"An accident?" I asked, dreading the answer.

"She heard a noise in the night. There was a loaded gun in the house. Now she talks to angels."

"Did Fred ask you for professional advice?"

"He just needed to talk. It's been hard on him. He loves her, but he's frustrated by the changes in her. Eileen's death brought back a lot of unpleasant memories, which is probably why she's confused."

I felt a surge of compassion for the woman and her husband, regretting my earlier, hasty judgment of them.

I forced myself to consider everything else I'd learned that evening. There were still so many pieces of the puzzle missing.

"Do you think Beach would let me look at Eileen's belongings? I'm sure the killer—or someone—got rid of the incriminating page on that writing tablet, but the information I dredged up tonight might still be of use to Beach. And I might get more by touching Eileen's stuff."

"Haven't you had enough for one day?"

"I want to get it over with. You're the one who wanted to go home as soon as possible."

He glanced at his watch. "It's 10:15."

I got up and headed for the door. "I'll call the station to see if he's still there. If it's a go, I'll meet you in the living room in five minutes, okay? Or I can go by myself if you'll loan me your car."

He shook his head. "I'd better go, too. But I've had too much to drink. You'll have to drive." He threw me the car keys.

TWENTY

When I called the police station, Beach seemed surprised to hear from me and asked if it could wait until morning.

It couldn't.

The roads were nearly deserted, which suited me fine. When I have a headache, Headlights penetrate my brain like knife thrusts. I was glad it took less than ten minutes to get to the police station.

Despite the hour, Beach was waiting for us. We sat on plastic chairs in the reception area and he listened patiently while I told him everything I'd learned that evening—avoiding how I'd obtained some of the information.

"It'll be interesting to hear what Mr. Dawson has to say about his expected windfall. I wonder if she even has a clue about her husband's intentions."

"You and the chief can tag-team them. It's likely one of them will crack."

"And it'll be interesting to hear what Ms. Ross has to say about being blackmailed. More likely, all three will deny everything. Unfortunately, without proof, everything you've told me is just hearsay."

We followed him to the same interrogation room I'd been in the evening before. Spread out on the metal table were Eileen's suitcase, a travel tote, and a briefcase. Beach jerked a thumb toward it. "Go for it."

I opened the briefcase first. It contained maps, a magazine, several travel folders, and a yellow legal pad—the one I'd seen in the vision. No indentations marred the remaining pages, indicating more than just the sheet Eileen had written on had been removed. It was disappointing, but not unexpected. "Maybe I should look at the fireplaces when we get back to the inn."

"And the barbecue," Richard added.

The travel tote, complete with shampoo, deodorant, and toothpaste, was of no help. Richard looked over the bottles of medication.

"Are you familiar with those?" Beach asked.

"I've seen the same combinations before for cancer treatment."

The black, soft-sided suitcase beckoned. I exhaled, sweat already dampening the back of my shirt.

"What's wrong?" Richard asked.

I gestured toward my chest. "I've got this weird feeling in my gut. Like I shouldn't touch it."

"You're the one who asked to see it," Beach reminded me.

"Yeah."

Putting on a brave front, I unzipped the case and threw back the lid. A swell of emotion pounded me. Overwhelmed, I wasn't immediately able to identify it. My breath caught in my throat as my eyes welled with sudden tears.

"Jeff?" Richard asked.

I stumbled into a chair and forced myself to breathe evenly. Eileen's neatly folded, terry cloth robe—the last thing she'd ever worn—sat atop her other clothes, radiating wave after wave of despair.

"What is it?" Beach asked.

"Betrayal." I covered my eyes with my hand, massaging my aching temples.

"Get beyond it," a detached Richard advised.

I nodded—reached for the robe, and settled my left hand on it. Conflicting images filled my mind. Laura. Mouthing epithets. In the clearing behind the inn. Then a younger, more vulnerable Laura, crying. The images strobed back and forth, making me dizzy.

"Eileen ... argued with Laura. But she didn't look the way she does today. Her hair was darker. It must've been years ago. Why am I'm getting something from so long ago?"

"Can you zero in on what happened Friday night?" Richard asked.

I shut my eyes, swamped by more painful memories. Zack—his eyes wide in anger. Pushing Eileen. Demanding money. Blaming Eileen. Eileen's terrible guilt.

"Eileen ... talked to Zack. She argued with him."

"About what?"

"Money. I don't know when. It could've been Friday. I'm not sure."

"What else?" Beach asked.

Eileen's lingering emotional baggage poured relentlessly out of the suitcase.

The hot tub. Eileen's hand clutching the tumbler of scotch, gulping it, the amber liquid dibbling down her chin. A voice. Quiet. Menacing. Unintelligible. Skyrockets of pain. Then, blissful nothingness.

I let out a shaky breath.

"All I'm getting is betrayal. She felt she had no reason to live. Then she was dead. Floating in the hot tub."

"Murdered," Beach said. "But who did it?"

I shrugged, my head pounding. I reached into my jeans pocket and pulled out the prescription bottle.

"No," Richard said, taking it from me. "That's it for tonight. Sit back and relax."

I did as I was told, and watched in silence as he closed the suitcase, zipped it shut, and set it in the corner of the room farthest from me.

Acute defeat settled over me. "Sorry, Beach. I thought maybe I could get to the bottom of this if I saw—touched—Eileen's stuff."

He shrugged, obviously as disappointed as me. "You tried. It looks like I go about this the old-fashioned way."

Exhaustion pulled at me. But there was still so much that needed to be said—to be asked. I forced myself to think about other things. "What's Stowe's drug problem like?"

"Not good. It's a transient population—upper-middle class to wealthy people who like to party. Why?"

"Adam Henderson grows and sells marijuana on the side. You might want to look into that when you get a chance."

"Did he try to sell you some?"

"No, but he sold it to at least one of the other guests."

"Are you telling me this to get back at him for pushing you down the stairs?"

"I could've pressed charges if I was that pissed. I'm just telling you what he does to make money on the side."

Beach scowled. "Anything else?"

"Yeah, what's this about Ted Palmer being arrested for joyriding?"

"He mentioned it to you?"

"He thought you'd already told me. Either that or he wanted to tell me himself before I found out some other way." That struck me as odd. "How did he think I'd find out?"

"Does anyone at the inn know about this psychic stuff you do?"

"I don't think so. Maggie could've told Susan, but she knows I like to keep it quiet."

"I can see why. Anyway, Palmer's never been in trouble since his arrest almost eleven years ago. But he still could've been the one who forced you off the road.

Wouldn't you have known that?"

"Not necessarily. I tap into emotions. If he wasn't bothered by nearly killing us—I wouldn't pick up on it. And whoever killed Eileen obviously isn't obsessing over it and feels confident he—or she—won't get caught."

Beach frowned. "Two days ago I would've laughed if anyone told me I'd believe a psychic. Now...." He stared at the floor. Suddenly I was getting something from him.

I couldn't take much more.

"What is it, Beach?" I asked, anticipating his question.

"My sister—is she...?" His expression was one of hopeful dread.

"I don't know about the hereafter. I only got what you felt about the accident. You're being too hard on yourself. How old were you, six?"

He nodded. "I caught a bass. Karen was so excited. She tried to help me land it and fell in. Neither of us could swim. The dock was two feet higher than the water. I couldn't reach her. By the time I got help, it was too late."

He fell silent, radiating remorse.

I felt like a creep intruding on his misery.

My head threatened to split. "I—I have to go," I said, then Richard was at my elbow, helped me from the chair and guided me out the room.

"Wait," Beach called after us, and handed Richard a large brown envelope.

Before I knew it, we were outside, standing in the parking lot. Above the mercury vapor lights the sky was inky black and dotted with stars. My breath came out in a wispy fog. There'd be a frost by morning.

"Come on," Richard said, steering me toward the car. "I'm taking you back to the inn and putting you to bed."

"You make me sound like a bad little boy."

"Well, you certainly don't know your own limits." He got in the car, tossed the envelope in back and buckled himself in. "Seat belt," he reminded me.

I didn't have the stamina to argue. I fumbled with the belt. "Beach ought to chat with Kay Andolina," I said, sinking back in the seat. "She's the one who talks to angels."

Then we were on the road heading north. Except for a few of the village's hot spots, the place seemed deserted, shut down, asleep.

I was shutting down, too.

TWENTY-ONE

I awoke to the sounds of car doors and trunks slamming. Opening one eye I looked at Richard's travel clock: 7:36. His bed was empty and the shower was running. I heard another slam, realizing the departing guests were probably already loading their cars. That way they could eat as soon as the kitchen opened and hit the road for home only a day late.

It took a minute or two for me to realize my headache was nearly gone. I thought back to Richard's posthypnotic suggestion and felt myself instantly relax. Why hadn't we thought to try this during the past six months?

The water stopped running and a few minutes later Richard emerged, dressed in Dockers and an Izod shirt, his graying hair tousled. "Good morning, roomie."

"Roomie?"

"Yeah. I never had one before. Unless you count my lady friends."

I sank back on my pillow, too lazy to get up. "I had twenty-three roomies in my barracks at Fort Gordon. It wasn't much fun as I recall."

Richard turned to the mirror and combed his hair. "I offered to send you to college, but you had to prove you were a grown-up and enlist." At least there was no animosity in his rebuke.

"Why am I back here with you, anyway? I've got a room of my own, you know."

"Hey, it was all I could do to drag you in from the car last night. Once you're out of it, kid, you're dead to the world. And I swear, when you sleep, you're as still as a corpse. It made me want to put a mirror under your nose to see if you were still breathing."

"I'll try to be more animated in future."

"Are you getting up?"

"Yeah. I've got to call the insurance company about my car." I didn't move. I thought of my charred, demolished Chevy. "Damn. It was a wreck, but it was *my* wreck. And paid for."

"We'll start looking again once we get home. At least you weren't too badly hurt, and Maggie's going to be all right, too."

I thought about that five-inch tear in her leg.

"Can we go home tomorrow?" Richard asked, grabbing a pair of socks from the dresser drawer.

"God, I hope so."

"Good. I'm running out of clean clothes."

I didn't bother to tell him that I already had.

I showered and dressed and was ready to head for breakfast by 8:10. We passed through the bar on the way to the dining room. All evidence of the party the night before was gone. The rug had even been vacuumed, a testament to Susan's good housekeeping.

As I expected, Jean and Michele Dubois and Doug and Alyssa were already breakfasting. I poured myself a cup of coffee, glanced out the window, and saw Sgt. Beach crouched by the backyard barbeque, accompanied by the same photographer who'd taken shots of the crime scene three days before.

"Rich?" I nodded toward the window.

Richard noted the sergeant's presence. "He didn't waste time getting here."

"We took our coffee out to the patio."

"You're up early," I said.

Beach looked up at me. "Unfortunately, I couldn't get a warrant just on your say so, but Mrs. Dawson signed a consent to search form, letting me look at the fireplaces and barbecue."

I gestured toward the ash pit. "Did you find anything?"

"Ashes from the tablet in the barbecue here. Nothing in the fireplaces inside. It doesn't point the finger at anyone, but it confirms your story about incriminating evidence."

I sipped my coffee. My story. That irked me—Maggie's the writer, not me.

"We want to head home tomorrow. Is that okay?"

He shrugged. "Are you willing to come back to testify—that is, if we solve this?"

"Sure. I want to know how it all turns out. I have a vested interest, if you know what I mean."

"If you come up with anything else, give me a call."

"You got it."

I followed Richard back to the dining room. We paused by the coffeemaker for a warm up, then sat at one of the empty tables. Moments later, Nadine came out from the kitchen.

"Zack's making huevos rancheros and blueberry pancakes. Can I interest either of you in them?" Her voice was a monotone. Definitely no joie de vivre.

"I'll just go through the buffet," I said.

"I'll have the eggs and whole wheat toast, please," Richard said. She nodded and headed back for the kitchen.

"What're we going to do about getting home?" I asked.

"How about we drive the rental car to Burlington and take a flight to Buffalo?"

"What about all that camera equipment upstairs?"

"It'll have to go as excess baggage. I wish we could fly

straight home from here, but there's no way Maggie could do it in a Cessna with her leg the way it is. And, to tell you the truth, I'm in no hurry to get back in one of those rattletraps."

I tried—and failed—to suppress a smile.

"I'll call the airlines and make reservations after breakfast," Richard volunteered.

"Okay." I looked toward the kitchen and food. "Well, my stomach calls."

As I crossed the threshold, the tension in the kitchen hit me like a slap in the face. There was no conversation today. Adam's dishonesty and the fact that he'd attacked me had not been enough for Zack and Susan to fire him. He was busy scrubbing pots at the large sink. I tore my gaze from him. Anger had deadened my appetite, but I grabbed a couple of sausage links and a spoonful of eggs before heading back into the dining room.

I dropped the plate with a clunk, making Richard jump.

"Is something wrong?"

"No." I sat down and started shoveling scrambled eggs into my mouth.

Nadine reappeared, her smile tight as she placed Richard's breakfast in front of him. "Enjoy."

He looked at her retreating figure, then back to me. "Did the whole world suddenly get pissed off when I wasn't looking?"

I swallowed, spoke quietly. "Adam's still here. Maybe if he'd pushed a paying guest down stairs he would've lost his job. Damn that Susan."

"How do you know it wasn't Zack who gave him another chance?"

"Because he's been screwing Susan for months!"

I stopped chewing. I hadn't known that juicy little fact before that moment, but it made sense.

"My, you're just full of surprises," Richard said.

I looked away, my anger smoldering.

"Jeff, calm down. There's nothing you can do about it."

"That still doesn't make it right."

Richard refrained from commenting, picked up his fork, and started eating his breakfast. He was halfway through his eggs, and I was polishing off the last sausage on my plate when the Andolinas came in and sat at a table next to the window overlooking the garden. Kay smiled shyly and waved at me. I gave her a self-conscious smile and halfhearted wave in return.

"Do you think she really believes I'm her son?" I muttered under my breath.

Richard took a quick look over his shoulder. "I doubt it. But apparently you do look a bit like him. He had dark hair and dark eyes. It's only been six months. Hopefully she'll come to terms with it and won't try suicide again."

"Suicide?"

He nodded. "Two months ago. Pills. Fred decided she needed to get away. They came to Vermont on their honeymoon thirty-four years ago. He thought it might be good for her to return."

Again I felt a pang of guilt for my hasty judgment of the woman. "Boy, people really do confide in you."

"I told you, they'll tell doctors things they wouldn't tell their best friends."

"I take it you got no such revelations out of Laura?"

He shook his head, taking a sip of coffee. "She's a real ice queen."

Beach came in through the garden door and headed for the Andolina's table. He spoke with them for a few moments, and I guessed he was giving them permission to leave, too.

Dipping my hand in my pants pocket, I came up with Maggie's cell phone. "Guess I'd better go make my call."

I went outside on the patio to call my insurance company and report the accident, telling them where to send the adjuster to look at the remains. I'd have to fill in the paperwork back home, and I made a mental note to remind Beach to give me a copy of the police report.

Richard was saying good-bye to the Canucks as I came back to the dining room. They gave me a wave as they headed up the stairs one last time.

"Lucky bums," Richard muttered.

"Tomorrow, bro."

"It can't come soon enough for me." He got up from the table. "It's my turn to make calls."

I sat down to nurse another cup of coffee and wait for Richard, wondering how we'd kill time before visiting hours at the hospital. As it turned out, I didn't have to. I was on my third cup when Richard finally reappeared. He sat across from me, his expression grim.

"I couldn't get us home from Burlington without a four-hour layover in Albany, so we're driving to Albany. I had a little trouble with the car rental agency. They didn't want me to take the wagon to New York, but it's all straightened out."

"How much is this going to cost you?"

"Don't ask."

We split up, with Richard heading for Susan's office to tell her of our checkout plans, and me to my room to finish straightening up and pack. I had a feeling there might not be a whole lot of time to do so later.

It amazes me how I don't analyze funny feelings that deal with seemingly insignificant things. If I did, I'd save myself a lot of trouble in the long run.

I came downstairs to collect Richard, rounded the stairwell and saw Patrolman Morris, the first cop to arrive at the murder scene, standing guard outside the door to Susan's and Zack's apartment. His expression said no nonsense tolerated. I nodded a terse hello, turned the corner and knocked on Richard's door. He was ready, shrugging into his jacket.

"It looks like Beach is pushing Zack and Susan."

"Both?" he asked.

"One or the other or both."

He pulled the door shut and followed me outside.

The day was hazy and cool—almost clammy. Rain was in the offing and I was glad I'd thought to grab a jacket.

I followed Richard down the steps to the car and noticed the vacancy sign was out. Susan had wasted no time trolling for new customers. Across the lot, Ted spoke to the lady cop while a crying Laura sat in the back seat of a patrol car.

"Do you think she's been arrested?" Richard asked.

I shook my head. "No handcuffs. My guess is she'll be taken to the station for a little chat like Maggie and me the other night. Let's get out of here. Just thinking about that gives me the creeps."

We made it through the village in record time, thanks to the nearly deserted streets. The mass exodus after the Labor Day holiday was only a pause in the tourist trade. In another couple of weeks when the leaves turned color the entire state would be jammed with sightseers and tour busses.

We arrived at Copley Hospital at precisely eleven o'clock and headed for the elevators. My footsteps slowed as we approached Maggie's room and a dark, queasy feeling came over me. "Uh-oh...."

"What's wrong?" Richard asked.

"I'm not sure." I moved ahead, knocked at the door-jamb and looked in. "Hello?"

Maggie was waiting for us all right, only she was dressed and sitting in the room's only chair, with a pair of crutches propped against the wall beside her and her bag packed. I didn't need to see that her face was shadowed with misgiving; I could feel it radiating from her.

"What's going on?" Richard asked.

"My insurance company says I'm well enough to leave."

If there's one topic in medicine that sets off Richard's seldom-seen anger, it's insurance companies dictating patient care.

"What did your doctor say?"

"He said there was no real reason for me to stay. But no stairs."

"Which means you can't go back to the inn," I put in. "It's just as well. I don't want you going back there—it's not safe. I don't feel safe there."

"I'll talk to the head nurse," Richard said. "I don't think you're ready to leave. And I'll pay for you to stay, if that's what it takes."

"No, please," Maggie begged. "I want to get out of here. Can't we just go home?"

"We've got plane reservations for tomorrow," Richard said. "Would you mind staying at one of the motels in town?"

"It looks like I don't have much choice."

We called for the nurse, who arrived with a wheelchair, and within minutes we were on the road—complete with flowers, crutches and teddy bear in tow—and on our way back to Stowe. We stopped at the first motel along the strip that sported a vacancy sign. Clean and comfortable, its ground-floor location made for easy accessibility.

Sensing he needed to play doctor, if only to reassure himself Maggie could navigate on her own, I left Richard to help her get settled, while I hit the deli across the street.

Twenty minutes later, Maggie sat propped up on one of the beds, her injured leg resting on a pillow, while I doled out sandwiches and drinks. Richard and I settled on the room's two chairs, looking like mismatched bookends as we squirted packets of horseradish sauce on our beef hoagies.

"What happens next?" Maggie asked, and then took a bite of her sub.

"I didn't know you were getting out of the hospital, or we could have gone home today," Richard said. "Those reservations are for a four o'clock flight out of Albany— tomorrow."

"Then I take it Sgt. Beach says we can go."

"Yeah, but we still don't know who killed Eileen," I said.

"What else can we do?" Richard asked.

"I know a lot more about the players in this little drama, but I'm no closer to knowing who did it. And I'm getting really tired," I admitted.

Maggie took a good, hard look at me. "Jeff, you look terrible. What happened?"

"The Great and Powerful Resnick knows all—except his own limits," Richard said. "We ought to hire him out for parties: 'Have your past read.' It might be funny if it didn't cost him so much."

"Would you mind not talking about me like I'm not in the room. I didn't ask for this to happen to me. I feel like a broken radio that only gets an intermittent signal."

"You seemed to have been adjusting your signal just fine last night."

"Can we talk about something else?"

"Like who killed Eileen?" Maggie suggested. "I'm assuming you made progress at the party."

"Ted. It's obvious it was Ted," Richard said.

"So what's his motive?" I asked. "People usually only kill to save their necks or to gain something—like money. If Eileen had money, she wouldn't have been blackmailing Laura. I might believe Ted killed Eileen for Laura, but how would she get him to do it?"

"How did Eileen find out Laura was even with Ted?"

Maggie asked. "And what's the big deal anyway? It's not a sin for a younger guy to be with an older woman."

She had that right. "It depends on the age of the couple." I filled her in on our little hypnotism experiment the night before.

"Whoa. Screwing with little boys. That's just plain nasty."

"It depends on the age of the boy. I imagine quite a few thirteen year olds would be thrilled to have sex with an older woman despite what some shrinks and the law say. But at age ten—that's really pushing it. "

"I didn't think a boy that young could even—" She hesitated. "Get it up."

Richard cleared his throat, but said nothing.

"Then how about Susan as a suspect?" Maggie suggested. "Adam thought she qualified."

"And she's a good one," I agreed. "He might have had good reason to suspect her and try and protect her." I told Maggie about my revelation at breakfast. She didn't seem surprised.

"She and Laura sure like them young." She shook her head. "I suppose it's understandable if Zack prefers older women over her. Do you think he knows about her and Adam?"

"Maybe he doesn't care. Then again, Eileen thought Zack wanted to buy her out for a two hundred and fifty grand. The inn is worth a lot more than that. If they can get those remaining rooms finished, they'd make out like bandits during a good ski season."

"Yes, and a decent lawyer would negotiate for better than that for her," Richard pointed out.

"I don't think she'd take a deal. I think she likes being an innkeeper," I said.

"Why do you say that?" Richard asked.

"The inside of the Sugar Maple is Susan's domain—and it's immaculate. Out back there must be five or six different gardens that, until recently, look like they've had a lot of care. I'm assuming that was Zack's interest. Didn't you say he had a landscaping business at one time, Maggie?" She nodded. "Everything was kind of shaggy when we arrived. The shrubs by the sign at the edge of the road are in desperate need of trimming. The outside of the inn is where tourists get their first impression of the place."

"You're right. Susan was so proud of that Triple-A shingle. She said they worked hard to get it."

"Sloppy gardening isn't a motive for murder," Richard pointed out.

"No, but it shows Zack's interest in the place has waned. Maybe he had other interests he wanted to pursue."

"You did say he'd do anything to get the money. Perhaps he'd lie about leaving Susan to get it. What if he had some other purpose in mind that even Eileen didn't know about?"

Something about that rang true. "Maybe he just got sick of playing first mate to Captain Susan. I mean, think about it. He had what amounted to a yacht and he sold it for Susan and the Sugar Maple Inn. What if he just wants to sail away and out of Susan's life? "

Richard shrugged.

Maggie frowned. "I still think Susan's the killer. She was livid when she told Eileen to leave. I can tell you from experience, it's humiliating to know your husband is catting around—be it with another woman or another man."

"But is that a motive for murder?"

She shrugged. "Maybe not. I still love Gary. A part of me always will."

"Yeah, but you're not a coldhearted bitch like Susan, either."

"Did she even know Eileen and Zack were lovers?"

Richard asked.

"I don't know. Maybe she knew and didn't care, especially if young Adam had been servicing her. But when she argued with Eileen, she didn't know we'd come down to the pool and were listening. If Susan was angry enough to kill Eileen, wouldn't she have hit her then?"

"I suppose she could've gone back to kill her later," Richard suggested. "But it doesn't seem likely." He balled the papers from his lunch and tossed them at the wastebasket across the room. Missed.

"Let's get back to Zack," Maggie said. "Maybe Laura wasn't going to come up with the money and Zack and Eileen argued. Murders often happen in the heat of passion."

"And the passion had definitely cooled between them."

"Another reason for murder," Richard said, retrieving the papers and disposing of them. "Do you think it was Zack who burned those pages in the barbecue?"

"I'd lay odds. He showed up after Susan—just as the police arrived on Saturday morning. That would've given him almost ten minutes to go through Eileen's room and remove anything incriminating."

Maggie frowned. "Did they ever determine what the murder weapon was?"

"Technically Eileen drowned, but I don't think they came up with the blunt instrument that knocked her out first. And it wasn't the plastic scotch bottle, either. Even full of liquid, I'm not so sure it was rigid enough to fracture her skull."

"That would depend on the force of the blow, but I tend to agree with you," Richard said, and Maggie handed him her leftovers for the trash.

She adjusted the pillow under her leg. "They've all got motives for killing the poor woman."

"But there has to be one crucial piece of evidence

that's missing. And somehow you know about it," Richard said.

"Why do you keep saying that?"

"Why else would someone come after you and Maggie? There's no reason—unless you know something incriminating about the killer."

"Well, I don't have a clue what it could be. And it can't be that important or they—he or she—would've tried again."

"They might—tonight," Richard said.

"Why?"

"Because we let it be known we're leaving tomorrow."

That statement troubled me.

I looked down at what was left of my hoagie and sank back in the chair. As Richard had said, I probably did know something so simple it was invisible to me. But what?

I glanced at my lady across the room. She looked weary. I felt weary. "Are you okay, Maggs?"

She nodded. "I guess."

"You both look like sleep refugees," Richard said.

I glanced at my brother. "You don't look that hot, either."

"Okay—it's unanimous. We're all tired. Tomorrow night we'll be home in our own beds."

I gathered up the mess in front of me and stashed it in the brown paper sack our lunch had come in.

Beds.

Bedroom.

Bedroom closet.

The prescription bottle in Zack's closet.

"Here's something I forgot to mention. When I was nosing around in Zack's and Susan's apartment, I found a prescription bottle hidden in some shoes in the closet."

"What was it for?" Richard asked.

I spelled it for him.

Richard looked up sharply. "Are you sure?"

"I think so What is it?"

He laughed. "It's generic Viagra."

"Are you sure?" I asked.

"As sure as I know my own name."

"Then that must mean that without a little blue pill, Zack's rather useless in bed."

Richard nodded.

"No wonder Susan went looking for greener pastures," Maggie commented

I sipped the last of my coffee. "Or maybe it was the only way he could do it with Eileen. It might be the only way I'd have been able to do the same."

Maggie giggled. "Okay, if Laura wasn't going to pay Eileen, that left Zack without money for a new boat. Do you think that's enough of a motive for him to kill Eileen?"

"I don't think it was Zack," I said.

"I'll second that," Richard said. "It's Ted. It's got to be Ted."

"But if Susan found out about Zack and Eileen—" Maggie started.

"If she was angry about it, she'd be radiating some pretty strong emotions."

"Ah, but as you pointed out to Sergeant Beach," Richard said, "there's the guilt factor. If she didn't feel bad about killing him, she wouldn't be radiating any kind of guilt or remorse. And you don't pick up on everything everyone feels."

I nodded, conceding defeat. "You're right. Susan's a blank slate to me. Then, I guess we're back to square one."

"So what's our next move?" Maggie asked.

"Go home. We can't hang around here forever."

"What time shall we leave tomorrow morning?" Richard asked.

"We should be on the road by ten at the latest."

"No problem for me," he said.

"Me, either," Maggie seconded. "I've been waiting to go home almost since we got here."

The quiet lengthened.

Maggie broke the silence. "What's in that envelope?" she asked, pointing to her stuff piled on the dresser.

"Beach handed it to me last night," Richard said.

I grabbed it, tore open the flap, and withdrew the contents: a copy of the accident report on my car, along with a bunch of eight and a half by eleven inch sheets of inkjet images of what I'd taken of the inn, as well as the memory card. "Not bad."

Richard looked over my shoulder and Maggie craned her neck. "I told you they'd come out good. I can't wait to see the rest of them," she said.

"We can look at them tomorrow night on the computer. How's the article coming?"

"Pretty good. I can probably finish it by the weekend and we can email the whole thing off next Monday."

"Your first sale," Richard said to me.

I crossed my fingers. "I hope."

Maggie tried to stifle a yawn.

"I think someone needs her rest," Richard said.

"Why am I so tired?" she asked.

"Blood loss, trauma. Need I say more?"

"I suppose you guys are going to take off?" she said, sounding grumpy

"Just to give you some peace and quiet."

"I guess you're right. But I feel like I'm missing out on all the fun."

"Believe me, there's been a serious lack of so far on this trip," Richard said. That, at least, made Maggie smile.

Richard grabbed his jacket and headed for the door.

"Give me a minute, will you, bro?"

He smiled. "Sure. See you later, Maggie." He closed

the door behind him.

"Are you coming back tonight?" she asked.

"I don't know, Maggs. I'd like to find out who killed Eileen before we leave. If I can, I'll be back to spend the night with you."

"Jeff, let the police handle it. It's what they get paid for."

I put the envelope on the bedside table. "I know."

"And don't take any stupid chances."

"You worry too much."

"After all that's happened, I think it's justified."

I opened my wallet, disappointed to find only eleven dollars. I took out the two bills and crushed them into Maggie's palm. "In case we miss you for dinner, there's a diner on the other side of the office. It's open 'til eight. If they've got room service, use it."

"What about tomorrow morning?" she reminded me. "Are we really going to leave?"

"Yes."

She studied my face, looking skeptical. "Why don't I believe you?"

"We will." I gave her a quick kiss. "I gotta go."

"If you're going to be too late, at least call me."

"I will." I kissed her again, longer, more intensely. When I pulled back, her expression was still unhappy. "Get some rest," I ordered, and headed for the door.

Her voice stopped me. "I love you."

"I love you, too, Maggie." I shut the door behind me, feeling like a jerk—knowing she'd be crying before I got to the car.

TWENTY-TWO

The clouds grew darker, reflecting my mood. That attitude wasn't going to win me any popularity contests with Richard or anyone else I came in contact with. I got in the Buick, buckled my seat belt, and avoided my brother's gaze.

"Is everything okay?" he asked.

"No."

He exhaled loudly. "Should I change the plane reservations?"

"Not yet."

"What does that mean?"

"I don't know."

"But you're getting a funny feeling we're not going home tomorrow, right?" he persisted.

"I don't know."

He glared at me, his voice tight. "Are we going back to the inn?"

I nodded, preoccupied with thoughts of Maggie and worried about what awaited me.

He started the car, and then headed for the lot's exit. "Here's something you haven't thought to do: revisit the scene of the crime."

"The hot tub?" I asked.

"I haven't seen you go near it. Is there a reason?"

"I don't think so. Except, Brenda told me it's a breeding ground for germs."

"It is," he said. "But nobody's been in it since Eileen died, right?"

"Not as far as I know."

"Then it's probably all right. There're health codes the inn has to follow. It's probably pumped full of chlorine every day. Maybe you can soak up some residual vibes." He tore his gaze momentarily from the road and looked at me meaningfully.

"I suppose I could have a look." Not exactly an enthusiastic response, but I wasn't really worried about germs. My insight tends to warn me about unpleasant experiences. I had a feeling visiting the hot tub might be one.

Richard braked as we approached the inn. Unfamiliar cars lined the driveway—new guests?—as well as Ashley Samuels' junky-looking van. The vacancy sign was down, another indication Susan's balance sheet would improve. Despite the cluster of cars, the place was devoid of people.

We bypassed the front door, skirted the garage and headed for the back gardens. Like the rest of the place, the pool was deserted. Because of cool temperatures, there weren't even any towels laid out—or perhaps the deputies' presence earlier had disrupted the inn's routine. Still, steam from the hot tub curled into the clammy air. I stared at the crystal clear water and wondered what Zack's utility bills were like.

Richard gestured toward the tub. "Okay, peel off."

I looked up at him. "Peel off?"

"Yeah."

I took in all the windows that overlooked the pool and hot tub. Until that moment I'd never considered myself a bona fide prude.

"I don't think so."

"You haven't got anything I haven't seen before," Richard said.

"Give me a break."

"Did you bring swim trunks?"

I nodded.

"Put them on. I'll ask Susan for a couple of those big towels and meet you back here," Richard said.

The weather, or perhaps just my mood, really wasn't conducive to hot tubbing, but he had a point. And, if nothing else, it would probably be my last shot at learning anything else about the murder.

When I returned a few minutes later, he was waiting by the hot tub in one of the chairs he'd pulled up. As promised, two large fluffy towels sat on the empty chair and he'd set the tub's timer for fifteen minutes.

Without a word I kicked off my sneakers, peeled off my jacket and stuck one foot into the water. "Jesus, it's hot!"

"You'll get used to it."

Richard's supposedly helpful comments bugged me. There he sat, fully clothed and dry, unmindful of the chill air.

Easing myself into the steaming water, I realized I was a couple of inches shorter than its last occupant. The water came up to my chin as I positioned myself where I'd last seen Eileen alive. Richard watched, fists jammed into his jacket pockets.

"I can't help remembering what Brenda told me about germs."

"Don't be paranoid. Besides, these things have filters. They've probably already strained off her finger- and toe-nails, and all her sloughed-off skin cells."

"What?"

"What do you think happens to a body in water?"

I stared at him.

"I'm joking," Richard said. "Eileen wasn't in there long enough."

My mouth hung open. Realizing it, I shut it.

He gestured at the water. "Concentrate."

Pondering the final minutes of Eileen's life was the last thing I wanted to do, but the faster I got it over with, the faster I could get out of the hot tub and back into dry clothes.

The churning water mesmerized me, making it easier to clear my mind. My eyes slid shut and I thought back to Friday night—the night of the murder.

My breathing slowed and deepened. The stench of chlorine actually helped revive my memories. The warm evening breeze. The hum of an air conditioner somewhere in the background. A mosquito buzzed my ear. Maggie's voice was an echo, teasing me. And then there was Eileen. It was all too easy to slip into her melancholy memories. The absolute hopelessness she'd felt sucked at my soul like a yawning abyss.

"Everything was ... falling apart."

"How?" Richard asked.

Numbness.

"She was ... so damned drunk."

I thought about what Kay Andolina had said to me when I was unconscious: Look within. Looking within brought back the image of the mountains. What the hell did that have to do with anything? I was definitely on the wrong track.

I replayed my mental video of Eileen in the hot tub. Poor unhealthy, unhappy Eileen. Drunk, alone, and unloved.

Something inside me twisted, and a familiar pain snaked through my skull.

"She .. .wondered if she should just...." I gestured with my hands, letting them sink beneath the surface of the swirling waters.

"Suicide?"

I squinted up at him. "You were right. Eileen wanted to die."

"And someone hit her with a blunt object, granting

her wish."

"Yeah. If they'd been a little patient, they wouldn't have had to resort to murder."

Someone had stood over Eileen and delivered the fatal blow. She'd been hit hard enough to knock her out and then she'd drowned. Beach had said something about blood loss, too. Had Eileen argued with her killer first? If so, no one had heard them. Yet the blow had been delivered in anger, I knew it—felt it.

I closed my eyes, dove under the water and let myself float. Bobbing for long moments, I listened to the muffled hum of the tub's motor, the sound of rushing water in my ears. Nothing else came to mind. Once Eileen lost consciousness she was gone.

I stood up, pushing the hair from my eyes.

"Is that it?" Richard asked.

"Yeah. The last thing I want right now is a skull-pounding headache from all this crap." He handed me a towel. "I'll be glad to get home. I don't want to do this any more."

"But you said your funny feelings would follow you if you didn't put them to rest here."

"Yeah ... I did." But I also had a feeling I was close to discovering the truth. "Can I use your shower again? I hate the smell of chlorine."

"Sure. Give me your key and I'll go get your clothes."

I finished toweling off in the chill air, stuffed my feet back into my Nikes and clomped back into the inn, wondering why I felt so ill at ease, not wanting to discover the reason.

Richard's bathroom was spotless. I was impressed with the amenities included with the best room in the inn, things I'd been too out of it to notice on other occasions. Two large, thick bath towels hung over a brass warming rail. A small wicker basket on the vanity offered shampoo, lotion, a comb, toothbrush and a disposable razor. Yesiree, paying customers were treated like royalty—whereas the hired help were of no consequence. My irritation with Susan flared anew and I stepped into the shower to douse it.

Richard tossed my clothes on the vanity and shut the door.

As I showered, I thought about Susan's standards of cleanliness, not a speck of dust marred any flat surface or the thousands of knickknacks that decorated the place. With such a small staff, it meant Susan had to be doing as much of the dirty work as Adam and Nadine.

I thought about all the extra touches: the sherry on the bar at night; the bath sheets laid out by the Jacuzzi; the sumptuous breakfasts; the fresh cookies, and the bottomless coffee pot in the dining room.

Though more than my budget could handle, Susan's prices weren't exorbitant for the accommodations she offered her guests. And the little extras, like the toiletry baskets in each of the guest bathrooms, were nicer than what I'd seen in higher priced hotel chains. No doubt they'd helped her earn the coveted AAA three-diamond rating.

I felt an unexpected pang of sympathy for her. Much as I disliked the woman, I was pretty sure Susan wasn't a murderer.

Minutes later I emerged from the bathroom, dropped my socks and sneakers and stopped before the mirror to use Susan's complimentary comb. Richard watched in silence from the loveseat.

Pocketing the comb, I picked up my shoes and took the chair nearest him, and put on my socks. "I keep thinking about what you said—that I know something that'll nail the killer."

"Did you figure it out?"

I stuffed my feet into my shoes. "On the night of the murder, the ice bucket behind the bar was empty, so I had to get some from the freezer. I stopped at the sink and a funny feeling came over me. I thought I should touch the dirty glasses, but I didn't want to because I didn't want to know."

"Know what?" Richard asked.

"That's it. I don't know. It's just ... I'd shaken so many hands and learned so much crap about the people here, things I wasn't prepared for and didn't want to know, that I couldn't face anyone else's emotional garbage. If I had, I probably couldn't have prevented the murder, but maybe I could've prevented all that's happened since."

"Jeff, you can't take on that kind of responsibility."

"That sounds very logical—very sane. Meanwhile my gut's telling me to keep asking questions, keep looking."

"Okay, let's try and unlock that memory you can't get at with a little word association. I'll say a name and you say the first thing comes to mind."

It sounded stupid, but I was game. I sat back in the chair. "Shoot."

"Eileen."

"Sick and unhappy. But there's so much more."

"Just the first thing you get," he scolded. "Zack."

"Anger."

"Ted."

"Conceit."

"Why?"

"Because he thinks he's God's gift to women. Are we still playing?"

"Laura?"

"Aloof."

"Susan?"

"Bitch."

"Adam?"

"Liar."

"Why?"

"Because he lied. He lied about when he found the

body. He lied about being at the inn on Friday night."

"Wait a minute. You said he lied about being there on Saturday, the night he tried to plant the scotch bottle in your room. Was he there Friday—the night of the murder—too?"

I thought about it for a moment. "I think that's when he sold Doug the pot."

Richard stared at the carpet, thoughtful. "Could it be that with so much going on with the most obvious suspects, you've completely ignored someone who directly threatened you?"

"Adam? Why would he want to kill Eileen?"

"You tell me."

I thought about it for a moment. "Okay, he admitted he pushed me down the stairs, but we don't know that he can hot wire a car."

"And we don't know he can't, either."

That made sense. More than I wanted to admit. That all-too-familiar queasiness invaded my gut.

"Do you think he could be protecting Susan like he claimed?" Richard asked.

"I don't know what to think."

"Maybe we'd better have a little chat with Susan."

I grabbed my jacket and followed him to the living room. As expected, we found Susan in the hole in the wall she called an office, tapping on her computer keyboard.

"Susan? Do you have a minute?"

She turned, looked at me over the top of her half glasses. "A minute."

"I want to ask you about Adam."

Something in her expression flickered—anger, annoyance?—then was gone. She looked at me suspiciously. "What about him?"

"Do you think he's capable of murder?"

Her eyes widened. "What?"

"You heard me.

"He's a nice kid."

"Nice kids don't push people down a flight of stairs."

She turned in her chair. "Don't you think you're over-reacting?"

"Don't you get it? He tried to kill me."

She looked back at me, her eyes narrowed. "You don't know what you're talking about."

"Oh no?" Sudden insight filled me as images of them together assaulted my mind. "How about you and Adam in that hole of a room you stuck Maggie and me in? How about the two of you screwing on a blanket in the woods?"

"Jeff—" Richard warned.

Susan's glare grew menacing, her words deliberate— her tone icy. "I've had enough interrogation for one day. I want you out of my house. Now!"

"Jeff, let's get some coffee."

My defiant stare made no impression on Richard, so I pivoted and walked off. He quickly caught up with me, snagged my arm and steered me toward the stairs to the lower level.

"I don't want coffee."

"Yes, you do," he said and gave me a shove.

I headed down the steps. "The last thing I need right now—"

He jostled past me on the stairway. "Shut up."

Surprised by his tone, I did as I was told.

The lower level was deserted, and I reluctantly followed my brother into the empty, spotless kitchen.

"What the hell was that all about?" he demanded. "Why tip your hand? She could be in this with Adam."

"I don't know," I said stupidly. "She pisses me off."

"Letting your anger get the better of you isn't going to solve this."

"Now look who's talking about solving it."

He leaned again against the center island, resigned. "Let's drop it. Instead, tell me what you were doing when that funny feeling came over you Friday night."

I leaned against the sink, trying to overcome my annoyance. "I went to the bar to get ice. The bucket was empty, so I came in here."

"Show me what you did."

Dutifully, I trudged to the freezer, opened the door, saw a new, ten-pound bag of ice.

Déjà vu.

I closed the freezer door with exaggerated care. My gaze traveled around the room, like it had Friday night. Again, my eyes were drawn to the sink.

"I felt like I should pick up the glasses."

"But you didn't."

I shook my head, puzzled by the anxiety—the dread—building within me.

"Go ahead—do it now."

"What's the point?"

"Humor me."

I stepped up to the deep porcelain sink, reached for one of the glasses, but stopped, frowning. "Maybe it wasn't the glasses...." My gaze shifted up from the sink to the antique cooking utensils decorating the wall. "Something's different."

Before Richard could ask, a commotion overhead interrupted us. A herd of heavy footsteps clomped across the wooden floor. I heard muffled voices. The words were indistinct, but the tone was angry.

In an instant, I sprinted for the lobby. Topping the stairs, I pushed my way through a crowd of new guests just in time to see one of the uniformed cops hauling a handcuffed Susan through the front door, with Beach bringing up the rear.

"Wait," I yelled, but the police ignored me. "Beach, she didn't kill Eileen."

He turned, annoyed. "How do you know?"

"I just do."

"Not good enough. If you come up with anything solid—call me."

They shoved Susan into the back of a patrol car, while Ashley snapped pictures as fast as her flash could recycle.

"I'll call the lawyer, honey, and see you at the station," Zack called, and rushed back inside the inn, heading for the office.

Richard and I watched from the porch as the patrol car pulled out of the driveway and headed south toward the village. Ashley stood in the drive, her camera still slung around her neck, scribbling in a spiral notebook.

"Ashley, what's going on?" I called.

"Just what it looks like," she hollered and started for her van.

I jogged to intercept her. "They're arresting Susan for murder?"

"Yeah. I've got to get back to the office. It'll be my by-line on page one."

"They're going to let her go—she didn't kill Eileen."

She turned away, ignoring me. "What are you, psychic?"

"Yeah, I am."

She climbed behind the wheel of her van and started the engine.

Richard came up behind me. "Do you know for sure Susan didn't kill him?"

"Yes. C'mon, I want to show you something."

The throng of curious bystanders had thinned by the time we reentered the inn. Richard followed me back to the kitchen, where I pointed at the wall of antiques. "Look at the potato mashers."

His gaze traveled along the shelf where some dozen or so antique, heavy wooden mashers stood. They were more or less cylindrical with tapered handles. Each worthy of the description blunt instrument.

"So?"

"One of them was missing Friday night."

"Which one?"

I went to take one, but he grabbed my hand. "Wait." He took out his clean handkerchief and picked it up by the slender handle. "There probably aren't any fingerprints, but just in case." He rolled the masher in the cloth, noting a mark on the side.

"Is that blood?" I asked.

"Hard to tell. It would have to be tested in a lab. Do you think it was Adam who did it?"

"I'd have to touch it. And I can't ... not until the cops look at it."

"You'll have to call Beach."

"And say what? That I think Adam smacked Eileen in the head with a potato masher?" I hefted the primitive utensil; it weighed about a pound, but was capable of delivering a deadly blow. "That sounds kind of stupid, don't you think?"

"Not if it's true."

"But I can't prove it. It's just hearsay." We stared at the masher. "Put it back. It isn't going anywhere. I can tell Beach about it later."

Richard stretched to put the masher back on the shelf; this time I stopped him. "Just in case, why don't we exchange it with that one over there." I pointed to a duplicate.

He switched mashers, angling the murder weapon so the dark smudge faced the wall. "Now what?"

"We could confront him."

"He's a murderer. Why make yourself a target?" Richard asked.

"Maybe he didn't mean to kill Eileen."

"Or push you down the stairs, or crash your car—?"

My half-hearted attempt at devil's advocacy instantly vanished.

"What are you doing?"

We both whirled. Adam stood in the doorway, a sack of groceries in his arms, his expression clouded with anger. My stomach knotted: how much had he seen and heard?

"Just admiring the antiques," I bluffed.

"Bullshit! Get away from there."

We backed away slowly—and into a corner.

"Look," Richard started reasonably, "we're just—"

"Shut up," Adam ordered, dumping the sack on the center island. Growing fury twisted his features. "What happened upstairs?"

"They arrested Susan for Eileen Marshall's murder."

"Shit!" He smashed his fist on the counter, making us flinch.

"What really happened that night, Adam?" I asked.

"How would I know?"

"Because you were there. You lied to Beach. You never work nights, but you were at the inn on Friday *and* Saturday nights. You parked your truck up on the adjoining property so no one would see it."

"Jeff—" Richard's voice was a warning.

"You seem to know a lot about what's been going on here."

It was time to hedge. "No more than the cops."

"Yeah, then how come *you're* asking these questions, not them?"

Uh-oh.

"You know, Mr. Resnick, I think you know just a little *too* much." He grabbed a knife from the island's cutlery rack, its eight-inch blade glinting under the fluorescent light.

He moved closer.

Cornered, there was nowhere for us to go.

I lashed out with my sneakered foot, catching his left arm, but instead of knocking him off balance, he whirled and lunged forward, slashing the sleeve of my heavy denim jacket. I fell back against Richard, my right hand clamped to my bleeding forearm.

Adam loomed with the knife. "That's the last stupid move you're going to make, *Mr.* Resnick—" He made the title an insult.

I swallowed, collecting some very bad vibes from our young friend.

Warm blood soaked my sleeve, dripping onto the linoleum. Adam nodded at Richard and tossed him a soiled kitchen towel. "You, doctor, take care of him."

Wary, Richard unsnapped my sleeve cuff, folded back the fabric, pried my fingers away from the wound, all the while keeping an eye on our assailant. He blotted the blood.

"It's not too bad, but it really should be sutured." He tore the towel in half, making a bandage out of it, tying it with a strip from the bloodied cloth. "Isn't that the same move that got your arm broken last winter?" he grated.

"Old habits die hard."

He winced at my word choice.

"Shut up," Adam ordered. "Now, button it up—I don't want anyone getting curious." He pointed at me. "Clean up this mess."

He tossed me a towel to wipe up my own blood. Queasy, I did as he said—anything to stall for time. I was about to dump the towel into the hamper when Adam tossed me a plastic trash bag.

"In there. I'm not leaving evidence behind this time."

The dumb shit didn't know spraying the area with Luminol would cause any trace of blood to fluoresce. Expensive—highly toxic—and probably out of the league of a small-town police force, but there'd be enough evidence to place me at the scene ... if anyone thought to look.

Adam grabbed the potato masher—the wrong one—and shoved it into his jacket pocket. "Now, the three of us are going for a ride. Doctor, you'll drive. And I'm going to hold a knife on your little buddy the whole way. Do anything stupid and you'll have his death on your conscience."

Still on my knees, he waved for Richard to back off, then grabbed me by my jacket collar and yanked me to my feet. The knife pressed into my side. He nodded toward the patio. "Outside."

With Richard in the lead, we circled the inn, staying close to the building. I'm not the hero type, and my throbbing arm was enough to convince me to wait for a better opportunity. I wondered if Richard would make some kind of move—do something—to give me that opportunity, all the while hoping there'd be a stray cop out front.

No such luck.

Adam stuck to me like a shadow, his left hand on my left shoulder, the knife pressed against my back. He steered us toward the side of the garage where his battered green pick-up was parked. My heart sank at the sight of a hunting rifle with a scope resting on the gun rack.

We were as good as dead.

TWENTY-THREE

The cool, overcast day had either driven everyone into their rooms or enticed them to leave for an early dinner. No one was around—no one looked out the inn's windows.

Adam shoved me against the side of the truck. He tossed Richard a set of keys. "Get in."

Richard opened the driver's door and climbed behind the wheel.

"Open the door," Adam told me.

I slid in next to Richard. Before I had time to reach for and slam the door, Adam piled in. He wrapped his left arm around my throat. The knife jabbed my ribs. "Toss the bag on the floor. Now, pull out and head north," he told Richard.

Richard shoved the key into the ignition. The engine roared to life. No one saw us pull out of the drive and onto the highway.

Hands clenching the wheel, Richard kept his eyes riveted on the road. I tried not to look at him or at Adam, but my gaze kept drifting from the knife, to the road, and back again. I felt I should do something, maybe elbow Adam in the stomach, but I knew he'd shove the blade between my ribs without hesitation. It was harder to wait, but it might be our best chance.

As always, Richard was a blank to me, but in this instance it was a blessing; I had my own fears to contend with. Adam exuded absolute confidence, without a shred of fear—which scared me shitless.

We traveled along the empty road, past motels, restaurants, and acres of forest in between, for two or three miles. I kept hoping Richard would do something—smash the truck into a tree—anything! But he drove like a grandmother, obeying all the traffic laws. I couldn't blame him; I wouldn't have gambled with his life either.

Adam broke the heavy silence. "Slow down. There's a road on the left that leads to the Mt. Mansfield ski area. Take it."

A gravel track appeared. Richard pulled onto it, slowing. We traveled a couple hundred yards until we came to a service road and a large empty gravel parking lot.

"Drive up there. Park behind that building."

Richard stopped the truck behind a small shed. Above a boarding ramp, a miniature cabin sat atop the world's largest pulley. He cut the engine and looked past me to our captor. "Now what?"

"Get out. Keep your hands where I can see them."

We waited as Richard got out, and then moved away from the truck, his hands raised in surrender. Adam shoved me facedown on the seat, pinned me, as he grabbed the rifle from the rack. "In case you were wondering, it *is* loaded."

Adam backed off, and I looked over my shoulder to see him toss the knife into the truck bed, and the gun trained on my face. Then he opened the glove compartment, took out a box of ammo, and pocketed it. "Get out."

I slid across the seat and got out. He nudged me with the barrel. "Over there."

With my hands in plain sight, I moved to stand beside Richard, who looked downright terrified. Just as scared, I couldn't offer comfort. Adam walked to the front of the truck, reached in the driver's side, grabbed the keys, pocketed them, and slammed the door.

He herded us closer to the shed, backed up to the door and smashed the glass with the butt of the stock, then reached through and opened it. I was sure he meant to kill us right then—but instead he groped for a key— turned it, and threw the main power switch. The ski lift jerked into motion.

"I know a nice quiet place at the top of the mountain, where nobody's going to find you. At least not for a very long time."

He motioned us over to the platform where a plaque overhead read: Wait Here.

"When the next seat comes up, get on."

I looked at Richard, who only shrugged. The metal chair came up from behind at mid-thigh, forcing us into it. Adam slapped the safety bar into place.

"I'll be right behind you," he warned, brandishing the rifle for emphasis.

"Jesus Christ," Richard muttered. "What the hell—?"

"Shut up," Adam shouted behind us.

The chair rose in the air, high above the ground, heading up the side of the mountain at a leisurely pace. We faced straight ahead, eyes intent on the scenery before us.

"What the hell are we going to do?" Richard grated.

"If Adam had any brains, he would've killed us the minute we got out of the truck."

"Well, the dumb ass sure outfoxed us, and the cops."

"Sorry I got you involved in this, Rich. God, I'm sorry."

"Apology accepted. Now get me out of it."

I tried to squelch my growing panic. I'd been skiing exactly twice in my life and never on this mountain. I had no idea how long the ride to the summit would take—but I knew we only had minutes to live if we didn't do something before we got to the top. I could see only one way out.

"We've got to jump."

Richard glanced at me, aghast, then turned to stare straight ahead once more. "We'll break our necks."

"It's either that or a rifle shot in the back."

Richard swallowed. "I'll take my chances jumping. When?"

"I'll tell you."

Frantic, I studied the terrain ahead. Boulders jutted through the thin topsoil directly underneath us, but a hundred yards farther up the mountain was a clear grassy spot with a drop of perhaps only fifteen feet.

"What about the safety bar?"

It would take split-second timing. Even with an injured arm, I figured my reflexes were still probably faster than Richard's. "I'll take care of it. Jump when I tell you. Don't grab the seat—don't hang on—or he'll have a clear shot at you. Try and roll when you land."

"We're going to kill ourselves."

"Have you got a better idea?"

He shook his head almost imperceptibly.

"Get ready." I moved my arms under the safety bar.

Richard closed his eyes. "Holy Mary, mother of God, pray for us sinners—"

"Now!"

The bar flew up.

We pushed forward into open space.

The rifle went off with a bang.

Richard rolled as he landed. I didn't. My left ankle hit solid rock with the force of a pile driver. White-hot explosions ignited before my eyes.

Richard grabbed my arm. "Move!"

He hauled me toward the trees and cover. The rifle thundered again, the dirt just inches from my feet exploding like a mortar blast.

Hopping and scrabbling, we darted into the safety of

the trees, where I collapsed on the moldering mat of leaves and dirt, breathless.

Adam faced backwards, balanced on the lift chair, re-loading, aiming the rifle. He fired twice, wide and high over our heads.

Panting, Richard plastered his right arm across his chest, fingers clutching the fabric on his left shoulder.

"Are you okay?" I rasped.

"I think I fractured my collar bone. It hurts like hell. How about you?"

"Ankle. I think it's broken."

"Let's see." He crouched down, helped me peel back my sock. It was too soon to see a sign of damage, and the light filtering through the trees was far from good. He grasped my ankle. The pain shot straight through to my skull. I fell back, my vision darkening until I thought I'd pass out.

"It doesn't feel broken," Richard said, still palpating. "But a sprain can hurt more than a break. Without ice, it'll swell up like a melon, too."

I leaned against a tree, still trying to catch my breath. "Talk about the walking wounded."

Richard pulled up my sock. He sat back on his heels, brushed his sleeve against his face, which came away bloody from a cut on his cheek. "Now what?"

My mind raced as my stomach roiled.

Adam.

There'd been no more shots. Had he jumped, too?

"We've got to get the hell out of here."

"And go where?" Richard asked.

"Back down the mountain."

"There's no one around for miles. We're both hurt and there's a maniac with a gun after us."

"Yeah, let's go."

"Sweet Jesus, how do you get me involved in these things?"

"Shut up and move!"

Richard hauled me to my feet and we shuffle-hopped through the trees and brush, every step exquisite torment. Richard's face was a grimace. Grunting with effort, we crept down the slope, breathless in a minute.

"Slow down," Richard commanded.

"Can't," I puffed. "We don't know how close he is."

"You're hyperventilating. You'll keel over if you don't slow down. Then we won't be going anywhere."

I leaned against a birch for support, noting how Richard's fingers dug into the fabric of his jacket as he fought to keep his injured shoulder immobile; his knuckles were paper white. Despite the chill air, we were both sweating.

"How's the shoulder?"

"Fine."

"Liar."

"So sue me."

I studied the terrain, picking a new goal: a large maple. "That's enough rest. See that big tree down there." I nodded toward the right and pushed myself up. Richard put his arm around my waist, steadying me, and we were off again.

Stumbling fifteen yards over uneven, boulder-strewn ground seemed like fifteen miles. I was hyperventilating again, my vision dappling.

Skittering into the trunk, I clung to a branch, closed my eyes, and dragged in deep lungsful of air. Richard was breathing just as hard.

"This ain't working."

"Shut up and breathe," he ordered.

I glanced at my watch; it was already after six—we had maybe an hour of daylight left. We'd been on the run less than five minutes and already my reserve of strength was just about gone. My dark denim jacket gave good camouflage, but Richard's buff-colored one may as well have been a flag of surrender. Survival was the name of the game, and if we stayed together neither of us would make it.

"You've got to go on without me."

Richard looked up sharply. "No."

"You *have* to."

"I can't."

"Rich, there's not much daylight left. It's our only chance. Go—get help! I'll only slow us down—get us both killed."

"I *won't* leave you!"

"What about Maggie? This nut case could think she knows about him, find her, and kill her, too. Don't you see, he won't stop with just us!"

The war between logic and emotion played out across his face. "Jeff, I—"

"Brenda needs you. You've got to go. Stay in the woods—but close to the ski lift so you don't get lost."

"I can't leave you here to die."

"It's a big mountain. Adam won't find me in the dark. Besides, I'll find a place to hole-up."

His worried eyes, filled with indecision, bore into me.

"Rich, you're wasting time."

He grabbed me in a fierce, one-armed hug. When he pulled back, he looked me in the eyes. "I'll be back for you. I promise. I love you, kid."

"Go!"

He turned, skittering down the slope without looking back. I watched as he half-ran, half-slid down the incline, and followed his progress until he was out of sight, hidden by trees and brush.

Then I was truly alone in that damnably quiet forest.

TWENTY-FOUR

Playing hero doesn't really suit me. I mean, I value my life as much as the next guy. By making Richard leave, I'd effectively ended it. But I'm not a quitter, either. And I'd had enough of that bastard Adam. He wasn't going to get rid of me without a fight.

I risked a look behind me, and saw no sign of him.

All right. The logical move was to try and follow Richard, but not directly behind him. If Adam caught up with me, I had to make it harder for him to follow—to track—Richard.

Move!

But I couldn't. Not with my head pounding, and my legs as insubstantial as jelly. I pulled out my prescription bottle, flipped open the top and spilled most of the pills on the ground.

Christ! Just my day.

I dumped two in my mouth, recapped the bottle and, with shaking hands, stuck it back in my pocket.

Think! Hadn't I learned anything I could use during my army training? But that training had been eighteen years before. What should I do next?

Move, stupid!

I glanced through the trees. The lift had stopped. That meant Adam had ridden to the top to cut the power, probably so it wouldn't draw attention from the locals or passing motorists. He was a thousand or more feet up the mountain from me. That gave me time. But Adam also had two good arms and legs and the rifle with a scope. There'd be a shack up top, stocked with rescue gear; ropes, flashlights—maybe even infrared goggles—everything he'd need to track me in the dark. And he didn't have to take the hard way down. He could follow the grassy slope under the chair lift while I had to stay in the woods.

He must have worked at the operation during the ski season. How else would he have known how to run the lift? As a local, he probably knew every inch of the mountain, too. And if he knew exactly where we'd dropped, it would make it that much easier for him to hunt me down.

Rest time was over.

I pulled myself up and hobbled to the next closest tree. The uneven, treacherous ground conspired to trip me with broken limbs, sticks, and exposed tree roots. I looked around for a heavy branch to use as a walking stick, but could see nothing suitable.

Get going.

I hopped from tree to tree but was soon confused. Was I zigzagging downward or was I just getting farther and farther away from the ski lift, my reference point? I didn't want to stray too far or I'd get lost and no one would ever find me ... at least not alive.

Déjà vu hit me with a vengeance: this was my vision—climbing the mountain—the one Kay Andolina had inspired with her talk of looking within. Only I was climbing down—not up.

Why hadn't I seen it as a warning? Where was the guardian angel she said watched over me?

I pushed myself away from the tree. I was not making good time. In fact, except for the loss of daylight, time seemed to be standing still.

Hop to a tree.

Rest.

Hop to a tree.

Rest.

I glanced at my watch. I'd gone maybe twenty yards in twenty minutes.

The light waned. Except for the sound of my labored breathing, the air was still. I hadn't heard footsteps or crashing sounds behind me. Then again, I'd probably feel the rifle blast before I ever heard it.

Hop to a tree.

Rest.

Hop to a tree.

It got old very fast. But I had to keep going, because when the light was gone I'd have to stay put for the rest of the long, cold night.

Rain had eroded a path among the birches. Though steep, it was relatively clear of obstacles. Inching my way down on my backside, I gained unwanted momentum. Little avalanches of pebbly dirt cascaded before me. Then I was skidding, tumbling, smashing into a stand of young pines.

Stunned, for long moments all that registered was the fire along my ribs.

After long minutes of pain-racked breaths, it hit me— I could still breathe. One small triumph at a time.

Get up. Get up, get up, get up!

Struggling to straighten, I pressed a hand along my right side. The pain flared, but I didn't pass out. Maybe that meant my ribs were only bruised—not broken.

One sore foot in front of the other.

Slower this time.

Drag to a tree.

Rest.

The light was nearly gone when I stumbled over a solid maple branch. Almost five feet long, the thicker, jagged end was about two inches thick. I stripped the

smaller branches and stamped it against the ground, testing its strength. It would do.

It was taking far too long to move from tree to tree.
Then like a soft sigh settling over the forest, it began to
rain—cold droplets filtering through the web of branches
overhead. The wind was rising, too. I fastened the top
button on my denim jacket. It was a useless gesture; I'd be
soaked in minutes.

That's when I really started to get scared.

My fingers were already going numb. My left, slashed
arm had gone stiff from holding it in the same position
for too long, and was too painful to straighten.

I blew on my right hand. My breath came out in a
fog. The temperature was dropping—fast. Already fifty
degrees or less. Cold and wet—perfect for hypothermia.

I had to keep moving. Once it was fully dark, I could
edge toward the ski lift's treeless corridor, maybe walk in
the grass. But to do that left me open for target practice.

I leaned against a tree trunk, only my ragged breathing broke the quiet. Adam could sneak up behind me at
any time—I'd never hear him. But maybe I could sense
him, like I had in the truck.

I closed my eyes, concentrated, and tried to home in
on Adam's aura. If there was ever a time when I needed
that damned, erratic psychic ability, it was then.

And it failed me.

Miserably.

I bit my lip, stifling the urge to scream.

It was time to face some harsh truths. It didn't matter
if Richard made it to help—no one was going to come for
me in the dark. It was too dangerous. And despite what
I'd told Richard, there was nowhere to hole-up for the
night; just the shelter of the trees—and I doubted I could
climb one.

Nope, I was stuck in the rain and cold for at least
eight, maybe ten hours. Depending on how cold it got,

chances were I might not make it—whether Adam found me or not. And it didn't look like I'd come up with any constructive way to conserve my already waning body heat.

A drop cascaded down my neck, soaking into my shirt. I pulled up my jacket collar, shivering—the body's instinctive response to generate heat.

It wouldn't be enough.

To move was to stay warm, but moving was getting too difficult. I looked up into the treetops, seeing nothing. Droplets cascaded down my cheeks. The thickening clouds gave no hope of moonlight or stars breaking through to give me an inkling of direction.

It was time to risk it all, go back to the edge of the forest and follow the ski lift.

I took off again. Slower this time.

I smacked into a tree, which set my ribs on fire again, and snagged my good foot in the forest litter.

I took a steadying breath. I *had* to keep going.

The lift should only be a few more yards.

It should be.

I glanced at my wrist. It was too dark to see the hands on my watch—no way to figure time.

Winded, I slumped against a tree, sank to the ground and pulled my good leg up to my chest, hugging it for warmth.

I was so friggin' tired.

I had to stay awake. To sleep was to die.

Me, dying?

I'd never been so close to the end of everything—not even when I'd been mugged.

A face from the past came back to haunt me. Shelley, my ex—dead—wife. Our marriage had ended six months before she was killed. That she'd found cocaine more attractive than me had badly bruised my ego.

I didn't like to think about it

What about Richard? I'd treated him with indifference for over twenty years before we became friends just six months before. Our past relationship had been tainted by his wealth and my own goddamned pride.

He loved me. He'd said it aloud, something I could never do. And he'd said it because he didn't want me to die without knowing.

Thanks, Rich. I owe you.

And dear, sweet Maggie. I thought she was my future. But if I didn't have a future....

Time out!

Thoughts like that would get me killed. I needed to think positively. I needed to believe I could actually get out of this mess.

But the dark thoughts multiplied.

A sprained ankle. An armed killer chasing me. A steady downpour and the temperature dropping. My odds of survival were just about nil.

Goddamn it! Think positive!

I shivered in my damp clothes. If Adam didn't kill me, I'd probably die of pneumonia. *It's an infection, you ass. You don't get it from being cold and wet,* some logical part of my brain told me, sounding an awful lot like Richard.

You need to kill time. Don't sleep.

Two times two is four.

Two times three is six....

How long had Richard been gone? He had to reach safety. Brenda was going to need him. I wasn't sure how or when exactly, but I knew. Saw her horror-stricken face etched with fear, worry—every negative emotion known to mankind.

Was it precognition? Would I be there to help? Or was I destined to be *her* guardian angel?

The rain came down harder.

The darkened landscape beckoned. Did I dare keep moving? If I fell and sprained my other ankle I'd be completely helpless when Adam found me.

So what? I could get all the way down the mountain and never see him. It was a goddamned big mountain. I could be safe and warm and dry. But no, there I sat like some scared schoolgirl.

Shit.

My tired, sore muscles protested as I pulled myself up and hobbled forward. Two feet. Four feet. Six feet....

Twigs broke somewhere behind me.

I froze—squeezed my eyes shut tight—and held my breath until I thought my lungs would explode.

Maybe I hadn't really heard the noise behind me.

A tidal wave of anger and hatred rolled over me.

Adam.

How the hell had he found me so quickly?

A bobbing flashlight shone some ten yards behind me. Flattening myself against the tree trunk, my hand tightened on my walking stick.

His anger grew nearer, stronger, like the burst of emotion I'd gotten from Maggie at the hospital. I couldn't let it overwhelm me. I steeled myself against his rage.

Despite the cold, I broke out in a sweat. I didn't dare move as I heard his carefully placed footsteps on the wet, slippery leaves.

Adam slowed, the beam of light sweeping before him.

Four feet from me.

Two feet.

Lunging forward, I smashed the branch over his shoulder. The rifle went flying, hit the ground and went off—the explosion fracturing the night.

Adam landed face-first, but rolled, coming back at me, swinging the long-handled flashlight like a club. I dove for his throat. The flashlight caught my slashed arm, and the pain sent me cringing.

Adam came at me again, blinding me with the light. I ducked, hearing a whoosh as the flashlight whipped over my head. I rushed him, knocking the light from his hand. We rolled, tangled in the brush. The coil of rope around Adam's shoulder came loose. Legs thrashing, one of his kicks connected with my swollen ankle, sending skyrockets exploding in front of my eyes. I countered with a knee to his balls—that killer move sending him into spasms of agony.

Struggling to my knees, I wavered, spit out pine needles and dirt, groped in the mud for the flashlight, then gathered up the rope. Grabbing his left wrist, I yanked it behind him, took the right and tied him, looping rope around his legs, too. Doubled over and gasping, I shoved Adam onto his back and searched his jacket pockets. I took the ammo and the flashlight's extra batteries, then tossed the wooden masher into the dark woods.

Winded, I sank back.

Now what the hell I was going to do?

TWENTY-FIVE

Holding the flashlight under my chin, I unloaded the rifle, listening to Adam's gasping breaths. The US Army had taught me to take any advantage and exploit it. It was time to do just that and shift to rescue mode. That meant making us visible.

Hunkering over to a tree, I used it for support, hauling myself upright. Exquisite agony coiled up my leg and through my body as I gingerly put weight on my swollen ankle. I breathed through gritted teeth, unwilling to let Adam know just how much I was hurting.

I wound the rope around my forearm, intending to use it like a leash. If Adam tried to make a run, I'd yank it taut and trip him. Hefting the flashlight in my left hand, I used the rifle in my right as a walking stick. I nudged him with the stock. "Get up. We're moving out."

"Where?" he croaked.

"To the grassy area under the ski lift."

"In the open—in the pouring rain?"

"You don't like the weather—talk to God. Move!"

Adam struggled to his feet, unable to fully straighten. Good. If he was hurting, it evened the odds.

My ankle screamed. I bit my lip to keep from grunting. Adam wasn't feeling so hot, either—at first. But in no time his stride lengthened.

"Slow down," I called, my shoulder snagging an unseen branch.

He did, for a couple of steps.

"You're hurting, man. That makes you easy prey," he taunted.

"Shut up."

The rope pulled tight again. "I said, slow down!" I jerked it hard, sending him face-first into the sodden ground.

I trained the flashlight on him as he struggled to his knees. Adam's face was screwed in fury, his anger near the boiling point. He turned without a word. We started off again.

We walked, brushing past trees, stumbling over roots and branches, only the feeble beam of the flashlight cut the gloom.

Minutes passed.

No sign of the clearing and ski lift. I must've lost my bearings in the dark.

"We're lost," he grunted.

"Shut up!"

"Hurt, lost. You're a dead man."

Not so far.

Suddenly we broke free of the trees. The rain came down harder without the canopy of branches and leaves overhead.

"Keep moving," I said

I walked him some twenty feet away from the trees.

"Sit."

"In the wet grass?"

"Sit!"

He sat. "I've got plenty of time—but yours is running out."

"Shut up!" I told him for what seemed like the hundredth time.

"You got hurt when you jumped off the ski lift."

"It didn't stop me from capturing you."

"Pure luck. It won't hold." Despite his bravado, I

knew he wasn't feeling quite as confident as he made out.

My ankle throbbed, so I moved behind him and sat in the cold wet grass. Dipping a hand in my pocket, I took out the bullets and reloaded the rifle.

"Have you ever fired a gun before?" he asked.

"An M-16. I figure at close range I can blow your head off."

That shut him up.

The downpour continued. I trained the flashlight on my watch: nine-fifteen. It was later than I thought. Only another nine or ten hours before rescue.

I took a breath to calm myself. No way would I let him know exactly how scared I was. On the other hand, he was pretty cool. Despite the current situation, he still felt the odds were in his favor. Much as I didn't want to admit it, they probably were.

Richard had been gone for three hours. If he'd found help, then he and the cops were probably down at the ski center at the base of the mountain. I couldn't see any lights—not even traffic on the road somewhere below the line of trees. Would they throw the master switch, bathing the ski lift in beautiful white light?

Not if Adam had sabotaged the system.

"You cut the wires, didn't you?" I said.

He looked at me over his shoulder, grinned. "Yeah."

My finger tightened on the rifle's trigger. "You son of a bitch."

He laughed. "I told you. You're a dead man."

"What's the point in killing me now? By now the cops know about you. They know you murdered Eileen. Why is it still so important for you to get rid of me?"

He glared at me, the flashlight's harsh beam gave his face an almost demonic appearance. "Do you have to shine that thing in my eyes?"

"Yeah."

He half-turned. "It ain't gonna last an hour unless you

turn it off. And those other batteries might give you another hour after that. Then it's just you and me and the dark—and it's a long time until dawn."

It was my turn to be quiet.

The problem remained: the temperature was dropping and my only source of heat was sitting in front of me, glaring at me.

"So where's the doctor?" he said.

"I sent him on ahead."

"Yeah, right. You got that bum ankle. He figured you'd slow him down, so he left you. Nice guy. No sense of loyalty. None of 'em."

He wasn't making any sense. "None of who?"

"All you queers are the same."

What was he talking about?

"Why did you killed Eileen?"

"Not that it's any of your business, but that old bitch and Zack were fucking around. She got what she deserved."

"Because she was fucking Zack or because she was fucking Susan's husband?"

He ignored my question. "That doctor ... he's a looker, ain't he?"

"Very good looking," I agreed; at least, Brenda thought so.

"He left you, practically helpless." Adam shook his head ruefully. "Just deserted you. No sense of loyalty," he repeated.

"On the contrary, I told him to go."

"Then that was plain stupid."

"At the time, it made perfect sense. Why should both of us end up gut shot by you." I glanced down at my watch: nine-twenty.

"He's kinda special to you, that doctor, huh?" His tone was snide with accusation.

"As a matter of fact, yes."

"Nadine told me about him and you. She makes up the rooms and said since your girlfriend's been in the hospital, you've been sleeping with him."

I bet she'd neglected to tell Adam that she'd had to make up both beds. That would've made the story just a little too mundane.

"So what if I was?"

"It's even sicker than Zack and Eileen."

Something was going on with him. I wasn't sure, but I took a guess.

"Eileen made a pass at you that night, didn't she?"

"Shut up!"

It was beginning to make sense. Eileen was so drunk I don't think she knew what she was doing in those last few minutes. Coming on to me ... and then Adam. Had the idea of balling an old lady actually been appealing? Was he capable of rape? Why not—he was capable of murder.

"I hope you're not too homophobic, Adam, because you've got something I need."

I crawled nearer, shoved him down onto the ground, and turned him onto his stomach. His fear escalated as I yanked the rope, tying his feet, looping it back around his hands so he was trussed like a Thanksgiving turkey. Then I nestled close, wrapping my left arm around his shoulder.

"Get away from me, you pervert," he shouted, trying to squirm away.

Grabbing a hank of his hair, I jerked his head back, cutting off his air, his left ear inches from my mouth.

"Listen, you dumb shit, three times now you've almost cost me my life. I'm not going to die of exposure because of you. So, if you don't want me to cave your head in with the rifle butt, you'll shut up and settle down, because I intend to suck up every therm of heat your body can generate between now and the time somebody finds us come dawn. Do you understand?"

Strangled noises escaped his throat. He tried to nod, but I didn't loosen my grip.

"Good." I let go and he gasped for air.

Reaching behind me, I snagged the flashlight, holding it in my left hand. Another weapon in my arsenal. I could use it as a club if I had to. I switched it off.

"Now, we're just going to lie here quietly and wait until morning. Right?"

Anger and humiliation rolled off him in waves—warming me like a space heater. I basked in it—draping myself across him to take full advantage of his body heat. But all those sensations pummeling my psyche made my head pound. I didn't kid myself; Adam was just as dangerous as he'd been with the rifle in his hands. He was younger than me and I was cold, wet, and bone tired. And hugging a murderer wasn't my idea of bliss, either.

Survival mode, I reminded myself.

I was determined to survive.

A barrage of conflicting messages and emotions continued to assault me. I waded through the miasma of memory and sensation and after a while, things began to clear. The snippet of a vision I'd picked up in Zack's and Susan's bathroom suddenly made sense.

"You saw them—Eileen and Zack—in the hot tub together, back in April."

He answered easily, unconcerned with how or where I'd gotten my information. "I was helping Zack with the renovations. I left my tools on a Friday and I needed them for another job. I had a key, so I came inside, but I couldn't find Zack. I wandered out back and saw him in the garden—screwing old lady Marshall by the hot tub." He shuddered at the memory.

But that wasn't all I got.

"Eileen hired you," I murmured in disbelief."

"So what," came his cool reply.

"She hired you to...." I couldn't quite understand it, had to concentrate. "... to break up Zack and Susan. You were screwing her to break up their marriage."

"You don't know nothin'!"

Ted's words to me that day during the dining room photo shoot came back, sickening me: *Older broads are grateful for anything they get in the sack.* Was Susan so love starved that Adam's attention seemed like a godsend?

"What did Eileen offer you?"

"Money. But I stopped taking it back in June. Susan's worth more than a mercy fuck. She's teaching me the business. I'm not gonna be washing dishes the rest of my life."

More likely he'd be staring at the walls of a jail cell, I thought. "So why didn't you kill Zack, too?"

"He never bothered me. All he thinks about is getting back his goddamn boat."

"Then why kill Eileen?"

"She was going to tell Susan everything. How I took money from her—how I sold pot to the guests. She pissed me off being so damned smug."

"Tell the truth. She pissed you off by making a pass at you. Isn't that what really happened?"

Adam's anger flared. "I was walking up from the creek, heard the way she talked to Susan. I was fed up with her and all her shit. So while you guys were in the pool, I ducked in the kitchen—grabbed the masher. I was just gonna scare her. After you left, she said those things to me and I got mad, so I whacked her. Big deal. I figured the cops would think she smashed her head on the side of the hot tub. And they would have, if you hadn't gotten so damned nosy."

My anger boiled. Despite her character flaws, I could identify with Eileen feeling betrayed by someone she'd loved. That this callous little bully snuffed out her life disgusted me.

The night wore on and I had no desire to speak with Adam again, though it became a game to eavesdrop on his emotions. And I let his anger feed mine, which helped me stay alert. Because something Richard said came back to haunt me: *Once you're out of it, kid—you're dead to the world.*

I couldn't afford to fall asleep.

Occasionally Adam would move, either trying to get more comfortable or testing to see if I was still awake, but a sharp tap with the flashlight quickly reminded him who was in charge.

Time dragged.

Eventually Adam's body went lax, and my psychic pipeline to him shut down as he dozed off.

Cold rain rolled down my face. I shifted position, unwilling to listen to Adam's thudding heart. I'd never felt so uncomfortable—so ridiculous. But this was survival, I kept reminding myself. Unpleasant as the situation was, it was the only way for me to survive. I could suffer a little indignity for the privilege.

I switched on the flashlight and glanced at my watch: 12:43. That left five or six hours 'til daylight. I was so damned cold. Yet despite being stiff and achy, I let myself hope.

Maybe—just maybe—I'd live through the night.

TWENTY-SIX

My head dropped for what seemed like the thousandth time, waking me with a start. Turning my face to the clear sky, I stared at the stars. Hadn't I been warmer sometime during that endless night? My head lolled and I took in the shadowy trees across the clearing. The rain had stopped and a brilliant moon illuminated the gloom.

Closing my eyes, I rolled onto my side, drew my knees up to my chest, wrapped my arms around them and tried to warm myself.

Something rustled nearby.

My eyes snapped open as I rolled onto my stomach, terror pumping adrenaline through me.

Adam saw me. He wiggled free from the last of the rope and made a spectacular dive for the rifle.

I lunged at him, grabbed the barrel with one hand, pushing it away from my face and toward the trees.

Eyes feral, Adam shoved me backward, his anger feeding him incredible strength. Fingers still locked around steel, I yanked him with me, sending us rolling, end over end down the slope.

A gunshot shattered the night.

I let go, still tumbling backward and smashed into something hard and unyielding. White light exploded behind my eyes, blinding me as I bounced off and fell facedown in damp earth.

My lungs didn't seem to work as celestial noises, like I'd heard when Adam pushed me down the stairs, rang through my ears. A voice or a sound like nothing on earth echoed through my ears—and this time it wasn't Kay Andolina.

I must be dead.

But I wasn't.

Was I crazy, or had I simply blacked out?

Time wobbled.

I coughed, then took a few deep, sweet breaths and lay still.

Eons later, I stared at the still-dark sky, aware of strained muscles I hadn't known existed. I waited, wondering if I'd ever muster the strength to roll onto my side.

Adam lay crumpled by one of the ski lift's concrete supports. We'd both hit it—my shoulder, by the ache in it—his head, by the blood staining his pale face. I watched him for long minutes while assessing a whole new set of aches and pains. My right hand didn't want to close. Broken? Nerve damage? I worked at flexing it until finally I could almost make a fist.

I'd live.

No longer winded, I made it to my knees, dragged myself yards up the soggy hill until I found the rifle, and then painfully inched my way back down the wet grass toward Adam.

He hadn't moved. Was he dead? Quite frankly, I didn't give a shit. I hefted the gun's cold steel barrel. It would've been so easy to reload, gut shoot him and leave him as carrion. Instead, I reached for Adam's throat, felt for a pulse. It was weak, but there.

I'd lost the flashlight, but there was moonlight enough to see my watch: 4:18. The sun would rise in about two hours or so. The long grassy slope lay before me. I might be able to hunker down the hill on my ass, maybe even work up a decent sweat doing so. I didn't have to wait for rescue, I could go find help myself.

But I knew I wouldn't. I was too damned tired.

I considered my options. I could just leave Adam crumpled against the concrete support, but his breathing sounded strained. Wasn't there some kind of law about withholding aid? I almost laughed. What a crazy idea that I could go to jail for letting him die—after all he'd done to me....

Using the last of my energy, I hauled him away from the pillar and out into the open. He still had a pulse—he was still breathing. The rope was somewhere above us on the slope—I had no way to secure him. Instead, I sat on his ass. Only this time I held the gun cradled on my lap, ready and willing to use it if he roused.

I wondered what Richard would say. He'd felt guilty not waiting for help and moving an injured Maggie from my wrecked car. But I wasn't a doctor, and instead was blissfully ignorant of further damage I might've caused the kid. Killer, I reminded myself. Richard would've moved him with great care, to avoid the risk of further injury or death. He would've figured out some way to keep him warm and alive....

I shrugged. *C'est la vie.*

The adrenaline rush that had warmed me wore off. I couldn't even shiver—which was not a good sign.

Spilling the ammo into my palm, I counted the remaining bullets: twelve. Okay. One last-ditch effort. I fired three times—a distress signal—the recoil knocking me back to the ground.

The echo of the blasts died away and I waited in the still darkness.

Nothing.

Maybe there was nobody out there to hear it.

I swallowed my disappointment. I'd try again—maybe in half an hour. It gave me a goal, because without that I had nothing to occupy my mind.

I was so damned cold, I couldn't feel any emotions at all—there was just nothing left inside of me.

Worse, I didn't even care.

It took a long time for the sky to brighten over the hills to the east, staining it a milky orange. Its beauty eluded me as I stared at the shadow-drenched silhouette. The rifle lay across my lap, my index finger resting lightly on the trigger, the ground around me littered with shell casings.

And I waited.

I was good at waiting. I'd been waiting...forever?

"Jeffrey Resnick. Can you hear me? It's Sergeant Beach."

The voice registered, but the words weren't making much sense.

"Resnick! Put the gun down."

Where had the sound come from?

Something clicked inside my head. A bullhorn.

Okay! Rescue at hand.

I looked around me, couldn't even tell if Adam still breathed. Well, if he was dead, that was okay too. Everything was just fine with me.

"Resnick, put the gun down!" the voice commanded again.

Put the gun down.

Put the gun down—where?

It was a perplexing problem.

"Put. The. Gun. Down."

Down? On the ground?

I set the rifle on the grass beside Adam's prone body, folded my arms across my chest and waited. From out of the trees came a swarm of uniformed police and fireman. I squinted up at Sgt. Beach who had stopped in front of me.

"It's okay now," he said. "You can give up your prisoner."

Strong arms lifted me off Adam and placed me on a blanket. Stuporous, I sat there, while warm hands worked on me.

"He's alive. Head injury. Hypothermia for sure," a fireman said of Adam.

Someone peeled off my wet jacket and shirt, wrapping a dry blanket around my shoulders. Someone else cut off my mud-caked jeans. Then I lay on the ground and watched the sun creep higher over the Green Mountains while a firefighter splinted my sore foot.

A buzz of voices asked questions with no meaning. I longed to sink into oblivion. Then a single voice penetrated the fog around my brain.

"Hey, kid. I told you I'd be back for you."

My eyes cracked open to see Richard's worried face. Groping fingers found his hand. I used what little strength I had to squeeze it before my eyes slid shut. All I wanted to do was sleep—because now I could.

ABOUT THE AUTHOR

The immensely popular Booktown Mystery series is what put Lorraine Bartlett's pen name Lorna Barrett on the New York Times Bestseller list, but it's her talent -- whether writing as Lorna, or L.L. Bartlett, or Lorraine Bartlett -- that keeps her in their hearts. This multi-published, Agatha-nominated author pens the exciting Jeff Resnick Mysteries as well as the acclaimed Victoria Square Mystery series, and now the fantasy series Tales of Telenia, was well as many short stories and novellas to her name(s). Check out the links to all her works here: http://www.LLBartlett.com

You can also find her on Facebook, Goodreads, Pinterest, Google+, and Twitter.

ALSO FROM NEW YORK TIMES BESTSELLING AUTHOR

L.L. Bartlett

Don't miss ...

Cheated By Death

Jeff Resnick is definitely out of his element when he and Maggie take a working vacation at a quaint Vermont inn. But the moment Jeff crosses the Sugar Maple Inn's threshold, his sixth sense warns him that someone is about to meet a violent death. His anxiety intensifies when he travels on one of the local roads and he is nearly overwhelmed by feelings of impending doom. With their own lives at stake, Jeff uses all his wits and skill to bring a ruthless killer to justice before he becomes the next victim.

Lightning Source UK Ltd.
Milton Keynes UK
UKOW06f2201180817
307520UK00022B/303/P